Twins? Im[possible]

Georgia stared at both men. It wasn't that they looked a lot alike. They were *identical*. They were the same height, and they had the same muscular, rangy frame with the wide shoulders that gave them a deceptively burly look. Their hair was the same thickness, the same color, so close to black a crow couldn't tell the difference. They wore it in the same way. Their eyes were the same hue of brown; their eyebrows arched at the same place. They both sported thick mustaches over beautifully shaped mouths that had been carved by the same master sculptor.

"Who is this, Georgia Lee?" her fiancé asked. "What the hell's going on?"

"It's you," she said, then added, "I mean, I thought it was you. I guess I don't know who he is. And neither does he—he has amnesia...."

Dear Reader,

The hustle and bustle of the holiday season is just around the corner—and Special Edition's November lineup promises to provide the perfect diversion!

This month's THAT SPECIAL WOMAN! title is brought to you by veteran author Lindsay McKenna. *White Wolf* takes yo on a stirring, spiritual journey with a mystical Native America medicine woman who falls helplessly in love with the hardene hero she's destined to heal!

Not to be missed is *The Ranger and the Schoolmarm* by Penny Richards—the first book in the SWITCHED AT BIRT miniseries. A collaborative effort with Suzannah Davis, this compelling series is about four men...switched at birth!

And bestselling author Anne McAllister delivers book six in the CODE OF THE WEST series with *A Cowboy's Tears*—a heartfelt, deeply emotional tale. The first five books in the series were Silhouette Desire titles.

The romance continues with *The Paternity Test* by Pamela To when a well-meaning nanny succumbs to the irresistible char of her boss—and discovers she's pregnant! And Laurie Paige serves up a rollicking marriage-of-convenience story that will leave you on the edge of your seat in *Husband: Bought and Paid For*.

Finally, *Mountain Man* by Silhouette newcomer Doris Rangel transports you to a rugged mountaintop where man, woman a child learn the meaning of trust—and discover unexpected happiness!

I hope you enjoy all that we have in store for you this November. Happy Thanksgiving Day—and all of us at Silhouette would like to wish you a joyous holiday season!

Sincerely,

Tara Gavin
Senior Editor

Please address questions and book requests to:
Silhouette Reader Service
U.S.: 3010 Walden Ave., P.O. Box 1325, Buffalo, NY 14269
Canadian: P.O. Box 609, Fort Erie, Ont. L2A 5X3

PENNY RICHARDS

THE RANGER AND THE SCHOOLMARM

Silhouette®

SPECIAL EDITION®

Published by Silhouette Books

America's Publisher of Contemporary Romance

This book is for Tara, who came up with a great and fun idea.
Thanks. For Zachery, my dark-haired, blue-eyed, soon-to-be-
a-heartthrob grandson for lending me his name.
Love you, Zach! And for Suzannah—good friend, writing
partner, travelin' buddy. I miss you.
Special thanks to Karen Taylor Richman for her keen eye and
for keeping "all our ducks in a row."

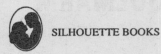 SILHOUETTE BOOKS

ISBN 0-373-24136-4

THE RANGER AND THE SCHOOLMARM

Copyright © 1997 by Penny Richards

Books by Penny Richards

Silhouette Special Edition

The Greatest Gift of All #921
Where Dreams Have Been #949
Sisters #1015
*The Ranger and the Schoolmarm #1136

Previously published under the pseudonym Bay Matthews

Silhouette Special Edition

Bittersweet Sacrifice #298
Roses and Regrets #347
Some Warm Hunger #391
Lessons in Loving #420
Amarillo by Morning #464
Summer's Promise #505
Laughter on the Wind #613
Sweet Lies, Satin Sighs #648
Worth Waiting For #825
Hardhearted #859

Silhouette Books

Silhouette Christmas Stories 1989
"A Christmas Carole"

*Switched at Birth

PENNY RICHARDS,

of Haughton, Louisiana, describes herself as a dreamer and an incurable romantic. Married at an early age to her high school sweetheart, she claims she grew up with her three children. Now that only the youngest is at home, writing romances adds an exciting new dimension to her life.

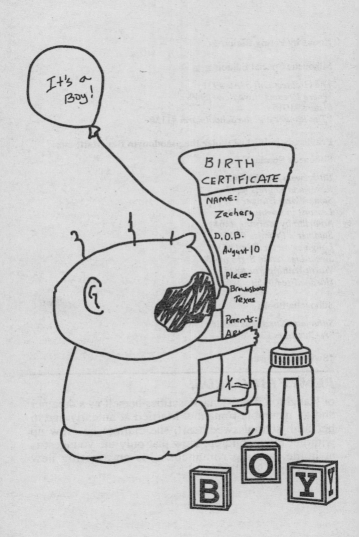

Chapter One

"As God is my witness, I'll never step foot on an airplane again."

The heartfelt statement, along with the loud roar of the jet engines, nudged Georgia Williams from a light sleep. The voice was young, feminine, definitely thankful, and the rip-off of the familiar line from *Gone With The Wind* was delivered in a passionate, faux Southern accent.

Sabrina, Georgia thought with a smile. Sabrina Noble was one of her nine French students—all girls—who had accompanied Georgia on a ten-day tour of France just before school let out for the summer. Sabrina longed to be an actress and had the drive and ambition to do it, a trait Georgia sometimes envied.

"Geez, I'd kill for a Big Mac," said plump Meredith Jarvis.

Georgia looped her fine strawberry-blond hair behind her ear and sat up, casting a halfhearted smile over her shoulder.

"*Français, s'il vous plaît,*" she said, entreating her charges to speak French as she'd had to do several hundred times a day during their trip.

"C'mon, Miss Williams!" Meredith moaned as the plane bounced and the brakes squealed at touchdown. "We're home now. Baseball, hot dogs, apple pie and Chevrolet—remember?"

"Point taken," Georgia said, smiling.

They were home. Home, where all things were familiar...and predictable. Georgia pushed away the uncharitable thought. It wasn't that she didn't adore her friends, but it had been exciting to meet new people in France, to be stimulated and challenged by their conversation and points of view.

Paris had awakened something inside her. It was impossible to visit the Louvre or watch the lovers strolling down the streets with the fanciful names without falling under the spell of romance, which was the very soul of the city. A restlessness and hunger she didn't understand filled her. For a brief time, she had even considered trying to find a teaching position and staying. Now that she was about to pick up her normal life again, the thought was even more appealing.

She sighed again as the plane shuddered to a stop and the passengers, including her charges, began to gather their belongings from the overhead compartments.

"I can't wait to get home," Meredith said.

Home. Georgia closed her eyes again. Home for her was the same small house in Aledo, Texas, where she'd grown up, the house her parents had deeded to her when they retired from careers in education and moved into an apartment so that their plans to see the world wouldn't be interrupted by yard work and maintenance.

"I can't wait to sleep in my own bed."

Bed. Her bed was the huge four-poster where she'd been conceived. It was empty. Frustratingly empty.

"I can't wait to see Joey. I'm gonna lay a big juicy kiss right on those sexy lips of his," drawled sultry Kat Bensen, whose lush auburn hair and green eyes gave credibility to her sex-kitten image.

Unlike most of her female classmates, Kat was a throwback to a time when women were women and men were men, both sexes knew their place and liked it that way. At seventeen, she had the male mentality figured out and had honed testosterone manipulation to a fine art. Who needed women's lib, she'd once asked Georgia with wide-eyed candor, if you had eyelashes like hers?

Who needed it, indeed, Georgia thought with a rush of rebellion that would no doubt infuriate her feminist sisters. Personally she had more freedom than she knew what to do with. She was looking forward to having a man to take out the garbage, to get up and start her car on cold mornings, to by golly bring home the bacon— or in Jake's case, the beef.

Jake. A wave of something closely akin to despair washed over her. She and Jake had been engaged for two years now. They planned to tie the knot on June fifth, a little less than a month away, but strangely, every time she thought of her approaching nuptials she could almost feel a hangman's noose around her neck.

Guiltily, she shoved away the traitorous thought. Jake was a good man. A *wonderful* man. He was kind to animals and small children. Rich as Midas. And handsome as a Greek god—if you liked your Greek gods big and burly and booted, which was standard for the Greek god type in Texas.

More important, Jake loved her—plain little Georgia Lee Williams. He was willing to end her reign as Aledo's resident old maid and give her the thing she'd dreamed of for so long: a home, complete with an adoring husband and two point five kids—more if she could talk him into it. There would finally be a man to snuggle up to in bed.

The thought should have brought a tingle of excitement. Instead, it elicited another sigh. Jake was rich, good-looking, had a heart of gold and was highly eligible in every way. The problem was that he didn't make her heart go pit-a-pat. His kisses didn't leave her breathless and wanting more.

Stop it, Georgia! The familiar voice of her conscience spoke up. *Jake is salt of the earth, rock solid, the original Steady Eddie....*

Yeah, but that translates to boring. Her heart tossed in its two cents worth.

Maybe *boring* wasn't quite the right word, Georgia thought, seeking a peaceful compromise with her warring id and ego. It's just that Jake was so...so predictable! Compared to the routine of Jake's life, her own staid existence was wild and decadent. She did at least travel whenever she could and held season tickets to the Dallas symphony, not to mention she visited the occasional art gallery and attended the infrequent summer barbecue given by her colleagues.

As she'd told him before she left, if only—just once—Jake would do something outrageous or completely unexpected. If he'd go out on a limb and make an effort to surprise her...whisk her off in the Lazy L helicopter to Tulsa for dinner, or surprise her with tickets to a—she gave a delicate shudder—country music concert! She could handle Garth, Reba and the Mavericks...in small doses. If he'd just do *anything* to prove to her that he didn't take her or their relationship for granted, she might be able to muster up some enthusiasm about hitching herself to him for the rest of her life.

The night before she left for the trip, she'd asked him if he'd like to go to Paris with her. He said he'd already been. Surprised, she asked when. He'd smiled that guileless smile of his and told her he'd bought a prize heifer from a guy in Paris and drove up there to pick her up—Paris, Texas, that is.

She hadn't seen the humor in his teasing and told him so. She had told him a lot of things that night....

"That was a bad joke," he said. "I'm sorry."

Hurt, angry and filled with frustration, Georgia kept her gaze focused on her steak. "I'm not so sure this is a good idea."

"What's not a good idea, sugar?"

She looked up and met his gaze. "The wedding."

The bite of rare beef on Jake's fork paused on its way to his mouth. He smiled. He had such a great smile. A sexily shaped mouth and white teeth beneath a mustache that mirrored the dark thickness of his hair.

"Don't go gettin' cold feet on me, Georgia Lee."

She put her knife and fork down and clasped her trembling hands in her lap. "Is that what it is?"

"I've had a few shaky moments myself," Jake admitted, popping the bite of steak into his mouth.

The admission surprised her. "You have?"

He nodded as he chewed.

"Do you ever feel like something's missing?"

He swallowed. Frowned. "Missing? Like what?"

"Excitement," she said, putting her forearms on either side of her plate and leaning toward him with an earnest expression in her blue eyes. "Jake, we won't be married for another month, but we already act like people who've been together twenty years."

For the first time, he looked ill at ease. "We've known each other a long time. We're comfortable together, that's all."

"Comfortable?" she said, her voice rising. She shook her head. "We're not just comfortable. We're in a rut. Dinner here on Monday. My place on Wednesday. A burger at the Bearcat on Friday. A rented movie on Saturday. Church on Sunday. Just once, I'd like to do something different!"

He blinked, and a hurt look entered his dark brown eyes. "Different? Like what?"

"You're a smart man. Think about it."

He did...for all of ten seconds. "You're right," he said with a nod. "There's no reason we can't drive to Dallas some Friday night for dinner and a movie."

Something inside Georgia snapped.

"That's not what I mean!" she screeched, shoving her chair away from the table. Jake's fork clattered to his plate. His mouth fell open, and his eyes widened as if the devil incarnate stood before him.

"I mean *different.*" Her voice grated like two rocks rubbing together. "Like a...like a—" She clutched the sides of her head and struggled to think of something. Inspiration struck, and she threw her hands up into the air.

"Like a picnic down by the creek with bread and wine and cheese." Her eyes sparkled and satisfaction filled her voice.

Jake's heavy eyebrows drew together.

She snapped her fingers when another idea hit. "A ride on horseback in the moonlight." On a roll, she pointed a finger at him. "Or—or going skinny-dipping in the tank and making love under the stars. Now *that* would be different."

"Georgia Lee!" he said, his face red.

"We've been engaged two years, and we have never been to bed together, Jake. Why? Don't you want to make love to me?"

His face turned redder. He swallowed. "Of course, I do."

"Then why haven't you?"

"Well, hell," he said, showing his first sign of irritation. "That should be obvious. Because I respect you."

Even she heard the bitterness in her laugh. "You respect me? Tell the truth, Jake. You haven't taken me into your bed because little mousy Georgia Lee with her funky Annie Hall wardrobe doesn't excite you."

"Now look here, Georgia, that's enough!" he yelled, scraping back his chair and rising to his full six feet, three inches. They stood there mere feet apart, the distance between them an ever widening chasm.

"I love you, and you love me, and we're getting married in June, and that's the end of this nonsense."

The pained expression in his eyes pricked her tender heart. Shame filled her. What kind of ungrateful wretch was she? He was right. She did love him—who didn't? And she would marry him, because she would soon be thirty and her chances of being swept off her feet were lessening by the second. Marrying Jake might not be exciting, and her life with him might not be a thrill a minute, but it was darn well better than the alternative.

At least she wouldn't have to sleep in that lonely bed anymore.

With a soft "I'm sorry" she rounded the corner of the table and put her arms around him. His heart beat out a strong steady rhythm beneath her ear. His arms went around her reluctantly. She pressed closer, then closer still.

"I'm leaving early in the morning, Jake. Take me to bed."

She felt him stiffen. He didn't say anything for several seconds. Then he took her shoulders in his big hands and set her away from him, so that her hands rested on his denim-clad hips.

"Don't tempt me this way, sugar," he said, his voice low and husky. "I'm only a man. If I took you to bed, I'd have to look your daddy in the eye come Sunday morning. I still remember how he looked at me when I was a kid and got sent to the principal's office. I swear, that man could make the devil squirm."

Georgia had been the recipient of that look herself. The fact that Jake remembered it after all these years was a testimony of its effectiveness. She nodded in defeat and released her hold on him. "I'll help you clean up, and then I'd better get home and get some sleep."

He hadn't let her clean up, but he had driven her home soon afterward, leaving her on the front porch with a thorough and pleasant but less-than-earth-shattering kiss on the lips. She'd left the house before daylight the next morning and had only talked to him once since then, a quick call to remind him of the day and time of her arrival at the Dallas/Fort Worth airport and to ask if he would be meeting her there.

Jake said he'd be vaccinating cattle that day. He'd see her that evening when she got in, though. Maybe, he'd suggested, they could go grab an Elaine Burger from the Bearcat Café.

Pushing the memory away, Georgia picked up her carry-on bags and stood, waiting to find a break in the line of people exiting the aircraft. She wasn't sure why his refusal to come and meet her hurt so much. She'd known what he'd say before he said it. Jake hated traffic, hated everything about the city.

She'd hoped the conversation—or argument—they'd had before she left town would make a difference in how he looked at their relationship, that he would care enough about her to take her concerns to heart and do something about them. Obviously, the discussion had made minimal impact on her hardheaded cowboy, and she was back at square one.

She'd also clung to the hope that the trip to France would change things somehow, that absence, as the old saying claimed, would make both their hearts grow fonder. She didn't think that had worked, either.

She had come to realize one basic truth while she was away—Jake was a loner who didn't need her or any woman for anything but the most obvious, and he was too much of a gentleman to even pursue that. He had a routine that conformed to the seasons of planting and breeding and mending and fixing and whatever it took to maintain life on the Lazy L Ranch, and he liked it that way—plain and simple.

When she married him, he would work as diligently at maintaining her as he did everything else on the ranch. She would be allotted her time, her place.

With another sigh, she followed Kat out into the

throng of people waiting for their loved ones on the plane. The prospect didn't do anything to cheer her.

The man leafing through the latest Dean Koontz novel with apparent disinterest was big and burly and booted with a thatch of dark brown hair and a thick mustache. Anyone giving him a casual glance would assume he was absorbed in the book.

They would be wrong.

His dark eyes—clear and sharp—moved frequently over the crowd, as if he was looking for someone, as indeed he was. He was looking for a woman, a particular woman with red-blond hair. He had a little surprise for her....

"Stay close until you see your parents, girls," Georgia cautioned. "And when they find you, come and tell me so I'll know I've been relieved of my duty and can mark your name off my list."

Her directive met with several moans of dismay. "Sorry, but this is a big city, and there are a lot of wackos out there. I'd hate to get you back safely from a foreign country just to lose you in our own backyard."

For the next few minutes, Georgia was busy seeing that her charges were reunited with their parents and telling them she'd see them in school in a couple of days. When the last name was checked off, the last hug and thanks accepted and the last goodbye said, she drew a relieved breath.

Now she was ready to go home to her empty house and her lonely bed. Though it was only four-thirty, she was ready for a long hot bath, a cup of chamomile tea, a silly sitcom and an early night.

She was gathering her shoulder bag and cosmetics case when she saw Jake. They were separated by a throng of people, but there was no doubt that it was Jake standing in a bookstore several yards away, engrossed in a book.

Her first thought was that he'd told her he wasn't meeting her. Her second was that he must have taken their talk more seriously than she believed. His usual Western attire had been left at the ranch, all but his boots and hat, which he wore with a nondescript gray sport coat and slacks.

Changing the way he dressed wasn't exactly what she'd had in mind, and the cut of the clothes didn't do much for him, but it was a start, and at least he was making an effort. Her weariness vanished. With a broad smile curving her lips, she left the waiting area and started through the crowd.

She was halfway to him when he looked up, and his dark gaze panned the people milling around him. As he made eye contact with her, Georgia gave him a smile bright enough to put the Texas sunshine to shame. His gaze lingered for a heartbeat, but instead of the return smile and wave she expected, his glance swept past her, and he gave his attention back the book in his hand.

Georgia stopped dead still in the midst of the teeming throng. Maybe he hadn't seen her, she reasoned. After all, she was standing in a sea of people.

"Hey, lady, move it."

The command came from a glowering man with a beard and backpack. With a mumbled apology, she started toward Jake, who at that moment put the book back on the rack, stepped out of the store and headed her way.

"Jake!" The sound of her voice, or maybe the motion of her hand, snagged his attention. She smiled. He scowled, and his gaze shifted past her. He was probably out of sorts because he'd driven into the city and was now having to fight his way through a crowd just to get to her. Jake would rather be in the middle of a herd of cows than a herd of people any day.

With a scant two yards separating them, Georgia was all set to fling her arms around Jake's neck when he made an abrupt cut to his right and walked right past her.

She couldn't believe it. When she recovered enough to turn around, all she saw was his broad back disappearing in the crowd. What was going on? Shifting her cosmetics case to her other hand, she brushed at her too-long bangs and started after him, uttering the appropriate apologies as her elbows and bags parted the crowd, like Moses parting the Red Sea.

Her fingers curled around his biceps. She planted her size seven Mary Janes and pulled on his arm with all the strength of her one hundred twenty pounds. "Hey, Jake, didn't you see me?"

Uttering a profanity, he half turned. He looked as if he wanted to kill her. The smile on her lips died.

His attention was focused on someone in the crowd as he said harshly, "I'm not Jake, lady, okay? Now would you please let go of me?"

Georgia was aware of the passing people staring at them, but she was too puzzled by Jake's strange behavior to be embarrassed. Without another word, he jerked his arm free of her hold and walked away.

Her cosmetics case clattered to the floor at her feet. Georgia watched him go, her mouth sagging open in shock. What was the matter with him? Was he drunk?

He wasn't acting like her Jake at all. It was almost as if he was playing a part. The thought echoed through her mind. A sudden understanding dawned.

Jake was pretending not to know her.

She'd heard about couples who got into role-playing, pretending to be someone they weren't to spice up marriages gone stale, but she'd never imagined that Jake Lattimer would be the kind of man to go that far. She wanted different. He'd give her different. More than pleased that she'd underestimated him, Georgia grabbed her makeup case from the floor and started out after him again.

This time she donned a jaunty smile and darted around in front of him. "This is great, Jake!" she said, walking backward through the crowd, heedless of the people in her way.

Jake's purposeful stride faltered, and he stopped in his tracks. Almost snarling, he reached out and took her by the shoulders to set her away from him. He was looking over the top of her head when he spoke. "Look, sunshine, I'm not interested in getting picked up right now. Maybe later, huh? Now get the hell away from—oh, *damn!*"

Before Georgia could do more than register his comments, he took one hand off her shoulder and reached inside his jacket, shoving her aside with the other. She fell against someone, taking him down with her and landing on her hip with a yelp of pain.

Jake glanced down at her for no more than a second before something that sounded like a gunshot jerked his attention away again. Piercing feminine screams and masculine cries and curses filled the air.

What in the world was going on? Georgia wondered, her mind racing wildly. She saw a foot encased in a pointed-toe boot come toward her, and with a shriek of her own, she ducked and covered her head with her arms—too late. The boot found its mark, a fireworks display went off inside her head, and everything went black....

"Come on, precious, open your eyes."

The plea was uttered by a grating feminine voice and was accompanied by sharp stinging on her cheeks. Georgia wanted to comply, but she couldn't seem to get her eyelids to do what her mind was telling them.

"Try the water, Myra. It works every time."

Something wet slapped Georgia in the face. She gasped, and her eyes flew open. Two elderly ladies—one tall and spare, the other short and dumpy—knelt beside her, concerned looks etched on their rumpled faces.

"I told you it would work, Myra," the plump one said with a pleased smile, pressing a dry paper towel into Georgia's hand.

Georgia was too confused to be concerned about the water dripping from her face to her dress. Her questioning look moved from one woman to the other. "What happened?"

"Who knows?" Myra, the tall rescuer, said, getting to her feet and offering her stout friend a helping hand. "Someone shot at someone else, and all hell broke loose—if you'll pardon the expression. There was running, more shooting and some fistfights. When the dust settled, they took four or five guys off in a police car. One man got hurt in all the hubbub. There's an ambulance on the way."

It all came rushing back. "Jake!"

Disregarding the buzzing in her ears and pain in her

head, Georgia struggled to her feet, only to discover that her legs might not hold her. She clutched her head, swaying dizzily.

"Grab her, Ruthie. She's going down!"

Georgia felt an arm go around her waist. "Just take it easy, sweet thing," Ruthie said.

Unable to do anything else, Georgia did as she was commanded. After she drew a few slow breaths, the room steadied. Except for a cluster of peace officers and security guards huddled around a prone figure on the floor and a few lingering gawkers, life in the airport was getting back to normal.

"Thanks," Georgia told the two women. "You've been wonderful."

"Helping is our Christian duty," Myra said.

"Yes. Do unto others," Ruthie quoted with a warm smile and a pat on the hand.

"Who got hurt?" Georgia asked, straining to see beyond the clump of men to the man lying on the floor. Was he wearing a gray sport coat?

"Some Texas Ranger," Myra offered.

A rush of relief brought another wave of weakness. Thank God! It wasn't Jake. But if it wasn't Jake, where was he? Had he lost sight of her during all the scuffle? Was he looking for her?

The arrival of the paramedics interrupted her thoughts. The circle of men moved back, giving the medical team room to maneuver the collapsible gurney closer. For the first time, Georgia had a clear view of the victim. The rugged profile was as familiar to her as her own features.

Myra and Ruthie had been misinformed. That wasn't a Texas Ranger lying there. It was Jake, as still and pale as death. With a whimper of fear, Georgia broke free and pushed her way through the crowd. The paramedics popped up the gurney and started wheeling Jake off to God knows where when she cried, "Wait!"

The medics stopped, and a dozen men turned to stare at her as she ran toward them. A Fort Worth police officer stepped between her and Jake and held up a warning palm. "Stay back, ma'am."

"Stay back? That's my fiancé, and if they're taking him to the hospital, I'm going with him."

"Fiancé? Zach isn't engaged." The comment came from a middle-aged man with jowls who sported the badge of a Texas Ranger.

"His name isn't Zach. It's Jake. Jake Lattimer. And I assure you he is engaged. To me. See?" She held out her left hand. The gaudy emerald-cut diamond flashed in the sunlight.

"So you have a ring. No offense, ma'am," one of the security guards said, "but Pete here could have given you that ring for all I know."

She pointed to Jake. "This man gave me this ring."

"Okay, lady, whatever you say."

"I'm tellin' you, this is Zach Rawlings," Jowls said. "I've known him for at least five years, and he *isn't* engaged. He doesn't even have a steady girlfriend."

Georgia could feel the heat in her cheeks rising along with her anger. What was the matter with these imbeciles? Jake was hurt, and they were standing here arguing with her as if she had no idea what she was talking about.

"For goodness sake, Officers, the woman knows whom she's engaged to!"

Georgia turned and saw that Myra and Ruthie had followed her. The elderly ladies were clearly intrigued by the situation.

"Thank you, Myra," she said.

"Certainly, my dear."

"Do you have a picture of the two of you together?" Ruthie asked. "That should convince them."

"Yes!" Georgia said, smiling her gratitude. As she rummaged in her oversize purse for the photo of her and Jake his dad had taken a few weeks earlier, she tried to explain the mix-up.

"This really is my fiancé. He's just pretending to be someone else," she said, finding the wallet and searching through the plastic sleeves for the right picture. "I told him things between us were getting a little stale…I mean, things just weren't very exciting, you know?"

The law officers swapped raised-eyebrow looks.

Georgia was too wrapped up in what she was doing to notice. "Anyway, I asked him to do something different—something to surprise me and put some spice back into our relationship."

"Hell, lady," the ranger said, "maybe we'd better take you to the hospital with us. To the psycho ward."

Georgia flung him a caustic look and pulled out the picture she was looking for. "Here!" she said with a triumphant smile, waving the photo in front of the doubter's nose.

He looked from the snapshot to Jake and back to Georgia. Passed it to the next man.

"Maybe he's leading a double life," one man suggested with a wide smile.

Jake? A double life? That was laughable. Pretending to be someone else as he had today was a real stretch. He had neither the personality nor the time to pull off a double life-style.

"Looks like the same guy to me."

"Well, it might look like the same guy, but it isn't,"

the ranger said in a voice that said that was the end of it.

"Well, if it isn't the same guy, it's his twin."

"Hey, fellas, I don't care who the guy is," one of the paramedics said. "We've gotta get him to the hospital."

"I'm going with him," Georgia said, crossing her arms, raising her chin and giving them a look that would have made her daddy proud. The ranger's gaze wavered and fell.

"Hell, let her go," he said. "I'll call Will. He's on vacation, but he can get this straightened out."

"I hope someone does," the paramedic said. "Let's roll."

Georgia thanked the two women again, ripped the corner with her name, address and phone number from her checking account deposit slip and told them to call her some time. Then she hurried after Jake before they changed their minds and made her stay behind.

Three hours later, Georgia sat beside Jake's bed, watching him sleep. When they first arrived at the hospital, he'd been whisked off somewhere to be examined, while she'd stayed behind to give the woman in emergency room admissions Jake's pertinent information.

After a little more than an hour, she was told that he had suffered a concussion during the fracas at the airport. He would be fine and could probably go home the next morning, but he'd have to take it easy for a few days. She'd drawn a sigh of relief.

During the interminable hour when she hadn't known the extent of his injuries, she'd been weighed down with tremendous guilt. As she'd prayed, she'd made a deal with God. If He would let Jake be all right, she would never again think of him as boring or inadequate in any way. She would marry him on June fifth and be proud to do so. She'd also promised God that she'd be a good wife and a loving mother to Jake's children.

When she learned that his injuries weren't serious, she'd breathed a sigh of relief and squared her shoulders. God had kept His promise. She'd keep hers.

Assured that Jake was out of danger, she'd caught a cab to the airport, picked up her car and driven to the hospital. It occurred to her that she should call Ben, Jake's father, but she remembered that during her last conversation with Jake, he'd told her that Ben would be in Wyoming visiting his sister for a few days. Since Jake was in no danger, telling Ben about the incident wasn't so pressing. Once she got Jake settled in at the ranch, she would locate his father and let him know what had happened and that everything was okay.

Since her decision an hour ago, time had dragged. She was starving, but her hunger was running a poor second to her weariness. The aftermath of the long flight was beginning to get to her, not to mention the ordeal at the airport and the fact that she had a pretty good sized goose egg on her head. She closed her eyes. She would just sit here and rest for a few minutes, and then she'd go to the cafeteria and see what they had to offer.

A soft groan awakened Georgia. Dusk had crept into the corners of the room while she slept. Automatically, her gaze moved toward the bed. Jake's eyes were open.

Filled with thanksgiving, Georgia pushed herself to her feet. He must have seen the movement out of the corner of his eye. He turned his head toward her with a grimace and another groan. Was it a trick of the light, or was that a question in his dark eyes?

"Hi," she said, urging a brilliant smile to her lips.

Something flickered in Jake's eyes. "Hi."

She leaned over to kiss him, and the woodsy scent he'd worn for years enveloped her. The familiar aroma evoked a plethora of memories from the past, all of them good ones. Blinking against a sudden rush of tears, she lowered her mouth to his. His hand moved to the back of her head, and he returned her kiss with a fervor that left her breathless.

Shaken, she pulled back, her disconcerted gaze meeting his. She didn't recall Jake ever kissing her like that. She certainly didn't remember responding the way she had just now.

It's just relief. They were both grateful that he was all right, that's all. As her mother always said, there was nothing like a crisis to put things into perspective.

"How do you feel?" she asked, hoping the innocent question hid her confusion.

"My head hurts like hell."

Her fingers brushed tenderly at the short hair near his temple. "That's to be expected. They say you took quite a blow."

"What happened?"

"You don't remember?" Her eyebrows drew together in a frown.

He shook his head.

"You don't remember being at the airport?"

"No."

"You don't remember seeing me there?"

He shook his head again.

A disturbing thought crept into her mind. "You don't remember any of it?"

His half smile was as much frightened as it was wry. "Not only don't I remember anything. I don't have the foggiest idea who you are. Or who I am, for that matter."

The next morning after the doctor had made his rounds, Georgia loaded Jake into her car and headed for the Lazy L. He dozed while she drove.

He had amnesia.

Stunned by his startling admission last night, she'd buzzed for the nurses, who summoned the emergency room doctor who'd treated him. The young resident had told her that amnesia was sometimes the result of a blow to the head, or that it could be psychologically induced by seeing something that was too painful to face. He had assured her that it was a temporary condition, that all Jake's tests looked great and that he could go home the next morning as planned. No doubt the familiarity of his surroundings would jog his memory sooner or later.

Sooner would be better than later, as far as she was concerned, so Georgia had spent all of Jake's waking hours telling him about the life he didn't remember. So far, the only things she managed to trigger were more questions and a permanent frown of puzzlement.

Forty minutes after leaving the hospital, Georgia's Ford Taurus bumped over the cattle guard at the gates of the Lazy L. Beside her, Jake eased himself into a sitting position and looked out one window and then the other, clearly fascinated by the grazing cattle, the sprawling Texas-style farmhouse and the half dozen outbuildings that comprised the Lazy L.

"All this is mine?" he asked, his dark eyes filled with astonishment.

"It will be when your daddy dies. You're his only heir."

"Unbelievable."

It was a lot to comprehend, Georgia thought, recalling Ben telling her he owned over four thousand acres and half that many cows.

"It won't be long before you remember everything," she said, smiling at him. "And if you don't, you'll get the hang of it soon enough."

"If you say so."

"You will. The doctor says that even though you've forgotten some things, you'll remember a lot, like how to ride a horse...things like that."

Jake didn't say anything else, and in a couple of minutes, she pulled into the circle drive and stopped in front of the house. She opened her door and got out, rounding the front of the car to help Jake, who was still a little shaky on his feet.

She had just slammed the car door shut when the front door of the house burst open and a big, burly man stormed down the front porch steps.

Georgia stopped, and her mouth fell open.

"Where the hell have you been, Georgia Lee? I've been worried sick!" Without waiting for her answer, he continued. "You were supposed to be home last night, damn it! You could have at least called. I suppose it would be too much to..."

Georgia couldn't have answered if her life depended on it. She wasn't even listening. Stunned beyond words, beyond coherent thought, she looked from the man bearing down on her, blood in his eye. Her fiancé, Jake.

Then she looked to the man whose arm she was holding. Her fiancé, Jake?

Chapter Two

The man who'd just come from the house and was giving her what for, the same man who'd given her the diamond engagement ring, the same man Georgia had thought was boring, pulled up short, both verbally and physically, when he saw the man standing beside her. His rugged face wore a look of stunned disbelief, an emotion Georgia was fast becoming familiar with.

She cast another look at the man she'd seen at the airport and mistaken for Jake, the man everyone said was a Texas Ranger, the man who had kissed her until she was dizzy....

Even though he had no memory, his face wore a curious expression. He might not remember who he was, but he wasn't stupid. He'd shaved before they left the hospital, and he had to be aware that he and the man standing on the flagstone sidewalk were more than look-alikes.

"What the hell?"

"What's going on?"

Uncannily, the deep husky tenor of their voices even sounded alike.

"Oh...my...gosh." Georgia added her own wonder to the stunned and somewhat disgruntled queries that couldn't begin to express the shock that held them all in a tightfisted grip.

As she looked again from one man to the other, she remembered one of the men at the airport saying that if the picture she'd showed them wasn't Jake it was his twin.

Twins? Impossible! Everyone knew Jake was Ben and Retha Lattimer's only son and that he'd been born just weeks before Ben bought the first parcel of land outside Aledo that would eventually become the Lazy L. But if they *weren't* twins, what other logical explanation was there?

It wasn't just that the two men looked a lot alike. They were identical. They were the same height, and they had the same muscular, rangy frame with the wide shoulders that gave them a deceptively burly look. Their hair was the same thickness, the same color, so close to black a crow couldn't tell the difference. They wore it the same way, cut short and parted on the same side. Their eyes were the same hue of brown. Their eyebrows arched at the same place. They both sported thick mustaches over beautifully shaped mouths that had been carved by the same master sculptor.

"Who is this, Georgia Lee?" The irritation in the voice of the Jake who'd given her the expensive diamond ring sliced through her mental comparison. "What the hell's going on?"

"It's you," she said, and immediately realized how

ridiculous the explanation sounded. "I mean, I thought it was you when I saw him at the airport."

"Why on earth did you think it was me? I told you I couldn't make it." His voice held a definite edge.

"I know, but when I saw you—him—and he was dressed differently I thought—" her face turned pink "—that maybe you'd had second thoughts about our conversation the night before I left."

This time it was Jake who turned pink. "So you just latched on to a total stranger and brought him here because he looked like me?"

"Not because he looked like you, because I thought he *was* you."

"He didn't bother to tell you any different?"

"We didn't have a chance to talk. I was trying to get through the crowd, but there was a police...sting, I guess you could call it, and you got hurt. I mean *he* got hurt. But I thought it was you," she hastened to add again.

A sound from the man at her side drew her attention. No help there. He was glancing back and forth from her to the other Jake, looking more at a loss than ever. And if that hint of gray lurking beneath his tan and the perspiration dotting his temples were any indication, he also looked ready to pass out.

Jake crossed his arms over his chest and jerked his head toward his other self. "Does he talk?" he asked with studied sarcasm.

Georgia nibbled on her lower lip. "Not much."

As if the question were a cue, the man at her side, the man she now supposed must really be a Texas Ranger, asked, "Can we go inside? My head is splitting."

Jake looked none too pleased by the request but was

too much a Texas gentleman to turn away an injured animal, much less a human being who was his spitting image. "Sure," he said. "Come on in."

Georgia and her charge followed him inside, through the wide hallway, more commonly known as a dogtrot to Southerners and Texans. To the left, they entered the spacious, Western-style living room with its massive oak and brick fireplace, its worn burgundy leather couches and the colorful turtle-themed pillows. Native American rugs covered the pegged hardwood floor. The walls were smooth stucco, painted a creamy white. Howard Turpning paintings shared the walls with a Remington and a Russell or two. It was a homey, masculine room that had tapped into the Southwest look long before that decorating scheme became vogue. On the Lazy L, the look of the West was a way of life, not a fad.

Georgia directed Jake's look-alike to the sofa while Jake paced, casting the stranger covert, curious glances. Jake number two—*Zach*—closed his eyes and leaned his head back.

"I see Georgia's back and brought company."

The cheerful observation came from Rosalita, Jake's thirty-something housekeeper, who entered the room with a wide smile. She and her husband, Ernesto, lived in the servants' quarters at the back of the house. Ernesto took care of the landscaping and outdoor maintenance. Rosalita took care of Ben and Jake.

"Hi, Rosalita," Georgia said, smiling. "You're looking particularly happy this morning."

"I just found out I aced my English test." Rosalita aspired to getting a teaching degree and was taking classes in Fort Worth two mornings a week.

"Wonderful! How's Leza?" Georgia asked.

Leza was Rosalita and Ernesto's four-year-old daughter. She was a beautiful, brown-skinned child with huge dark eyes surrounded by sinfully long eyelashes—a gift from her mother—and a mane of ebony curls she inherited from her father.

"She's great," Rosalita said. "Growing like a..." Her voice trailed away when the man lounging in the corner of the sofa lifted his head and turned to look at her.

"Madre de Dios!" she said, making the sign of the cross and looking from one man to the other.

"Unbelievable, isn't it, Rosie?" Jake said.

"What's going on, Jake?"

"That's what we're trying to establish. Do you mind showing Georgia's new friend to the guest room? He looks a little under the weather. And make a fresh pot of coffee, will you? I have a feeling it's going to be a long morning."

"Sure thing, Jake," Rosalita said. "Sir, if you'll come this way...."

"Thanks, Rosalita," Georgia said, as the man beside her pushed to his feet. "And his name is Zach...I think."

After the two disappeared, Jake pinned Georgia with a hard look. "Well?"

"Well, what?"

"I believe we've established the fact that your friend isn't me. Before he almost fainted on us, you were about to explain why he hadn't bothered to tell you that himself."

Georgia twisted her fingers together in her lap. This was getting worse by the minute. "He didn't tell me because he doesn't know. He has amnesia."

The inquiry in Jake's eyes made a quick transformation to disbelief. He closed his eyes briefly, shook his head and eased down in the worn chair next to the fireplace. "Amnesia? From getting hurt at the airport, I presume." She nodded. "Do you have any idea who he is?"

"Zach something. At least that's what the Texas Ranger at the airport said. He also said that Zach is a ranger, too."

"If that guy knew who he—" Jake jerked his thumb toward the guest room where the stranger had been taken "—was, why on earth did he let you bring him here?"

"Because I wouldn't listen," Georgia admitted, guilt settling over her like a shroud. This wasn't the first time her impulsiveness had landed her in hot water. Seeing the look in Jake's eyes, she drew on her best defense. "You saw him. If you'd been in my place, wouldn't you draw the same conclusion I did?"

Jake scraped a big hand down his face.

"Why don't you back up and start at the beginning," he suggested. "Maybe once I have a handle on what happened, we can figure out what to do next."

While Georgia did her best to explain to Jake what had happened at the airport, the man with no memory lay in the guest room of the Lazy L, trying to ignore the pain throbbing in his head and battling a growing panic.

He had no recollection of anything Georgia had told him about the events that had transpired the previous afternoon and didn't recall any part of the accident that had knocked him silly. His last memory was of a bright, sunny smile, the same smile he'd seen on Georgia Williams's face when he awakened at the hospital.

Georgia, the woman who'd told him she was his fiancée when he said he didn't remember anything.

He felt out of touch, strangely empty. The past was a void. The present was comprised of a series of revelations that became more bizarre by the moment. The future was...well, incomprehensible. How could he contemplate going ahead when he had no idea where he'd been?

All he knew about himself was what Georgia had told him, which had been frightening enough. But now, to add to his general confusion, he'd learned that everything she said was untrue.

If he wasn't Jake, who was he? Georgia had told him about the ranger at the airport who said he was a Texas Ranger, too, and when he'd dressed that morning, he'd found a badge in his jacket pocket that verified the ranger part. But Georgia had been so *sure* he was Jake and that he was role-playing that he'd bought into it. He'd clung to her certainty like a talisman. After all, if the story the ranger told was true, wouldn't he remember something about that part of his life?

When he tried to concentrate on Texas Rangers and what it must be like to be one, all that came to mind was the name Chuck Norris. He didn't have the slightest notion who Norris was, but surely if he remembered the name there must be some connection to Texas Rangers. Maybe Chuck was a friend or a superior.

He sighed. It was more than unsettling to wake up with no memory of who you were and then arrive at the place you'd been told was home, only to find out that an angry man who could be your twin was really the man you were supposed to be, and everything you'd heard about your life was his life, not yours—

including the woman with the mouth as soft as a butterfly's kiss!

That, he realized, was the hardest blow of all. In some way he didn't understand, he'd gotten attached to the talkative woman with the sunny smile. He didn't mind not owning the ranch and the cattle. But whenever he thought of the kiss they'd shared in the hospital—which was more often than was comfortable—he felt a pang of sorrow to realize that she wouldn't be marrying him at all. Georgia would be marrying the real Jake....

"What do you think we should do about him?" Georgia asked Jake when she'd finished her tale.

Jake shook his head, which still spun with disbelief. "He can stay here until we figure out who he is, I guess. If I were you, I'd start calling ranger headquarters and see if they're missing a man. It shouldn't take long." Frowning, he smoothed his forefinger down the corner of his mustache. "I can't believe they didn't send someone to the hospital."

Georgia winced slightly. "Maybe they were looking for him but couldn't find him," she suggested, her glance skittering away from his.

"Why wouldn't they find him?" Though he asked the question, Jake was afraid to hear her answer.

"I told them he was you and gave them this address and everything."

Jake shook his head. That was just like her. Georgia was one to leap before she looked. "You'd better get on the phone," he suggested. "He probably has family worried about him."

Her eyes widened with dismay. "I hadn't thought about that."

Knowing she'd worry herself sick over the mess she'd made of things, Jake tried to ease her mind. "I'm sure his people will understand the mix-up. He should be back with them by this afternoon at the latest."

Georgia nodded and raised her troubled gaze to his. "What are you going to do about him?"

"What do you mean?" Jake asked, even though he had a sneaking suspicion he knew what was coming next.

"What are you going to do about the fact that the man lying in your guest room is you made over?"

He shrugged. "Coincidence. They say everyone has a double."

"Coincidence! Jake, that man doesn't just look like you, he could be you. I can't see *anything* different about the two of you. You even sound alike. How do you explain that?"

Jake chewed on the corner of his mustache. She was right, but he had no answers for her, none that made sense, anyway. "What do you make of it?" he asked instead.

She sighed. "I don't know. I mean, if I had to guess, I'd say that you're identical twins, but that doesn't fly, because everyone knows you're Ben's only child. Unless you were adopted," she added, almost as an afterthought.

"Adopted! Are you crazy?" Jake said.

"Well, the only other scenario that comes to mind is that he saw you, wanted your inheritance, had years of plastic surgery to make himself into your image so he can knock you off and take up your life."

Jake felt the heat of indignation in his cheeks. "That's ridiculous!"

"Exactly," Georgia said, her voice as gentle as his

mother's had been when she'd been trying to explain a tough concept to him. She rose from her place on the sofa and went to him, sliding her arms around his waist and looking into his troubled eyes. "You need to call your daddy and tell him what's happened, Jake. Maybe there's something about your past he and Retha never told you."

At Jake's insistence, Georgia contacted ranger headquarters and found out that yes, indeed, they were missing a ranger, one Zach Rawlings, who'd been hurt during the incident at the airport the day before.

Certain that the woman who'd latched on to him was crazy, no one had paid any attention to the name she'd used when she'd tried to convince them that Zach was her fiancé. By the time Will James, Rawlings's partner, had been called back from his fishing trip on Toledo Bend to set things straight, Zach Rawlings had disappeared. Not a hospital in the Dallas/Fort Worth area had any record of him having come through their emergency room.

By the time the older ranger had slept on it and finally remembered the name of her fiancé, he was long gone from the hospital. Headquarters assured her that Will James would drive out to the ranch that evening to verify Zach's identity.

Georgia hung up, thankful that at least one part of the mystery was all but solved, but a bit sorry that Zach Rawlings would soon be gone.

At Georgia's insistence, Jake dialed his aunt's number in Wyoming while Georgia helped Rosalita with lunch. He thought her idea about him being adopted was the height of lunacy, but since he couldn't offer any explanation for the uncanny resemblance between him and Zach Rawlings, he had little choice but to humor her.

Like she said, all it would take was one short phone call to set everyone's mind at ease—hers, anyway. He might not know why the man in the downstairs guest room looked like him, but he did know that Ben and Retha Lattimer were his real parents.

Just hearing his dad's gruff voice made Jake feel better. Ben Lattimer was rock solid, salt of the earth, qualities that everyone said he'd inherited. `

"Good to hear from you, son," Ben said. "What's going on down there? Did Georgia make it back from France?"

"Yes, sir," Jake said, "but something really strange happened at the airport."

"Oh?"

Without further ado, Jake related Georgia's tale of what had happened to her after her plane landed. He finished by saying, "Evidently this guy's name is Zach Rawlings, and he's a Texas Ranger. One of his buddies is coming out late this evening to get him."

"And he looks a lot like you?" Ben asked.

"More than a lot. He's a dead ringer. Two peas in a pod. Spout a cliché, it fits."

"And he has no memory of who he is?"

"He claims he can't remember a thing."

"That's strange," Ben said. Something about the thoughtful note in his voice set alarm bells off in Jake's head.

"It's worse than strange. The whole thing is downright spooky." Then, subtly—he hoped—Jake dropped Georgia's little bomb. "Georgia says he's either some guy who's had plastic surgery so he can knock me off and take my place as your heir, or he's my twin. I told her you and Mom ought to know if you'd had twins.''

Jake laughed at the absurdity of the thought.

Ben didn't.

Jake heard a sigh. "Dad?"

"Stranger things than what Georgia has suggested happen every day," Ben said. "And there are a lot of wackos out there. I don't know who this man is, but I should come help you sort this all out. I'll be on the next plane home.''

Jake heard an unfamiliar heaviness in his dad's voice, and something else he couldn't put his finger on. Suspicion? Regret? Whatever it was, Ben sounded old and tired, suddenly.

"Don't cut your trip short because of this," Jake said. "It'll wait.''

"I don't think so," Ben said. Then, before Jake could reply, Ben hung up, leaving his only son filled with an unaccountable apprehension and wondering what the heck he was talking about.

Ben Lattimer pulled into the circle drive of the Lazy L late that afternoon, dreading the next hours, the next days.

When Jake had called him earlier and told him what had happened, Ben's mood and his heart had gone into a downhill spiral. He'd dodged this particular bullet long enough. The time had come to tell Jake the truth.

Ben's chest tightened. How could he tell Jake, the son he loved more than life, that the mother who had given birth to him on that rainy night in August wasn't Retha, but some teenager who'd gotten herself in trouble? How did you tell the son who looked up to you and trusted you that you'd lied to him for thirty-five years?

Ben knew he ought to have told Jake the truth years ago when his emotions were more resilient, but Retha hadn't wanted Jake to know the truth. Babies born out of wedlock weren't as commonplace back then, and adoptions were less standard. Retha had been afraid that the other kids would make fun of Jake if they knew, and, out of respect for her wishes, Ben had gone against his own better judgment.

But Retha had died ten years ago, and since then, Ben had no excuse for not telling Jake that he had been part of a private adoption in Brownsboro, Texas, that had been handled by a young attorney named Tom Barnette.

Now, with the advent of this stranger into their lives, the option of when and how to break the news to Jake had been taken from him. He should have known that the past would sneak up and bite them on the butt, as his daddy used to tell him, but Texas was a big place, and he and Retha had gambled on the chance that anyone or anything connected to that night would be swallowed up in the vastness of the state.

Ben wondered how the man Georgia had mistaken for Jake was related to his son and suspected that this Zach fella was an unknown relative with a strong family resemblance...maybe even a brother. Jake's biological mother had given birth to him at a young age, so it seemed only natural to assume that she'd have borne other children later.

With a heavy heart, Ben pulled the Jeep to a stop and went inside, sweeping the cowboy hat from his salt-and-pepper head as he stepped through the front door.

He heard voices in the living room and heaved a sigh of regret. He'd arrived too late to have a talk with Jake first. His Stetson in hand, Ben stepped through the doorway, his all-encompassing glance taking in the room's occupants. Georgia sat on the sofa. A stranger with a look of authority sat in the chair by the fireplace. One tall, dark-haired man stood in front of the fireplace. The other stood by the window.

Waves of disbelief eddied through Ben. Jake and the newcomer definitely shared more than just a striking resemblance—they'd been stamped from the same mold. It was Jake at the fireplace. He recognized him instantly, but only, he knew, because he wore his usual faded Wranglers and Zach Rawlings wore slacks.

The stranger who looked as if he were used to taking charge looked curious. Jake looked worried and irritated. The man who resembled Jake looked wary, uneasy, much the way Ben felt. Everyone in the room stared at him, waiting for him to say something—anything—that might shed a little light on the matter.

What he said was, "Dear God!"

Jake strode across the room, his hand outstretched, his eyes filled with turmoil, questions and a hint of anxiety. "Welcome home, Dad."

Ben used his son's outstretched hand to pull him into a brief, hard hug. It seemed imperative that he touch Jake—for both their sakes—to reassure himself that whatever this upset meant, nothing between them had changed and never would.

After Georgia hugged Ben, Jake introduced him to the other two men. The tall one by the fireplace was Will James, a Texas Ranger and Zach's partner, a man with a firm handshake and a direct, appraising look.

The man who, with a change of clothes, could pass

for his son was introduced as Ranger Zach Rawlings. The firm grip of his hand felt familiar in Ben's. Jake's hand. Zach's eyes were the same color as Jake's, the same shape. These eyes, too, held turmoil, questions…anxiety. Ben's heart constricted. Just as he'd wanted to reassure Jake, he now felt compelled to reassure Jake's twin.

Jake's twin. Without a doubt—though God only knew how it had come about—Ben knew instinctively that this man was indeed his son's twin. He felt a sudden pang of sorrow. Somehow, for some unknown reason, he'd been robbed of the opportunity to have two sons. Without conscious thought, he took Zach Rawlings's hand between both of his, giving it a reassuring squeeze. "Hello, Zach."

Surprise flickered in Rawlings's eyes.

"Sir."

Introductions over, everyone again looked to Ben, who cleared his throat and addressed Will James. "You know this man?"

"Yes, sir." James's gaze moved from one person in the room to another as he said, "His name is Zachariah Roman Rawlings. He's thirty-five years old. He's been a ranger and my partner for four years. Prior to that he was a detective with the Dallas PD. I tried getting hold of his former partner, hoping that seeing her would jog his memory, but she's involved with an undercover case and couldn't get away without stirring up suspicion."

Zach Rawlings's face wore an expression of fierce intensity, almost as if he was grappling with what he was hearing and struggling not only to remember but to make some sense of it.

"Any family?" Ben asked.

"Never been married." He looked at Georgia. "No fiancée. His mother died when he was fourteen. His dad drives a truck. Zach doesn't see much of him. From what little I've been told, I gathered they don't have a very good relationship."

"Did he ever mention having any siblings?"

"No, sir. He said he was an only child, but any fool can see that he and your son are identical twins, so it's clear that he was lied to for some reason," Will James said, aiming an accusatory look at Ben.

Ben frowned. "What are you getting at?"

James gestured toward Jake. "Is this your son?"

"It certainly is," Ben said.

"Well, then, if Jake is your son, then it's pretty obvious that Zach is, too."

Georgia gasped. Zach Rawlings squeezed his eyes shut. Ben looked gray beneath his tan. Jake swore.

"Are you implying that my parents had twins and gave one of them up?" Jake asked, his jaw set at a belligerent angle.

"Look, I know I have the subtlety of a bulldozer," Will James said, "but what we have here is pretty clear, at least to me." He gestured from one to the other. "Look at the two of you. I'll bet my pension that a blood test will prove beyond a doubt that you're twins, which means that either Zach's parents *or* Mr. Lattimer here gave up one child." He looked at Ben. "I guess your dad's the only one who knows the truth."

Jake had thought of little else all afternoon, and, since his dad had acted so strangely on the phone, he suspected James was right. But acknowledging that possibility brought up a whole set of new problems and questions he didn't want to contemplate.

Every eye turned to Ben, who looked directly at Jake and blurted, "Your mother and I adopted you."

The dull throb of pain that had been festering inside of Jake ever since Georgia had suggested that probability earlier in the day burst into a million shards of agony.

"Why?" Jake asked in a hoarse voice.

Ben crossed the few feet that separated them and put his hand on his son's shoulder. Too shocked to do anything else, Jake just stood there.

"Because your mother couldn't have any children, and she wanted one so badly. I know I should have told you sooner," Ben said, his voice quivering with nervousness and emotion, "but Retha didn't want you to know, and after she died, I never could seem to find the right words or the right time to tell you. The truth is, I hardly ever think about it."

"Why didn't you take us both?" Jake finally managed to mumble from dry lips.

Ben's eyes found Zach's briefly. "If I'd known there were two of you, I would have. But I didn't know."

"Will the real Zach Rawlings please stand up?" Zach said, doing just that.

Jake glanced at him in surprise. Rawlings hadn't said two dozen words all day, but now the man who might be his twin brother crossed the room and looked him square in the eye. The mouth so like Jake's own twisted into a wry smile. Jake saw his own pain reflected in the ranger's eyes.

"Look at the good side, hoss. At least you know who you are." Zach held his arms wide. "Look at me. I wake up from something I don't remember and find a pretty woman who says she's my fiancée standing over me. She tells me I'm Jake Lattimer, heir to a vast Texas empire with a wonderful father who loves me.

"I come here, find out I'm not Jake, I don't own any of this, I don't have a father who loves me, and I'm not engaged to the pretty woman after all. To cap that off, I find out that the mother I don't even remember isn't my mother. Talk about an identity crisis. I don't have any idea who the hell I am."

"No one said your mother gave you up," Jake said.

"No, but it doesn't make sense any other way. Why the heck would she just give up one of us, huh, hoss? Answer me that."

Shortly after Zach had added his two cents worth to the afternoon's revelations, the discussion ended. There was too much to think about. Too many questions to be answered. The problem was that everyone was afraid to voice those questions or hear the answers. Emotions were too close to the surface. Hearts were too raw.

After learning that there was no one to keep an eye on Zach while he recuperated, Ben had insisted—over Zach's objections—that he stay on as a guest at the Lazy L. Feeling that his friend and partner was in good hands, Will James had gone to finish his vacation, promising to check in on Zach in a couple of days.

Ben had told Jake he'd like a word with him after Georgia went home, and then he'd escorted Zach to the guest room, requesting Rosalita to fetch some of Jake's clothes so their guest could freshen up.

While Ben was seeing to Zach's comfort, Georgia and Jake walked down the long lane that led to the barn.

"He should have told me," Jake said, anger momentarily overcoming the pain.

"Probably," Georgia said, "but you have to remember that people weren't as open about illegitimacy and adoptions thirty-five years ago as they are today. Your mom and dad had their reasons for not telling you, and you owe it to your father to listen to those reasons."

"Oh, I owe it to him, do I?" Jake snapped. "Why? For adopting me?" He turned away and rested his forearms on the top rail of the corral fence.

Georgia put her hand on his shoulder. "No," she told him in a soft voice. "For loving you. For being a wonderful dad all these years. No *real* father could have loved you more than Ben Lattimer, and you darn well know it!"

Jake didn't answer for several seconds. "What kind of woman gives away her child? Her *children?*" he asked after several silent moments.

"Your mother probably wasn't a woman at all. She was probably a frightened young girl who got in trouble. Maybe her parents wouldn't let her keep you and Zach. Maybe she was poor and knew you'd have better lives with other people."

"The little bit Will James told us about Zach's life didn't sound too great," Jake said. "A father he seldom sees and no mother after the age of fourteen...."

"Then you were the lucky twin, weren't you?" Georgia said gently. "You got Ben and Retha."

"Why don't I feel lucky?" Jake said, turning to her and drawing her into a close embrace.

"Because you're hurt. Finding out you were adopted the way you did would knock the props out from under anyone. But you aren't a kid with a kid's emotional quotient. You're a man, old enough to understand all

the nuances of a situation like this. Old enough to understand the *whys*. And you're a strong enough man to
sort through it, deal with it, and get on with your life.''

"You've got a lot of faith in me.''

"I've known you a long time, remember?'' Georgia
said, smiling at him. "You're a good man, Jake Lattimer. A fair man. It might take you a little while, but
you'll come out of this a richer person.''

"How do you figure that?''

"Look at Zach. He's lost everything, even his memories of the people who raised him. You've still got a
father who loves you, memories of a mother who
thought you hung the moon—'' her arm made a wide
arc toward the grazing cattle "—all this.'' She looked
at him and smiled gently. "And today it looks like you
finally got the brother you always wanted.''

"I hate that you had to hear about the adoption the
way you did,'' Ben said to Jake at the dinner table that
night.

Knowing the two of them needed to talk, Georgia
had declined Ben's invitation to stay and had gone
home. Unfortunately, thankfully, the afternoon had
taken its emotional toll on Zach, who had requested his
dinner in his room.

"I'm sorry I had to hear it at all.'' Jake heard the
coolness in his voice.

"So am I. But I want you to know that your mother
and I never set out to deliberately lie to you. All we
ever wanted was your happiness. She felt that keeping
your adoption a secret was the best course to take. She
didn't want other kids making fun of you.''

Jake nodded. Knowing his mother, that explanation

was plausible, acceptable, but it lessened his pain only a little. "How did it happen?"

Jake saw tears in his dad's eyes. "I knew your mother had a congenital heart condition when I married her, but it didn't matter. I loved that woman more than anything." Ben shot him an apologetic look. "Don't take what I'm about to say wrong, son, but I loved her so much I could have been happy with just her."

He sighed. "She wanted a baby, but her heart condition made pregnancy a risk we didn't feel we could take. You remember how frail she was. But she *ached* for a baby. I guess as a sort of compensation, she started collecting those baby dolls that are all over her sitting room." Ben's mouth slanted in a wry grin. "Even after we got you, she kept on buying those damned dolls.

"Anyway, a couple of years before you were born, I'd gotten myself a young lawyer named Tom Barnette—"

"The same Tom Barnette who's running for senator?" Jake asked. "The same one who cheated you on that insurance deal?"

"The same," Ben said. "Retha and I had a little spread up near Brownsboro then, but the oil money was rolling in, and we were looking for a bigger place in this area. As a matter of fact, we bought the piece of land this house is sitting on while we were waiting for you to be born, and we moved here a week or so after we adopted you."

Jake had heard this part of the tale before. "What did Barnette have to do with me?"

"Your mother and I saw Barnette and his wife socially a few times, and he found out we wanted a child. He handled some private adoptions back then—you know, a financially sound family takes on some young woman's medical bills in exchange for the baby when he's born. It's a lot more common now than it was back then. It saves both parties a lot of heartache and a lot of time."

Jake nodded. "Go on."

"One day Tom suggested that Retha and I consider adoption as an option. After a lot of discussion, we agreed to be put on his list."

"Did you ever meet the girl?"

"No. Back then, there was no looking each other over to decide if you liked each other. There sure as heck wasn't any of this keeping in touch with the birth mother and granting her visiting rights, the way they do nowadays." Ben raked a hand through his hair. "I'm not sure which way is best."

Until now, Jake hadn't given it a moment's thought. But he would.

A reminiscent smile curved Ben's mouth. "I'll never forget when that pretty nurse came down to the waiting room and told us we had a baby boy. Your mother and I were thrilled. She'd convinced me that a child, especially a son, would enhance our lives, not become a wedge to drive us apart."

He met Jake's gaze squarely. "She was right. You were a joy from the first minute we set eyes on you. You've been everything a man could want in a son." Ben's eyes filled with tears. "You've always been a source of pride and joy to me, Jake, and no matter how we got you, in my mind and my heart, you're my son."

Chapter Three

Too emotionally undone to face an empty house, unpacking dirty clothes and tackling a mountain of laundry, Georgia bypassed her street and drove across town to her friend Carrie Adair's house.

She and Carrie had grown up together, roomed together in college and had maintained a close friendship even though Carrie had married fellow teacher Denton Adair six years ago. She and her friend now taught at different schools—Carrie at Aledo High, and Georgia at a private girls' school in Fort Worth.

With his gentle teasing manner and sometimes exasperating habit of looking at life as though it were one big cosmic joke, Denton, the school's beloved coach, was the perfect match for pragmatic Carrie, who taught algebra and trigonometry and took worry to the nth degree. She kept his feet on the ground. He often coaxed her into letting go and flying.

Georgia was barely out of the car when the assault began.

"Where the devil have you been? You were *supposed* to be home yesterday. Do you realize how worried we've been? I was about to call the cops!"

It was déjà vu all over again, only this time it wasn't Jake bursting through the front door and reading her the riot act, it was Carrie.

"Hi, Carrie, I'm glad to see you, too," Georgia said, putting her arms around her friend's stiff shoulders and giving her a brief hug.

Carrie's anger left her with a deep whooshing sigh, just as Georgia knew it would. She jerked her head toward the house. "I suppose it's another of your long stories. Come on in. Denton's had a brisket on the smoker for about ten hours, and you look like you could use something."

Georgia's stomach rumbled at the very mention of food. She'd been too uptight to eat much of the lunch Rosalita had prepared for them.

"Sounds great," Georgia said, following Carrie inside.

"Where have you been?" Carrie asked, taking up the hue and cry again. "I've been worried sick!"

"I've been at Jake's most of the day."

"Jake's!" Carrie squeaked. "Why didn't one of you call and tell me? When I didn't hear from you, I called him late last night, and he said he hadn't heard from you, either. We agreed to keep in touch."

"It must have slipped his mind."

Carrie looked at her as if she'd grown another head. The day anything slipped Jake's mind was the day hell would freeze over. "Jake's had quite a day."

Instead of commenting on the incongruity of the

statement, Carrie said, "When I found out your flight had landed and none of us knew where you were, I thought you'd been kidnapped or something."

Georgia bestowed a wan smile on her friend. "Actually, I did the kidnapping."

Carrie's eyes grew round with surprise. "Come again?"

Georgia gave another weary smile, knowing she'd have to tell her tale one more time. "It's a long story," she said as they entered a sunny kitchen decorated with green plants, sunflowers and deep cobalt accents. "Can we eat first?"

Something in Georgia's manner must have transmitted itself to Carrie. She nodded. "Sure."

"Where's Megan?"

"Out back with her dad," Carrie said, pulling a head of lettuce from the crisper drawer. She shoved it into Georgia's hands and gave her a gentle push toward the sink. "Salad," she said. "And hurry. I'm dying to hear this."

An hour later, Georgia sat at the Adairs' small kitchen table, looking from one disbelieving face to the other.

"You're putting us on, right?" Carrie said.

"'Fraid not. I guess you see why Jake didn't call and let you know I'd shown up."

"He did have more important things on his mind," Denton said. "So where is this Zach Rawlings guy now?"

"Ben insisted that he stay at the ranch until he remembers who he is, thank goodness." Georgia had been worried about him ever since the truth had come out. "I hated to think of him all alone with no idea of who he was, no family...nothing and no one to give him comfort.''

The sudden image of her holding Zach close and kissing the bump on his forehead drifted through her mind. The notion was tender and provocative and...wrong!

The picture vanished with the sudden surge of her heartbeats. Heat flooded her face. How could she be so disloyal to Jake? Just because Zach's kiss stirred her in a way Jake's never had didn't mean she should allow herself to indulge in traitorous—dangerous—fantasies. Hadn't she promised God that if He would only let Jake be all right, basically she'd never question her feelings or her marriage?

But it wasn't Jake who was injured at the airport. It was really Zach.

That was a trivial detail, she reminded her conscience. She'd *thought* it was Jake, and a promise was a promise, especially one made to God.

''Georgia? Are you all right?'' Carrie asked.

''I'm fine, why?''

''I asked you a question and you didn't answer. You just got all red in the face.''

''I'm sorry,'' Georgia said. She'd have to be more careful of allowing her thoughts to show around Carrie. Her longtime friend knew her like a book and had been known on the rare occasion to actually read her mind. ''What was it you wanted to know?''

''How long will Zach be at the ranch?''

''Who knows? I can't see him functioning too well on his own until he does remember. I mean, how could he do his job? Besides, I think he and Jake really ought to get to know each other.''

"You're assuming they are twins, then?" Carrie asked.

"If you saw them, you'd believe it, too. Physically, they're so much alike it's uncanny. But inside—emotionally—I suspect they're worlds apart."

"With the difference in their backgrounds, I'd say that's a safe presumption," Denton observed.

As if she hadn't heard her husband, Carrie asked, "How do you mean?"

"I don't know, exactly, but I get the feeling that Zach is more..." Georgia's voice trailed away and she shrugged. "I don't know...more passionate, maybe."

Carrie looked into Georgia's eyes for long seconds. "Denton," she said at last, "be a dear and put Megan to bed, will you?"

"Carrie!" Georgia cried, knowing it was too late, that Carrie had already picked up on *something* and wouldn't let it be until she'd picked Georgia's brain for every feeling she'd experienced during the time she was with Zach.

"Ah, I see a grueling fourth degree in your future," Denton said to Georgia as he pushed back his chair. "Given a choice between listening to you beg for mercy and telling Megan the story of the three bears for the ten thousandth time, the furry guys win hands down."

"Denton Adair!"

His massive shoulders lifted. "I love you, babe, but when you get that look in your eyes..." He shook his head and let the implication speak for itself.

Leaning over, he kissed the top of Georgia's head and offered her a thin smile. "Glad you're home safe and sound, kiddo," he said, giving her a brotherly pat on the shoulder. "Call me if she gets too rough. I've been known to wrestle her to the ground on occasion."

"Denton Adair, you can kiss where I can't!" Carrie said with an indignant huff. "I'm not *that* bad."

"My pleasure, Mrs. Adair," he said with a lecherous grin. "And, yes, you are." He grinned at Georgia and lifted Megan from her booster seat onto his shoulders. "Tell Mommy and Auntie George good-night, Meggie."

"'Night, Mommy. 'Night, Auntie George," Megan chimed, blowing them both a kiss.

Carrie and Georgia—who'd been dubbed Auntie George when Megan first started talking—bade the three-year-old good-night and threw kisses back.

As soon as her husband and daughter disappeared from the room, Carrie shook her head. "That man!"

"Is a wonderful man who loves you very much."

"Of course he does," Carrie said as if that were a given. "And the feeling is mutual. But that doesn't stop me from wanting to punch him in the nose sometimes." She shook her head again, sighed in resignation and pinned Georgia with a penetrating look. "Okay, now tell me what's up."

"I have no idea what you're talking about."

"You lie so poorly, Georgia," Carrie said brutally. "I can't imagine why you waste your time doing it with me, so save us both a lot of time and tell me what's going on with you and this Zach guy."

"Nothing's going on!"

"Well, there's more to this than you're telling me, that's for sure. What did he do, make a pass at you?"

"No!" Georgia's denial was sharp, emphatic. The look in Carrie's eyes said she didn't believe her for a moment and that if Georgia didn't fess up it would be a long night.

"Okay, okay," Georgia said. "He kissed me. Or I kissed him. I don't know which." Carrie's expression was inscrutable. "But it was when he was in the hospital and I thought he was Jake."

"That's understandable," Carrie almost cooed. "Under the circumstances, a kiss isn't anything to get your panties in a wad about."

Relief flooded Georgia. She smiled broadly. "That's what I've been trying to tell you."

"What does concern me is what exactly happened during that kiss. Now come on, tell me everything."

Dusk was creeping over the rolling landscape when Jake finished feeding the dogs and went to the barn to water off his prize mare that was due to foal in another four weeks or so. She was a registered quarter mare, and a hell of a cutting horse. He'd been offered a small fortune for her. Her foal should be worth a lot, too, if he could get it on the ground without any mishaps. Through the years, Jake had seen plenty of things go wrong bringing foals into the world.

Lucy, named after Lucille Ball because of her sorrel color, whickered softly as he let himself into the stall to top off her water bucket. She nuzzled his shirtfront, blowing softly. Laughing, he rubbed her silky nose and took a couple of sugar cubes from his shirt pocket. She lipped the treat from his palm, then rolled back her lips to show him her teeth and nodded, as if to give him her approval.

Laughing again, Jake moved to her side and ran expert hands over her ponderous belly. The foal moved beneath his palms, and Lucy whipped her head around to nip at her side, almost knocking him over in the process.

"It won't be long now," he said, giving her a final pat and letting himself out of the stall.

He was latching the mesh metal door when he realized the unhappiness and uncertainty that had driven him from the house had dissipated as he'd taken care of the mundane chores.

Maybe he *was* boring, but the smell of alfalfa and leather and sweating horseflesh stimulated him. Heck, even the scent of horse and cow manure was far from offensive.

As for art and music, Jake loved the unparalleled image of the stars at night when you were far enough away from the lights of the city to really see them. He'd never lost his fascination with the changing pictures of the seasons, never grew tired of hearing the sad melody of a dove's call, never failed to feel a sense of peace and satisfaction with the contented symphony of lowing cattle and bullfrogs at night, or a rush of something bittersweet when he heard a hard-lovin'-hard-drinkin'-stand-by-your-man kind of song.

Man-made spectacles were all fine, and, in their own way, impressive, but, unlike Georgia, he didn't need faraway places, symphony orchestras and highbrow art to stimulate him in any way. After a lifetime on the ranch, he was still awed by the power of a summer thunderstorm and humbled by the fragile advent of birth and the inevitability of death.

With his mom and dad's help, he'd come to appreciate the beauty in every aspect of the world around him. They'd taught him to respect the earth and every living creature, big and small. They'd taught him to be thankful for every breath he drew. He realized again, as he had so many times before, that he was very lucky to have the parents he'd had, even though they weren't his real mom and dad at all.

Some woman had given him life and then given him away. Zach, too, apparently. It was hard to comprehend that any mother could do that. Animals weren't so cruel and coldhearted. The only time an animal mother abandoned her newborn offspring was when they were old enough to make it on their own, or if they were weak at birth and bound to die. Strangely, he didn't find that cruel. It was the natural way of things. Survival of the fittest.

People were a lot more callous. He wondered if his birth mother ever regretted what she'd done. Wondered if she ever thought of him and Zach. Wondered who she was and where she lived and what kind of man his real dad had been.

Does it really matter?

The whispering of his heart brought his thoughts up short. It didn't matter. Not really. What Georgia had said was true. Ben and Retha had been the best parents a kid could have ever hoped to have. His biological parents couldn't have loved him more, or given more of themselves to their child.

Whatever had happened thirty-five years ago, he couldn't change who and what he was, boring or not. More to the point, he didn't want to.

While Carrie grilled Georgia and Jake was out tending to the livestock, Ben Lattimer sat at the desk in his suite at the back wing of the house, nursing a bottle of Corona and trying, as they all were, to come to terms with the news of Zach's existence and how it would affect their lives.

Ben had talked to them about having DNA testing done to determine whether or not they were identical twins, which would put an end to some of their questions...and raise more.

His heart ached for both of them. The very foundation of Jake's world had been shaken that afternoon. All that he believed in and held dear had been shattered by Ben's confession. Zach, too, must be hurting. Even though he was temporarily denied the memories of the woman he'd called mother, he was no doubt rocked by everything that had transpired in the past twenty-four hours, and when his memory came back, his real pain would begin.

Ben was glad he'd talked Zach into staying until his memory returned, or at the very least for a few days. It would give him time to heal, physically and emotionally, and it would give him and Jake a chance to get to know each other. Besides, offering Zach shelter during this time of need helped assuage the guilt eating at Ben.

As crazy as he knew it was, he somehow felt responsible for the mix-up, as if it were his fault Jake and Zach regarded each other like wary strangers, afraid of what the next comment might reveal, afraid that something else they'd trusted in might be taken away.

For his part, Ben had worked past the shock and was now experiencing more than a hint of anger. If Jake and Zach were indeed twins, they never should have been split up. As brothers, and especially as twin brothers, they had been denied a moral right to grow up together.

Whoever was in charge at the hospital that night should have told him and Retha there were two babies.

Just because they were only expecting to adopt one child didn't mean they would have turned down the second.

But they hadn't been granted that option, and because someone, somewhere, had taken it upon himself to play God, he and Retha had been cheated out of a son, Zach had been cheated of a mother and father who would have loved and cherished him, and both boys had been robbed of a brother.

Ben took another gulp of the beer. Who would have believed something like this could happen? More important, how could they get at the truth? Who would know? The doctor at the little country hospital in Brownsboro where Jake had been born? No. The storm had knocked out the phone lines that night, and the doctor hadn't shown up—Ben remembered that. The delivery had been left to the nurse on duty, who not only had to be pretty old by now but whose name he didn't remember after so many years.

Ben doubted if the hospital was even in existence anymore. Lots of small community hospitals had closed during the past twenty years due to mass migrations to bigger cities and lack of funding for new equipment.

Jack Campbell. Yeah, Jack, whom Ben had met in the waiting room that night might remember the nurse's name. But Jack had been three sheets to the wind. Chances of him recalling much of anything were pretty slim.

No, the only person who might be able to help find out what had happened was Tom Barnette, but Ben would just as soon talk to the devil himself than ask the rotten slimeball who'd soaked him for more than a hundred thousand dollars for anything—including a simple bit of information. He wouldn't give him the satisfaction of letting him know what a stir Zach's presence had caused.

Ben lifted the bottle to his lips. Still, if Barnette had any knowledge about twins being born to the woman, Ben owed it to both Jake and Zach to swallow his pride and find out. Slamming the bottle onto the gleaming desktop, he reached for the telephone. It was after hours, but he could leave a message. If Barnette had any guts, he would return the call. If not, Ben would track him down.

Though it wasn't dark yet, Zach lay in the queen-size bed of the guest room, his eyes squeezed shut, as if by keeping them closed he could keep the troubling images at bay. Ben telling Jake he was adopted. His own heart sinking at the realization that he was farther away than ever from knowing who he was. Sinking farther still when he learned that Georgia wasn't his fiancée, but his brother's, Jake's.

Brother. It was strange to think that Jake Lattimer was his brother, but even to Zach, any other explanation seemed absurd. Were there other siblings? According to Will James, there weren't, but all Will knew was that the woman who'd raised Zach hadn't had any children, which made sense, since she'd adopted him. But if his birth mother had had other children, there were half brothers and sisters he'd never get to know, that he might never be able to locate.

Zach's mind felt sore from thinking too much. It ached with the intensity of his concentration. But no matter how much or how hard he tried to remember, nothing came to him. He felt as if he'd entered the twilight zone.

He sat up quickly. He knew what the twilight zone was. Remembered watching reruns of a television show by that name. The show had dealt with unnatural occurrences, strange, unexplained happenings—like waking up with no memory and finding out you have a twin.

A noise at the door interrupted his thoughts. It sounded like Attila scratching, demanding in that superior way of his to be let in. *Attila.* Zach sucked in a sharp breath. He knew who Attila was. His cat. Not really *his* cat, but the blacker-than-Hades tomcat that had shown up on his doorstep the morning after he'd moved in to his new apartment, demanding entrance with a grating yowl that set both teeth and nerves on edge.

When he'd opened the door, the fifteen-pound, meaner-than-sin tom with half an ear chewed off had sauntered through the doorway with a nonchalance that still evoked both admiration and irritation. He'd headed straight for the kitchen as if he'd been there a thousand times before, scratching on the cabinet door as if he knew there was food there, and he by-damn wanted some.

Zach recalled with sudden clarity that he didn't like cats—then or now.

He remembered reaching down with the intention of putting the cat outside, but the dusky demon had set the nails of both paws in his hand and chomped down on the tender flesh between Zach's thumb and forefinger.

He'd let go of the sorry critter, who'd landed in a fuzzy heap at his feet and proceeded to lick its paws and wash its face, as if the minor skirmish had somehow dirtied it. Then, to Zach's amazement, the tom had gotten up, stretched and sauntered to the kitchen where it homesteaded until Zach relented and opened up a can of tuna, which the bad-tempered feline had scarfed down in record time, considering that the cat ate with a mincing delicateness that seemed incongruous with its battle-scarred demeanor.

Zach looked at his hand. There, just where he'd pictured the cat biting him, were the faint white scars that proved the whole scenario was not a figment of his imagination or a by-product of the pain medicine the doctor had given him.

Later, he'd learned that the cat had "sort of" belonged to the last family who'd lived in the apartment, but the day they'd left for Indiana, the cat was nowhere to be found, and the family had no choice but to leave the tom behind. According to a neighbor, the feline, called Blackie by the previous apartment dwellers and dubbed Attila by Zach, had no real owner. Attila was a free spirit, taking his pleasures as his mood warranted, roaming the neighborhood at will, with no one to hinder his stalking of unsuspecting prey, naive adversaries or willing female felines.

A relieved smile curved Zach's mouth. He might not remember much, but he knew Attila had been admired. Revered. Feared. He wondered suddenly if the cat was all right. He'd have to call Shelby and ask her to go by and check.

Shelby. That thought, too, caught him off guard. The name had popped into his mind as easily as his foot popped into his boot, but there was nothing to go with it. No face. No knowledge of how he knew her. Just the name and the certainty that Shelby was a woman, someone he felt close enough to that he could ask a favor of her.

The scratching at the door resumed, accompanied this time by a faint mewling that was too soft and refined to be Attila. The sounds dissipated the images filling Zach's head. He rose and went to the door, wondering what other memories were waiting to ambush him.

He turned the knob and the door swung open on well-oiled hinges. The cat that sashayed into the room was definitely not Attila, but a queenly Persian that pranced with airy steps across the carpet and leaped onto the comforter with the agility of a circus performer and the grace of a prima ballerina. With a purr of contentment, the feline settled on the pillow next to Zach's and looked at him with amber eyes filled with ancient wisdom and enviable confidence, as if to ask him what he was going to do about it.

Having gone more than one round with Attila, Zach chose the better part of valor and decided to do nothing. "I hope you've had a flea bath," he muttered as he shut the door and made his way across the room to the bed. The cat regarded him with a look of infinite boredom, lowered her head on her paws and closed her eyes.

Feeling exceedingly weary himself, Zach crawled into bed. The soft rumble of her purring soon lulled him to a deep and blessedly dreamless sleep.

Georgia lay in bed, her hands beneath her cheek, her teeth worrying her bottom lip, troubled by the things she'd admitted to Carrie. As Denton predicted, Carrie had been relentless in getting to the bottom line—how Georgia had felt during the innocent kiss she'd shared with Zach.

Finally, she had admitted that Zach—who she'd

thought was Jake—had kissed her in a way she'd never experienced with Jake. She'd admitted that the unexpected heat had surprised her and that she'd responded to the kiss with more enthusiasm than she'd ever felt with her fiancé.

At the time, she hastened to tell Carrie, she'd thought both reactions were good. It was only when she arrived at the ranch and learned that Jake was really Zach that the implications of what had transpired between them had hit her squarely in the heart and she began to analyze what had really happened.

In short, Zach's kisses excited her in ways that Jake's never had. She didn't know why, and it certainly didn't make any sense. After all, if she looked at them, they were exactly the same—from the way they spoke to their gestures. They both had the habit of smoothing their mustache with their forefinger. They even wore the same cologne!

So why did Zach's kiss make her toes curl when Jake's didn't? Was it because they'd both been glad he'd survived whatever had gone wrong at the airport? Was it because there was an aura of risk surrounding Zach? She had no idea. All she knew was that whatever it was, she had to put it out of her mind, because nothing could ever come of it.

She was Jake's fiancée, and she was marrying him in little more than three weeks. Even if she didn't plan to marry Jake, there was no way she would ever consider a relationship with a man like Zach Rawlings— no matter how good a kisser he was—because he was in law enforcement.

Her Granddaddy Avery had been a sheriff's deputy. A jolly, rotund man with a mustache, she had adored him. He'd taught her right from wrong and loved her as much as she loved him. If he thought she hung the moon and stars, he was the sun in her world.

And then one day when she was barely ten, the sun had gone out. Bill Avery had been gunned down giving what he thought was a routine speeding ticket to a kid in a beat-up Mustang. What he hadn't known was that the kid, who was crazy drunk and had just robbed a store in a nearby town, had no intention of letting the law stop him.

For months, Georgia had been inconsolable. Her parents had taken her into Dallas to some hotshot counselor who had finally managed to help her put her grief into perspective. But she had come away from those sessions with one thing certain in her mind—she would never allow herself to love anyone in a dangerous line of work. The chances of something happening were too great, as the news proved each and every day, as the incident at the airport proved....

As her mother always said, it was as easy to love a rich man as a poor one. If that was true, then it was also true that it was as easy to love a man in a safe line of work as one who courted danger, which was why Jake's proposal had held so much appeal. He was rich and had a safe life-style. What more could any woman want?

Kisses that make your heart race?

That might be nice, but lust wasn't what it was cracked up to be, as Georgia knew from the number of young girls who got pregnant and dumped, and by the number of marriages that were destroyed when the lure of passion enticed one or the other partner from the straight and narrow.

What she felt for Zach was pure infatuation,

prompted by the notion of a more adventurous Jake. She was happy with the status quo.

Liar.

She punched her pillow and flopped to her back. All right, then. Not exactly happy with the status quo, but satisfied with it. The emotions she and Jake shared couldn't be called blazing passion by any stretch of the imagination, but that was just fine and dandy. What they shared was warm and comfortable and comforting, unlike the moment of panic she'd felt at the airport when she'd seen the man she thought was her fiancé laid out cold.

"No, thanks," she said in a grim voice to the ceiling.

She'd take boring any day.

Chapter Four

The sunshine of the new day brought a measure of peace and hope to everyone on the Lazy L. Though still wary about how the advent of a twin into his life would change things, Jake awoke knowing he couldn't blame Ben and Retha for any part of this new development. All they'd done was love him and try to give him the best.

Ben awoke with new resolve to get to the bottom of things by insisting Jake and Zach have DNA testing and by following up on the call to Tom Barnette if the senatorial candidate hadn't returned his call by lunchtime. He also wanted to talk to both Jake and Zach and try to make them see what a blessing it was to have been reunited. It was amazing, he thought, that after only one day of knowing Zach Rawlings, Ben felt as if he'd found a long-lost son, another Jake....

* * *

Zach opened his eyes as a new dawn crept into his room. The cat still slept next to him. The smile that claimed Zach's lips was more of a wry grimace. It was the first time in a long time that he'd awakened to find a female in his bed. That knowledge came to him as easily as the name Shelby and the memories of Attila had the night before. He wondered why he couldn't remember who Shelby was and why he was reasonably certain there was no woman in his life. He came up with no answers.

Answers. That was his goal for the day. He had to find some answers.

Tired of being cooped up inside and able to move without his head pounding like a percussion band, he got up, showered and dressed in a pair of Jake's jeans and a cotton shirt. Then he headed for the dining room, where Rosalita was just laying out a breakfast buffet of silver-covered dishes.

When she turned and saw him, she jumped in surprise, her small hand flying to her throat. "You scared me out of a year's growth, Jake."

Zach's let a bemused smile answer for him. Jeez. If Rosalita, who saw Jake every day, couldn't tell the difference between them, who was he to argue with the theory that they were indeed twins?

"Everything's ready. Do you want orange or cranberry juice this morning?"

"Tomato juice, please," Zach said.

Rosalita frowned. "You hate tomato juice."

Zach relented. Toying with her was cruel. "Jake may hate tomato juice, but I happen to like it. And can you add a couple of dashes of hot sauce to it if it isn't too much trouble?"

Rosalita's shapely mouth fell open half an inch. "Mr. Rawlings?"

"'Fraid so, but call me Zach." He smiled at her, a smile so like Jake's, Rosalita crossed herself. "Weird, isn't it?"

"More than weird," she said. "I'm not sure I'll ever be able to tell you apart."

"Well, you won't have to worry about it in a few days. I'll be out of your hair in no time."

"Oh, you're no bother," Rosalita assured him. "Cooking for one more is no big deal." A sound drew her attention to the doorway, and Zach turned as Ben entered the room.

The older man paused in the aperture, his keen blue eyes taking in every aspect of Zach's appearance, from the top of his shower-damp head to the tips of the ostrich-skin boots on his feet.

"Morning, Zach," he said at last.

"Good morning, Mr. Lattimer."

Rosalita looked from Zach to Ben. "How could you tell?" she asked.

"It's in the eyes," Ben explained. "Jake has a calm, unconcerned look about him. Zach, here, looks watchful, almost wary."

"Which might be a negative given my chosen occupation," Zach said, dismayed by Ben's observation. "Maybe I need to find another line of work."

Ben smiled. "From what I hear, the last thing you should do is look for another job. Will James says you're one of the best in the business."

"What else did he say about me?" Zach asked, hungry to find out all he could about himself.

"Not much," Ben said. "You heard most of it." He reached out and squeezed Zach's shoulder. "Fill up your plate, son, or Rosalita will have our hides. There's plenty of time for talk.''

Ben was right. After not eating much the previous day, Zach realized he was starving. ''Don't you want to wait for Jake?''

''Present,'' Jake said, briskly striding into the room.

''Morning, son,'' Ben said as he began to fill his plate. ''Rest well?''

''Tolerably.''

Zach waited for Jake to go ahead of him, but with a sweep of his arm, Jake indicated for Zach to go first. Their eyes met in the mirror hanging over the buffet.

The look in Jake's eyes was watchful. Zach felt a strange stirring of something deep inside him that he'd never experienced before. Unless the tests Ben wanted them to have proved otherwise, and he didn't think they would, this was his brother. His twin.

A strange tightness filled his chest as something new and fragile began to well up into the emptiness generated by his amnesia. This man was part of him. They shared the same blood. Corny or not, he felt all the sappy things other people claimed to feel when they found their missing siblings—the sensation of finding a part of himself, a subtle but definite happiness he couldn't begin to explain.

But Jake hadn't wanted or needed a brother, and Zach's uncertain pleasure was tempered by the misgivings. Forging a relationship with Jake at this late date wouldn't be easy, but Zach knew it was something he wanted to pursue as much as he wanted to pursue finding answers about who he was.

''Company first.''

The sound of his brother's voice broke into Zach's thoughts. He offered Jake a smile. ''Thanks.''

Following Ben's lead, Zach heaped his plate high with sausage, potatoes fried with onion and green chilies, refried beans, tortillas and *huevos rancheros.*

"Dig in, boy," Ben said as Zach took a place on his left. "I can guarantee it's good."

They ate in silence for a moment before Ben asked Jake, "What's on your agenda today?"

"I'm going to palpate that dun mare and see if she's in foal. I've got to see to it that Alonzo and Jimmy start cutting that hayfield over by the creek, and I'm sending Miguel and Tony out to see if they can get a rope on that new heifer that broke out of the holding pen the other day." Jake shook his head. "She's as loco as they come."

"If they bring her in, take her straight to the auction," Ben said.

"I plan to. The last thing I need is a wild heifer." Jake picked up his fork and added, "Oh, I almost forgot. Georgia and I have a meeting with the choir director at the church at five-thirty."

If Jake and Georgia were picking out songs, the wedding wasn't far off. Zach didn't like the little jolt of pain that stabbed him at the mention of Jake's upcoming marriage to Georgia. The feeling didn't make a darn bit of sense, since he hardly knew the woman, yet it was undeniably there. But then, nothing had made sense since he'd awakened in that Fort Worth hospital and realized he had no idea who he was.

"When do you tie the knot?" he asked.

"About three weeks," Jake said. "June fifth."

"Gettin' the jitters?"

"I'm not. Georgia is," Jake said, rising to get another egg.

Zach felt a small thrill of satisfaction at Jake's admission. Was Georgia having second thoughts? Nah. Just because she had prewedding nerves was no reason to imagine she was about to throw Jake over. She was just getting cold feet. It happened all the time. Georgia was marrying his brother, and that's all there was to it.

The thought didn't do much to cheer him, but then he realized that he was probably hanging on to the memory of Georgia's kiss because he didn't have many memories to hold on to. Coveting wasn't his style. He knew that, even if he didn't know anything else. Heck, he might have a girlfriend somewhere. Just because he didn't remember one and Will said there was no one woman in his life didn't mean it was necessarily true.

Maybe Shelby was his girlfriend. Now that was something he hadn't considered. When Will James called to check on him, he'd ask if he knew who Shelby was. Georgia Williams might have the sweetest, softest lips he could remember tasting, but at the moment, he didn't have any memories of any other lips or kisses for comparison.

He dragged his thoughts back to the conversation at hand and realized Jake was telling his dad something else about his plans for the day.

"Do you need any help?" Zach asked Jake. "A little more of this sitting around and I'll go stir-crazy."

"I appreciate the offer," Jake said, "but you'd better take it easy until the doctors say you're over that concussion." He shifted his gaze to Ben. "Do you want to go look at those new heifers that came in while you were gone?"

"Maybe another time," Ben said. "I have a couple of phone calls to make, and then I thought I'd show Zach around the ranch." He smiled at Zach. "We can't have you thinking we're inhospitable."

"That's the last thing I'd think," Zach said. "I've been treated like the prodigal son."

Ben's pleased smile was accompanied by a chuckle. "The fatted calf is tonight. Jake and Georgia will probably grab something when they finish their meeting, but I've got some rib-eye steaks in the freezer that are so tender you can cut them with a fork."

"Maybe Georgia and I will join you when we're finished at the church," Jake suggested.

"Nonsense!" Ben said. "The two of you haven't had a minute alone since she got back, and I'm sure you have a lot to say to each other. Zach understands."

Zach's gaze drifted to his brother. Oh, yeah, he understood perfectly. Lack of memory didn't make him an idiot. He understood that there would be a lot more "doing" than "saying" to each other. He tried not to think about Jake and Georgia making love, and clenched his teeth together so tightly his jaw ached.

Zach noticed that Jake was watching him closely and fought to subdue the green-eyed monster that had reared up inside him.

"Have you remembered anything?" Jake asked.

"As a matter of fact, a couple of things did pop into my head last night," Zach said, thankful the conversation was headed in a new direction.

"I remember the name Shelby, but I have no idea who Shelby is. I also remembered that I have a cat...sort of. He isn't really mine, he just shows up at my place when he's looking for a handout or has nothing better to do, kind of like that female Persian of yours."

"Ah, you've made Elizabeth the Fourth's acquaintance," Ben said, smiling.

"She scratched on the door until I let her in. She

was bound and determined to spend the night in my bed. I hope you don't mind.''

''Elizabeth is like all females,'' Ben said. ''When she gets something in her head, you may as well let her do it, or she can make your life hell.''

''Hey, *muchacho!*'' Rosalita chided as she pushed through the swinging door with a trim jeans-clad hip. ''That's a sexist remark if I ever heard one!''

''But true,'' Ben said. He aimed a look at Jake. ''Don't you agree, son?''

''I plead the fifth,'' Jake said, pushing back his chair. ''Great breakfast, Rosie.''

''Thanks, Jake.''

Zach drew a shallow breath of thankfulness that the meal was over. His repertoire of subjects to discuss was limited to say the least, and his unwanted attraction to Georgia didn't make conversing with Jake an easy task. Maybe there was something to be said for staying in his room and reading after all.

The principal at Georgia's school had given the tour group a couple of days to rest up after coming back home. Georgia, who awakened with her determination intact and her sanity restored, spent the morning doing laundry, giving her already clean house a once-over and jotting down notes of everything she needed to take on her honeymoon trip to Colorado.

With the wedding just three weeks away, there was much to do and little time to do it. She had to drive into Fort Worth to try on her wedding gown in a couple of hours, and later that evening, she and Jake had to meet with the group of singers to finalize the order of the songs they'd chosen.

A lady from the church she attended had called to

set up an evening for a wedding shower. Valerie Campbell, the ex-wife of one of Ben's longtime friends, had agreed to come over from Louisiana and hostess a combination shower and brunch for the wives of the Lattimer friends and business associates, and Carrie was giving Georgia a shower for her teacher friends and sorority sisters.

There were so many showers planned that she and Jake might have to add another wing to the house just to display the gifts...which brought up another touchy spot. She and Jake would be living at the Lazy L, whose decor suited the life-style of its current inhabitants. While most of Georgia's things held no sentimental or monetary value, she did own a few antique pieces that had once belonged to her grandparents, things she didn't want to get rid of or put in storage.

When she'd mentioned her concern to Jake, he reiterated what Ben had already told her. She was to think of the house as hers. As the new mistress, she could change whatever she wanted. While Georgia didn't doubt the sincerity of the gesture, the thought of tampering with the home Retha had created was daunting.

Actually, the whole wedding ordeal was daunting, from ordering the invitations to the thought of writing all those thank-you notes. Coordinating a big church wedding took organizational skills that were far beyond Georgia's, not to mention nerves of steel. Ginny Williams had both. Georgia thanked God daily for her mother. If seeing to the arrangements was left up to her, she'd just tell Jake she wanted to call off the whole shebang and elope.

She could imagine Jake's response. A stickler for propriety, Jake would be too concerned about the trouble such a rash act would cause after everyone had already put so much time and effort into the planning of what the Fort Worth papers were calling the wedding of the year.

Sighing and looping her hair behind her ear, Georgia went to run a hot bath. She'd soak in some of her new French bath oil, conjure up thoughts of a Paris café and forget about it all...the wedding, Jake, and her troubling thoughts of Zach Rawlings...just for a little while.

To Ben's surprise, Tom Barnette returned his call at mid-morning. Unwilling to alienate a single vote, Barnette's hail-fellow-well-met persona was firmly in place as they exchanged trivialities. His cheerful garrulousness and pseudo-sincerity as he asked Ben what he could do for him, grated on Ben's nerves.

"Something strange has come up about Jake's adoption," Ben said. "There are a couple of things I wanted to ask you."

Barnette didn't reply immediately, but when he did, the joviality was still there, if not more so. "Don't tell me you want to send him back?" he asked with a hearty laugh.

"No," Ben said. "Jake has been a wonderful son."

"I'm glad to hear that, Ben. I truly am," Barnette said. "So what's the problem?"

"The problem is why you split up a set of twins." Ben didn't try to hide the cold outrage that had simmered inside him since he realized what had been done.

"Twins? What are you talking about?"

If Ben hadn't been so angry, he would have heard the incredulity in Tom Barnette's voice.

"I'm talking about not being given the chance to

adopt both boys, that's what I'm talking about. I know the adoption arrangement we had with you was for one baby, but hell, man, if Retha and I had known there were two, we'd have been tickled to have them both. We could have afforded it!''

"Now just you hold on a minute, Ben Lattimer,'' Barnette said, his ire rising. "I get the distinct feeling that I'm being accused of something here, but damned if I know what it is any more than I know what you're talking about when you start talking about twins.''

"You're saying you have no idea what I'm talking about?''

"I honestly don't know what you're talking about.''

When Ben didn't come back with another accusation immediately, Tom said, "Look, let's both just simmer down here, a bit. We're liable to have a stroke or something.''

Tom spoke in his best politician's voice. Ben recognized the smooth, comforting tone as the same one Tom had used to extol the virtues of one of his ventures when Jake was a toddler. The deal, which involved insurance and nursing homes, had cost both him and Jack Campbell a bundle. It was a tone Ben knew to be wary of. As far as he was concerned, honest was a word Tom Barnette should strike from his vocabulary.

"Maybe you'd better tell me exactly where you got the farfetched notion that Jake is a twin,'' Tom said.

Ben struggled to keep the irritation from his voice, which was hard considering the situation and who he was forced to deal with. "The notion isn't farfetched when you see two men standing side by side who look so much alike you can't tell them apart.''

Tom laughed, but the laughter lacked the raucous

note it had held earlier. "Come on, Lattimer, you know they say everyone has a double."

"Damn it, Tom, this is no simple look-alike situation. I'm telling you these boys are twins, and they've agreed to have DNA testing to prove it."

"You're that sure?"

"Damn right I am!" Ben said. "And if you saw them, you'd be sure, too!"

"All right, then. Why don't you tell me how you found this *twin* of Jake's?" Tom said. "I'm sure we can come to some logical explanation."

Ben explained what had happened to Georgia at the airport and about her bringing Zach to the ranch, thinking he was Jake. He told about Will James's visit and finding out that Zach had been raised by a preacher's daughter and a trucker.

"A preacher's daughter and a trucker, huh?" Tom said, a thoughtful note in his voice.

"So James claimed. Obviously," Ben went on, "the boys were split up at birth. I got Jake. This other couple got Zach. I want to know why. You handled the adoption. If anyone knows what went on that night, it damn well ought to be you."

"All I can tell you is that you and Retha wanted a child, and I knew you'd make good parents. I was the middleman, just like I was for the other adoptions I handled back then. I threshed out the financial details and made sure the paperwork was up to snuff. I handled one adoption the night your boy was born. Yours."

"You don't know anything about her having twins, then?"

"Good grief, man! I didn't make it a habit to go to the hospital when the girls went into labor. When one of the girls I was helping delivered the baby, the hospital called me so we could do the final paperwork. My job was to see that the *T*s were crossed and the *I*s were dotted. Once everyone signed in front of the notary, I was finished.''

Ben's anger drained away. Barnette had answered his questions without any hesitation. As much as Ben hated to admit it, he sensed Tom was telling the truth. Futility fueled his irritation. Now that he'd exhausted this lead, he was at a loss as to what to do next.

His frustration must have transmitted itself through the phone lines. Tom exhaled noisily. ''I'm telling you again that I don't know anything about any twins being born, Ben.''

''But it could have happened, couldn't it?''

''I suppose it *could* have, but—''

''How can we find out?'' Ben interrupted. ''Hospital records?''

''That dinky little old hospital closed down more than twenty years ago,'' Tom said. ''God knows what happened to their records.'' A note of eagerness crept into Tom's voice. ''The doctor might remember, though. Or he might know where the records were stored.''

''No good,'' Ben said. ''There was a hellacious storm that night, and they couldn't get hold of the doctor because the phone lines were down. A nurse delivered Jake, but I have no idea what her name was.''

''Hampstead,'' Tom said, his voice quiet and thoughtful. ''Lillian Hampstead.''

''Damnation! How'd you remember a name like that after all these years?'' Ben asked.

''She ran that home for pregnant girls there in

Brownsboro,'' Tom explained. ''I placed a lot of her girls' babies before I gave up private adoptions.''

''She's the key to this, Tom,'' Ben said, eagerness in his voice. ''If Jake and Zach are brothers, then something fishy was going on. This Hampstead woman should have let you know they were twins, shouldn't she?''

''She sure as hell should have,'' Tom said, his voice bristling with indignation.

''Can you get in touch with her?''

''I don't know,'' Tom said. ''If she's alive, she'd be older'n dirt by now. She might not remember a thing.''

''It's worth a try,'' Ben said. ·

''It surely is.'' After a moment's hesitation, Tom spoke again. ''Do you mind my asking you something, Ben?''

''Nope.''

''Why are you doing this?''

''Because if it is true, and there were twins born there that night, two sins were committed. The first was splitting up two brothers who shared the same womb, two boys who heard each others' hearts beating for nine months. The second was denying me and Retha a second son we would have loved as much as we loved Jake.''

Tom Barnette cleared his throat. ''Tell you what,'' he said in a gruff tone. ''I'll personally look into this for you—if you want me to. It may take a while, but I'll try and locate Lillian Hampstead.''

A faint feeling of alarm quivered through Ben. If history was any indicator, Tom wasn't the altruistic type. What was Barnette up to? Did he see some sort of potential in this for a big case? Or did he figure that if he put all the missing pieces together and blew the lid off some adoption scam, he'd come off looking like a hero and divert the voters' attention from the fact that he was under investigation for insurance fraud?

"Why would you want to do that?" Ben asked. "Don't you have enough on your plate with the campaign and everything?"

"I'm up to my butt in alligators," Barnette said, "but it's the least I can do."

"What do you mean?"

"Like you said, I handled the adoption. If something did go on that night that shouldn't have, I owe it to you to find out. I owe it to myself to find out. Because you're right. If they were split up, it would have been downright criminal...in more ways than one."

The creamy white satin and lace wedding dress was a picture straight from a Victorian dream. Fortunately, according to Ginny Williams and the shop attendant, the alterations made it a perfect fit, and Georgia forked over the last payment with a grudging sigh of relief.

Her mother helped her pick out shoes, a veil, hosiery and lacy, sexy, almost nonexistent underwear for the upcoming occasion. They treated themselves to a sinfully fattening dessert, then replete with chocolate, the two exhausted women drove home in silence.

Georgia dropped off her mother with a kiss and a heartfelt thanks. Then she went home and changed into wheat-colored jeans and a peach-tinted T-shirt and drove to the Lazy L to pick up Jake for their meeting with the choir director.

Rosalita answered the door. "Hi, Rosalita," Georgia said, smiling. "Is Jake ready?"

Rosalita rolled her dark eyes. "Ready? I don't think he's come up from the barn yet."

Georgia glanced at the marcasite watch strapped around her wrist. "I'd better go get him. We're going to be late if he doesn't get a move on."

"Why don't you go through the house?" Rosalita suggested. "I just made some fresh spiced tea. You can take a glass with you."

"That sounds wonderful!" She started after Rosalita but was hindered by Elizabeth the Fourth, who ran at her feet and swatted at her shoelaces with every step Georgia took. Finally, out of a combination of self-defense and fear that she'd step on the cat, Georgia picked up the feline and cuddled her all the way to the kitchen where Rosalita regaled Georgia with the story about Elizabeth demanding to be let into Zach's room where she'd spent the night in his bed.

The provocative image that flashed through Georgia's mind sent her pulse to racing. She squelched it ruthlessly. Minutes later, the cat exchanged for a frosted mug of mint-sprigged tea, she made her way down the long, glassed-in hallway that ran the length of the U-shaped house. She passed Ben's suite and let herself out onto the covered porch through the French doors near the guest room where Zach Rawlings was no doubt resting, sans cat.

A balmy breeze teased her hair and tempered the afternoon heat, making the walk to the barn an enjoyable one. In its own way, she supposed the Lazy L was as charming as Paris—just different. Cattle grazed to her right, and several yearling horses cavorted in the corrals next to the barn on her left.

As she entered the side door of the barn, a soft whicker from a nearby stall greeted her. One of Jake's prize quarter horses stuck its head over the mesh metal doorway and looked at her curiously...or was that expectantly? A quick glance into the stall proved that the horse hadn't been fed yet.

The sorrel colt, just over a year old, was one Jake planned to put in an upcoming sale. To prevent its coat from getting sunburned, Jake put the colt inside during the day and let it out at night to get the exercise it needed.

The horse whinnied again. Georgia chewed on her lower lip. *To feed or not to feed? That is the question.* She'd helped Jake feed before, and she knew how much of each grain to dole out, but on the off chance that he'd fed early because of their appointment, she ought to leave things alone.

As she stood there trying to decide what to do, she caught a movement from the corner of her eye. A mouse crouched next to the tack box that held Jake's grooming tools. Thank goodness it wasn't a snake! Before she could draw a breath of relief, the tiny rodent took courage in hand and sped out from its hiding place, straight at her.

With a squeal of terror, she jumped back, but one of her shoestrings had come undone, and the other foot had pinned it to the ground, causing her to lose her balance and sending her tumbling onto her tush. Thankfully, the tea landed a good three feet away instead of all over her. Drats! she thought as the furry creature sped off into the shadows. She'd probably ruined her new jeans.

With a grimace of disgust, she pushed herself to her feet and dusted off her hands. Then she bent over to tie her shoelace—no doubt undone by the sneaky Elizabeth—before it caused another catastrophe.

"You all right?"

The sound of Jake's voice sent her spinning around. Expecting him to be dirty and disheveled, she was pleased to see that he'd showered and was ready to go, which was good, since she'd have to stop by her place and change. He smiled and moved nearer, and she realized again, as she often did, that he was a fine specimen of a man. She smiled back. "I'm fine."

"You look fine," he said, his gaze moving over her face like a soft caress. "Damn fine."

The unexpected compliment took her off guard, and her heart hammered a little faster. It wasn't that Jake never complimented her—he did, and frequently. But seldom had she seen that heated look in his eyes. The few times she had, she'd expected him to carry her off to bed, but his chivalrous side had always emerged at the last minute, and she'd been left aching and disappointed.

"Turn around," he commanded, his voice a soft rumble as he moved between her and the stall.

It wasn't like Jake to demand anything. "What?"

"Turn around."

Georgia turned, obediently. She felt his hand brushing at her bottom, and bit back a small gasp of surprise. He was just brushing away the dirt, but she couldn't deny that the casual touch was disturbing. Was it her imagination, or had his hand lingered for an extra caressing second?

She turned and looked at him over her shoulder. The familiar woodsy scent of his cologne filled her senses. One massive shoulder filled her line of vision. Maybe it was the aftereffects of her scare by the mouse, but she suddenly felt all weak-kneed and quivery inside.

"Are they ruined?" she asked, more to cover the silence than because she cared.

"No." His hand moved over the roundness of her bottom again, and this time, unless she'd lost all sense of perspective, his touch was definitely a deliberate and lingering caress.

She sucked in a breath and floundered for something to say. What came out was, "Good. I'd hate to go pick out wedding songs with dirt on my jeans." As soon as the words left her lips, Georgia felt like screaming. Had that inane comment really come from her?

The comment brought a final brusque slap on the derriere. "All finished."

He straightened. She turned, reaching out and placing her hand against his chest. "Don't."

The look in his eyes was wary, cautious. "Don't what?" He took a step backward. Then another.

Relentless, she followed, until his back was to the wall...or rather the tack box. "Don't stop."

"Don't stop what?"

Georgia smiled at him and, putting both hands against his chest, she gave a little shove. He plopped onto the tack box, a look of surprise on his attractive face.

"You don't know what you're doing," he growled.

"Oh, yes, I do," she said. Knowing she'd lose her courage if she stopped and thought about her actions, she slung one leg over both of his, and sat on his lap facing him.

He reached out, took her shoulders in his big hands and opened his mouth to say something. She put her fingers over his lips to silence him, then cupped his lean jaw in her palm. Their eyes clung as she leaned forward.

His eyes closed.

Her thumb skimmed his lower lip.

The hands on her shoulders tightened, and a muscle in his cheek knotted beneath her palm.

Her mouth touched his, hesitantly at first, and then when she met nothing but passive resistance, her lips moved against his with a boldness that surprised her.

She actually felt the starch go out of him.

His grip on her shoulders gentled. "You're making a big mistake," he said, the words riding on the deep sigh that whooshed from him.

She shook her head, a smug smile curving her lips and dancing in her eyes. "No more reprieves, Jake. I've made up my mind."

"A *really* big mistake," he told her, before she leaned over and kissed him again.

This time he offered no resistance. A growl of need escaped him, and he dragged her against him so tightly that her breasts were flattened against his chest. She felt the hardness of his middle against hers. Even through his shirt, his skin felt hot to her touch, but not as hot as his lips that seared hers with a heat she'd experienced few times in her life. He devoured her parted lips with a hunger she was helpless to resist, a hunger that fueled an equal need inside her.

Driven by a desperation that was entirely foreign to her, she fumbled with the buttons of his shirt, almost sobbing in frustration when they wouldn't budge, almost sobbing with joy when they gave and her fingertips came into contact with his bare flesh.

His skin was smooth and firm, the muscles of his shoulders and chest and abdomen as finely sculpted as those chiseled by a master sculptor. Her hands caressed and explored while his mouth rained kisses on her lips, peppered kisses over her cheeks and chin, feathered kisses over her eyelids and trailed wet little kisses down her throat.

Georgia's thought processes seemed to have shut down. All she could do was give him back kiss for kiss while the heat inside her spread. The kisses grew longer, harder. The touches grew rougher, but a roughness spawned by need, not the desire to hurt. The sighs mutated to ragged, indrawn breaths gulped between kisses.

When his hands yanked her shirt from the waistband of her jeans, Georgia realized that she was no longer in control of the situation and wondered when and how she had lost it.

More to the point, when had Jake lost control?

The truth came to her on a whisper that soughed from his lips.

"I want you, sunshine."

It took the truth a minute to register, which was a testimony to her mental state. Jake never called her sunshine. He called her sugar. Had called her that for years. She dug her fingers into the wide shoulders beneath her hands and, wrenching her mouth free, pushed with all the strength of her one hundred twenty pounds.

For a minute he resisted, but when he realized she was trying to put some distance between them, she felt his hold on her loosen. His hands moved down her sides, over her hips and came to rest on her denim-clad thighs.

His eyes, watchful, wary, glittered with a hunger that set her heart to racing. His mouth was wet from their kisses, as she knew hers was. His chest, bared by the shirt she'd pushed aside, rose and fell as if he'd just finished a marathon.

He watched her, waiting, his thumbs moving in small, concentric circles against the insides of her thighs. Even through the thick fabric of her jeans, his touch generated a tingling awareness.

"What the hell's goin' on here, Georgia Lee?"

The sound of Jake's voice—and she knew it was Jake because no one else called her Georgia Lee—brought her nebulous suspicions into startling clarity. What had been going on was pretty obvious, she thought as she looked from the man whose lap she was sitting on to the man approaching from outside. Her heart plummeted, and a despair she couldn't begin to understand crept into her.

Zach Rawlings had tricked her, and she'd let him. She got to her feet so fast she almost landed on the dirt of the barn floor again and clasped her arms around her upper body protectively.

"You're not Jake."

Her voice held an accusation and horror at what she'd allowed to happen. No. At what she'd started.

Zach's gaze was unrepentant. "I tried to tell you."

And so he had. He hadn't tricked her at all, and that was the worst part. She was the one who had initiated those fiery kisses. She was the one who'd said she knew what she was doing.

Hot tears stung her eyes, and she pressed her lips together to stop their trembling. Once again, her impulsiveness had landed her in trouble. Bad trouble. A tear slipped down her cheek, and she swiped at it with a gesture that seemed more disheartened than angry.

"Georgia."

Jake. Jake coming toward her, fury etched on his features.

"What's going on here?" he asked, making a broad

sweeping gesture that encompassed everything from her disheveled appearance to Zach, whose shirt was still unbuttoned.

"I thought it was you," she said.

"The hell you did!"

His disbelief, though warranted, was the straw that broke the fragile back of her composure.

"The hell I did," she said. Gathering the scraps of her dignity, she turned without another word of explanation and headed for the door.

"Georgia." She'd taken no more than two steps when she heard her name again and felt a gentle grip on her upper arm. It sounded like Jake, but was it? She stopped but couldn't bring herself to turn around. All she wanted to do was go crawl into a hole somewhere and try to put the pieces of herself back together.

"If it helps any, I want you to know I'm sorry."

The apology had to come from Zach. She turned and looked at him, tears shimmering in her blue eyes like sunshine on the sea.

"Not as sorry as I am," she said. Jerking free, she ran out of the dim coolness of the barn into the May sunshine.

This time, they both let her go.

Chapter Five

One look at his brother's face and Zach knew there would be hell to pay. A man didn't go around messing with a woman like Georgia Williams behind the back of a guy like Jake Lattimer and not expect some fallout.

"Do you mind telling me what just happened here?"

The question was civil. Jake's tone might have been taken for curiosity...until Zach saw the hostility in the dark eyes probing his. He might have been intimidated by the fierceness of his brother's countenance if the blatant lust throbbing through him wasn't making Zach feel a bit quarrelsome himself.

His irritation—though for the life of him, he wasn't sure who he was mad at, Georgia for coming on to him or himself for not trying harder to make her understand he wasn't Jake—triggered a reckless insolence that Zach knew would aggravate, not placate, Jake. Still,

Zach couldn't scrape up the slightest tendency to suppress it.

With any luck, taking a pseudo-light approach might lessen the impact of what Jake had seen. As for Zach, he knew he'd remember those few moments of stolen kisses until the day they planted him six feet under.

He straightened his shirt, or rather Jake's shirt, and began to fasten the buttons Georgia had undone just moments before. "Don't be too hard on her. It was a simple case of mistaken identity."

"Yeah, sure. She thought you were me." It was a statement, not a question.

Meeting Jake's stony countenance without flinching, Zach unsnapped and unzipped the Wranglers that fit him exactly the way they fit Jake. He thrust in the tail of his shirt, buttoned the jeans and zipped the faded fly. "I'd say that about sums it up, hoss," he said, wondering how in the heck he'd managed to get himself into this predicament.

Jake's eyes narrowed. "You didn't even try to set her straight, did you?"

"I told her she was making a mistake, but she was a woman with a mission." Zach shrugged. "What your daddy said this morning was true. There's no stopping a woman once she makes up her mind about something."

Jake's hands clenched into fists. "Your attitude is pretty blasé, for a man caught cheatin' with another man's woman. Maybe that's because you're in the habit of it."

From the deadly look in Jake's eyes, Zach knew he had to do some fancy talking to get out of this one without another concussion to compound the one he'd gotten at the airport.

Zach didn't want to antagonize Jake. If the tests they were taking the next day proved they were twins, the last thing he needed was for some little strawberry blonde with a smile like summer sunshine and a hormone problem to come between him and the brother that he somehow knew he'd always wanted.

Abruptly, he dropped the casual, almost callous attitude and met Jake's gaze head-on.

"She thought I was you, Jake. I tried to tell her otherwise. Maybe I should have tried harder. We kissed a little—"

"A little! A few more minutes and you'd have been rolling in the hay!"

"No, we wouldn't," Zach said, not that that particular scenario didn't hold tremendous appeal. "She'd already figured out she'd made a mistake. She was fixin' to lay into me before you called her name."

Jake looked skeptical, but Georgia was his fiancée, and he loved her and wanted to believe what he heard. As well he should. It was, after all, the truth. Zach knew he'd feel the same way if he were in Jake's boots.

More disturbing was the knowledge that even though he was reasonably sure he wasn't the kind of guy who'd steal another man's woman, he knew that if a similar opportunity presented itself, he'd do the same thing. Zach flinched a little at the callousness of the thought. What was the matter with him? What was it about Georgia Williams that made him turn his back on the code of honor he somehow knew he lived by?

Feeling like the heel he knew he was, Zach said, "You're right. I should have tried harder to make her understand I wasn't you."

"Yes, you should have."

"I wouldn't blame you if you told me to get off the Lazy L and never come back."

"I'm thinking seriously about it."

"It didn't mean a thing to her, Jake."

Jake arched an eyebrow. "Didn't it?"

"No! You saw how mad she was," Zach said, wondering if Jake would ever relent. "You heard me apologize, and you heard her say she was sorrier than I was it happened." Zach's gaze held his brother's. "I'm sorry, too," he said.

Jake looked less than impressed, but the anger in his eyes faded a bit.

"I don't think I normally go around putting the make on women who are spoken for," Zach said. He hooked his thumbs in his belt loops and shifted his weight to one leg, a mirror image of the man standing ten feet from him. "I don't know what happened. Maybe it's the concussion."

"I'm going to let it slide this once," Jake said. "You may be my brother, but I want you to understand one thing. This is my ranch, and Georgia is my fiancée. We Lattimers have worked damned hard for and are damned proud of what we have, whether it's land, cattle or women, and we don't take kindly to squatters, wolves or thieves comin' in and trying to take what's ours."

Georgia stalked toward the house, alternately crying and cursing, albeit mildly, and wishing to heaven she'd never set eyes on Zach Rawlings. Life might have been predictable, but at least it wasn't like walking through an emotional minefield the way it had been since she'd blithely shanghaied Zach and brought his sorry carcass to the Lazy L.

She sucked in a sob and muttered another imprecation about the dubiousness of Zach's mother's lineage. How could he have kissed her that way when he knew darn well she thought he was Jake? What kind of pervert was he, anyway?

He tried to tell you.

Well, he hadn't by golly tried hard enough! They could both be excused for that kiss at the hospital—neither had any way of knowing Zach wasn't Jake. But this was something else altogether! It was one thing to steal a kiss, but what had happened between them in the barn had been far more than a kiss!

If Zach harbored any hopes of becoming a part of his brother's life—should the DNA tests prove beyond a doubt they *were* twins—he'd just blown it. Jake might not be on fire for her, but he loved her, and worse, he was as territorial as any of the wildlife that populated the ranch.

What about you, Georgia? What about your part in all this?

All right. She did start it. She did keep on when Zach tried to tell her she was making a mistake. She admitted she was *partly* to blame, but only because the libido that had been content to wait until her wedding night had gone awry the eve before she left for Paris—where, to make matters worse, she'd come into contact with all those romantic Frenchmen. That same libido had been knocked even more out of kilter by the kiss she and Zach shared in the hospital.

She wiped at a fresh rush of tears. If that little excuse for a kiss had skewed her emotions, only God knew what this latest passionate debacle would do to her. The frightening part was that *she'd liked it!*

She wrenched open the French doors at the back of

the house and ran headlong down the hallway to one of the two downstairs bathrooms that served visitors, slamming the door behind her. The face staring back at her from the mirror was familiar, but the distraught look in her blue eyes was as foreign to her as the tumultuous feelings Zach Rawlings's kisses inspired.

How could she have let it go so far? she asked herself as she got a washcloth from the linen closet to wipe the tears from her hot cheeks and mascara-wet eyes. Was she so desperate for excitement she couldn't tell the difference between the two men? She'd kissed Jake often enough during the past two years, and while they'd gotten into some fairly heavy necking on the rare occasion, his kisses had never set her on fire the way Zach's did. Why hadn't she recognized instantly that those mind-drugging kisses weren't Jake's?

You did.

The errant thought, whispered by her conscience, robbed her of breath. Her hand froze beneath the stream of cool water. No. She hadn't known. Not until he called her sunshine in that hoarse, husky voice. Not until he said he wanted her. She hadn't known until then. She hadn't!

But you suspected.

Staring at her reflection, Georgia shut off the water and squeezed the excess from the cloth, facing what her heart told her was true. Jake had never looked at her with those hot, hungry eyes. And, from the first moment her lips had touched Zach's, she *had* suspected. The moment Zach had taken control of the kissing, she'd *known*...at least on some level.

Georgia pressed the cool cloth to her hot face. If she'd known she was kissing Zach, not Jake, why hadn't she put an end to it? Why had she let things go as far as she had?

Because you liked it.

The answer, coming from her troubled conscience again, brought a fresh flood of heat to her face, but ashamed or not, it was the truth. She had liked it. Too much. In fact, she'd never suspected there was the capacity for such passion within what she considered to be her rather ordinary facade. Evidently, she *was* capable of feeling strong passions, but Jake wasn't capable of stirring them.

The moment the thought entered her mind, a terrible sensation of disloyalty came over her. It was a feeling she experienced often when her thoughts were filled with both Jake and Zach. Nevertheless, it was time to face the truth, no matter how unpleasant that might be, time to admit what she'd been unwilling to admit before now.

Zach Rawlings makes me feel more like a woman than I've ever felt in my life.

There. That wasn't so bad, she thought, releasing a sigh of relief. She'd faced her bogeyman and so far the world hadn't come to an end. Maybe admission really was the first step to recovery. Maybe the truth does set you free.

She regarded herself in the mirror and lifted a hand to touch her lips that were tender and swollen. There was no denying that Zach made her feel things an engaged woman should only feel for her fiancé, things that were wrong to feel for anyone else.

How could she feel this way when she hardly knew the man? Easy, her mind chided. She *did* know him...at least partly, because she knew Jake so well. No doubt the future would point out vast differences between them, but there would be undeniable similarities, too. But considering that they looked and sounded alike, it didn't make any sense that Zach's kisses made her heart race and Jake's didn't.

So what are you going to do about that?

"Nothing," she said aloud. She'd been all through this the night before, and nothing had changed. An unexciting and uninspired life with Jake was preferable to a life of fear and anxiety with Zach.

She laughed out loud, the irony-filled sound echoing off the bathroom walls. Here she was, weighing the pros and cons of a long-term, lasting relationship with Zach, all on the basis of a few mind-shattering kisses. If that wasn't the height of conceit! Just because she heard bells ringing and her toes curled when he kissed her was no sign he felt the same way. And even if he did, it didn't matter.

She would marry Jake Lattimer come June fifth, and that's all there was to it. This crazy obsession with Zach was nothing but her libido kicking up. She was ready for every aspect of marriage, including sharing a bed with her husband...especially sharing a bed with him. Whatever it was she thought she felt when she was with Zach was nothing but her needs looking for an outlet. Or infatuation. It would pass soon enough when she and Jake said "I do."

At least, she prayed it did.

As she expected, she got the third degree from Jake on the way to the meeting with the choir director.

"I told you I thought he was you," she said when he asked her again what had happened between her and Zach in the barn.

"That's what you said when you brought him home with you. It's wearing a little thin, sugar."

"Thin or not, it's the truth."

"Okay," Jake said, "I'll buy that you didn't know the difference at first, but do you mean to tell me that you couldn't tell the difference in the way we kiss you?"

Unable to dredge up an acceptable answer, Georgia sought refuge in irritation. "Jake, please!" she said, rolling her eyes toward him.

"Well, hell, Georgia Lee, how would you feel if you walked in on me and I was half-naked and another woman was all over me?"

Georgia closed her eyes and tried to imagine how she'd react if the shoe were on the other foot. Even though she had her doubts about her upcoming marriage to Jake, she was woman enough not to like that idea at all.

"Not so good," she admitted.

"I rest my case. It sure looked like the two of you were having a fine old time."

"I thought he was you, Jake," she said again, "and you know as well as I do that I've been trying to lure you into my bed for weeks. *I* rest my case."

"Touché," Jake muttered. "I guess if anyone's to blame, it's Zach. He knew better."

"There's no need to place blame on anyone. It just happened. It's over."

"I guess you're right," Jake said as they pulled into the church parking lot.

Georgia drew a relieved breath that their arrival had ended Jake's inquisition. She wasn't sure how long she could keep diverting his questions with exasperation or pretend that Zach's kisses meant nothing to her. After all, she was a French teacher, not an actress.

It took a private investigator the better part of the day to get a phone number for Lillian Hampstead, who'd left Brownsboro several years ago. To Tom's relief, they located her living in an apartment in Waco.

The quiet of Tom's office, which had closed its doors for the day, pressed in on him. He regarded Lillian's number with a thoughtful expression. Did he really want to do this? He shook his head. He had to. For his own sake, as well as Ben's. Resolutely, he reached for the phone and punched in the number.

He was almost ready to hang up when he heard a rattle on the other end, and an aging feminine voice said, ''Hello.''

''Is this Lillian Hampstead?'' Tom said. ''The Lillian Hampstead who used to live in Brownsboro?''

''Who's this?'' she asked after a slight pause.

''It's Tom, Lilli. Tom Barnette.''

''Tom!'' He thought he heard pleasure in her voice. And why not? They'd once brought each other lots of pleasure, even though Lillian was thirteen years older than him. ''Are you calling old friends to solicit votes, Tom?''

''I wouldn't turn them down,'' he said, chuckling. ''How've you been, Lilli?''

''Time goes on,'' she said. ''And mine's getting short.''

''I don't believe that for a minute. You'll always be that smart, sexy woman with the size-ten figure.''

''Well, I still fit into a size ten, but the sexy has given way to saggy, and the brain cells aren't what they once were, either.''

"Lilli, Lilli," Tom said, laughing again.

"It's true, Tom. I had to give up nursing a long time ago. I made a mistake with some medicine and..."

Her voice trailed away. Tom heard a quaver that had nothing to do with age. Though her brusque, no-nonsense manner often wasn't appreciated, Lillian had been a truly dedicated nurse, wanting the best for her patients and the young women she took in.

"None of us is getting any younger," he told her. "We just have to come to terms with that, I guess."

"Yes."

"Look, Lilli, I called because I'm looking for some information about one of the first adoptions you and I did together."

"That was a long time and a lot of babies ago, Tom."

"I know. Thirty-five years, to be exact." When she didn't say anything, he went on. "The adoption I'm talking about was for a rancher named Lattimer."

"I don't remember any Lattimers."

"Think," he urged.

"Why is this so important, Tom?"

"I spoke with Ben Lattimer this morning. I won't go into the details of how it happened, but it seems a man has shown up on Ben Lattimer's doorstep, who is the spitting image of the boy Ben adopted through me."

As Tom had done, Lillian laughed. "Everyone has a double."

"That's what I said. Ben thinks otherwise. He thinks they're twins and that they got split up at birth. Matter of fact, he jumped smack-dab in the middle of me, pretty much accusing me of doing something underhanded. I told him all I did was the paperwork, that the doctor there at the hospital would know.''

''That's right,'' Lillian said. ''He surely would.''

''The problem is that the doctor didn't show up that night. The phone lines were down because of a storm, and you delivered the baby.''

''Like I said, Tom, there were a lot of babies. The other nurses and I delivered a fair number of them through the years.''

''This is important, Lilli. You're the only one who'd know whether or not Jake Lattimer is a twin, and if so, what happened to the other one.''

''Are you insinuating that if there were twins born that night, that *I* separated them and adopted the other one out without telling you?''

''What I'm saying is that there's an election coming up, and I can't stand even the hint of another scandal.''

''You never could, could you?'' she said. ''You always looked out for number one, always arranged things so you'd come out smelling like a rose. Well, you listen to me, Tom Barnette.'' Her voice quivered with pious indignation. ''I wasn't the only nurse working that night or any other. Twins don't come along every day, not in a place the size of Brownsboro. Don't you think I'd remember?''

''That's my point. If it happened, just say so. I need to know so I can handle things at this end. Believe me, I'm not interested in causing you any trouble after all this time.''

''I don't remember any twins, and I certainly don't remember switching any twins.'' Her voice was firm, adamant.

Tom sighed. ''All right, Lilli. If that's what you say. But you might as well know that Ben Lattimer intends to have some DNA testing done. If you're lying, it's going to come out, and then there'll be hell to pay.''

After Georgia and Jake left for their meeting with the choir director, Ben and Zach dined on the steaks the older man had promised earlier that day. They'd spent a fair portion of the day together, Ben explaining the workings of the ranch and showing him the sights and their prize stock. Zach found Ben entertaining, intelligent and compassionate. He couldn't help envying Jake a little. Though the amnesia had robbed him of any tangible memories of his own father, he had a feeling he hadn't been as kind as Ben.

At dinner, Ben told Zach he'd been in touch with the lawyer who'd handled Jake's adoption to see if he could find out how a mix-up of this magnitude could have happened. He also said he'd made arrangements for them to have the blood work done. Zach wasn't sure if he should be comforted or disturbed by Ben's determination to get to the bottom of the mystery.

Zach didn't sleep well that night. Worries about not remembering his former life nagged him, as did the troubling memories of the kisses he and Georgia had shared.

His brief stretches of sleep were marred by distressing dreams of him and Jake coming to blows and Ben telling him to leave the ranch, but somehow it wasn't Jake he was fighting at all, it was his dad—whose face was hidden—and when Zach went back to thank Ben for all he'd done, the older Lattimer was gone, and Georgia was there in a chicken pen, wearing a wedding dress.

When he asked her what she was doing locked up, she said, ''Lattimer men don't like anyone messing with their women.'' He'd awakened then, but had fallen back asleep to dream more unsettling dreams.

He'd dreamed of a little dark-haired boy and a woman who, for some reason, reminded him of Georgia, yet other than having the same color hair, they looked nothing alike. Where Georgia's figure was slim, almost boyishly so, this woman's body was rounded, a few pounds shy of plumpness. Like Georgia, she was sweet and had a smile that could knock the birds from the trees.

In the fantasy, she pointed out a line of ants carrying food to their homes for the winter. She made him listen to the mournful song of a dove. She told him why there was lightning and thunder, when to plant potatoes, how eggs came from chickens.

She held him close and rocked in a squeaky wood rocker, and, with tears in her eyes, sang hymns to him. She taught him to pray and let him help crank ice cream on the front porch of a house in dire need of a painting. He didn't know her name, but when he awakened, he knew the woman in his dream was his mother.

Though he couldn't remember any distinct images, Zach knew he'd dreamed of a man, too, a handsome blond man with a mustache. Awake, with the picture fresh in his mind, he knew the man was his dad. That knowledge brought an unexpected rush of memories...the man with the mustache pulling up in front of the house that needed painting in an eighteen wheeler so black and shiny it reminded Zach of the patent-leather shine of the black widow spiders he often found beneath overturned buckets.

He recalled that his dad always smelled of liquor and Old Spice and remembered that the first thing he did when he came home from a trip was kiss his mama.

Then, with a sly smile, he'd tell Zach to go to his room and stay until he was told to come out.

Zach had known better than to disobey. He lay in his bed, a narrow twin cot with a faded brown chenille spread, and listened to the sounds that came from the other room, wondering what they meant, afraid to find out.

He remembered something else. He'd had an imaginary friend, Hoss. Hoss had been afraid, too. Hoss was the only one he could talk to, the only friend he had, the brother he longed for. His twin brother.

The recollection caused Zach to break out into a cold sweat. He'd called Jake hoss on more than one occasion since he'd arrived at the Lazy L, latching on to the name instinctively, because it felt right, somehow. Was it a coincidence, or one of those uncanny connections the medical and psychological communities claimed twins had?

Zach's head ached with the struggle to remember. But when his memory returned, there would still be a multitude of questions unanswered. He stirred uneasily beneath the single sheet covering him, as another torrent of recollections assaulted him.

He recalled that his dad didn't pay much attention to him, except to have him fetch him another beer or to do some chore or another. He remembered that if the task wasn't done to his dad's satisfaction, there was retribution in the form of a whipping.

Not overly fond of the leather belt used to discipline him, especially when he was drinking, Zach did his best to do the job right the first time. He remembered blaming Hoss for whatever went wrong, but he learned quickly that his dad didn't fall for that one.

He remembered, too, that his mother got furious at

any mention of his imaginary brother, and by the time he was six, Hoss had disappeared, except those nights when he couldn't sleep until he told Hoss all his tales of woe.

Zach knew his mama would listen to him if he had a problem, but she had her own problems, and he didn't want to add to her burdens. He had no choice but to tell Hoss how he felt, how much he hated his dad and how someday, when he got older and strong enough, he would make him sorry for things he did.

He liked it when his dad was on the road and there was no one in the shabby white house but him and his mama. When his dad was away, she smiled and laughed, but the minute his dad walked through the door, the light went out of her eyes, and the laughter died on her lips.

Zach had fallen asleep many nights listening to the sound of her crying after she and his dad argued and the argument had ended with his slapping her.

Now, lying in his borrowed bed in the Lattimer guest room and recalling the dreams, salvaging bits and pieces of his past from the rubble of his memory, Zach remembered their names.

"Abby." He spoke her name softly, almost reverently. His mother's name was Abby, and she'd been as pretty as a picture and as sweet as an angel.

His dad's name was Dwayne. His imaginary brother Hoss, he now knew, was the brother he'd been separated from at birth, the one whose presence he'd yearned for because they were so inextricably bound from the moment of conception. Hoss had been Jake's stand-in.

Staggered by the unexpected glimpse of his past, Zach scrubbed a hand over his face. When would the next memories come? What might trigger them? He didn't know, but he knew that he had to get back to the life he'd once lived and get the heck away from his brother's fiancée before he did something they'd both be sorry for.

Tom Barnette thought long and hard before he called Ben the next morning about his talk with Lillian Hampstead. She'd been outraged at his implications and resolute in her stand that she didn't remember splitting up any twins.

Why, then, didn't he feel any better about the whole ordeal? Her denial should have eased any worries he might have had, but he couldn't stop thinking about the injustice that had been done if Ben was right. But he was no magician. He couldn't pull rabbits out of a hat, and he couldn't conjure up proof that she lied any more than he could make a twin appear or disappear, no matter how much he might like to. All he could do was let this run its course and try to protect himself if it all came crashing down around him.

Reluctantly, he dialed Ben's number at the ranch.

"Did you find her?"

"I did. She's living in Waco now," Tom said. "She says she doesn't recall the night Jake was born, much less him being a twin. But she's pretty old, Ben. I told you she might not remember."

"Yeah," Ben said, his disappointment obvious.

"I know how you must feel."

"Do you, Tom? Do you know what it's like to be denied a child?"

"I know it must be hard, but have you thought that this DNA testing could only raise more questions and heartache?"

"Maybe so, but we're all adults and we deserve to know the truth. If your Nurse Hampstead is lying, I'm going to nail her miserable hide to the proverbial wall!"

"I don't blame you," Tom said. "If she's lying, I'll help you."

Chapter Six

Later that morning, Jake drove himself and Zach into town for the blood tests, complaining all the way. Zach learned that his brother hated driving in Fort Worth traffic, but since the Lazy L chopper was in the midst of its quarterly maintenance inspection, he had no choice. Zach wondered briefly what it would be like to have so much money he had a helicopter at his beck and call.

After having the requisite amount of blood drawn, Zach and Jake were told the results would take a minimum of ten days, but that two weeks was more realistic. Zach hoped the outcome was as painless as the actual testing, but he had an unexplainable feeling that they wouldn't be so lucky.

Even though things were more than a little strained between him and Jake, Zach asked if Jake would drive him to his apartment, so he could take a look around and see if anything jolted his memory. He didn't say it, but he wanted to make sure Attila was okay.

Jake agreed readily enough, and Zach figured that he agreed more out of curiosity about Zach's life-style as much as by a feeling of responsibility.

As Jake drove to the address on Zach's driver's license, Zach's troubled gaze searched each street, each strip mall, each storefront and each fast-food place, hoping for some recognition, but with no luck.

They located the apartment complex, a clone of many others in the area, with no problem. The sprawling buildings were stucco with wood trim, balconies upstairs, small porches on the lower levels, and the usual tasteful, if uninspired, landscaping.

Zach's armpits grew damp with an unaccustomed nervousness. Fighting a trepidation he didn't understand, he rolled down his window, welcoming the familiar scents and sounds of the city, so different from what he'd grown used to hearing and smelling at the ranch.

A listless creek meandered along the back parking lot. Trees with a tentative look—the hallmark of most trees in the city—grew to the water's edge. Children, unattended and, in his thinking, too small to be playing near the creek whose banks were swollen from recent rains, played there nevertheless, unaware and unconcerned by the possibility of danger.

Instinctively knowing the place was a favorite hunting ground of Attila's, Zach scanned the area for signs of the demon's presence but saw no black question mark of a tail twitching anywhere among the lush grasses growing to the water's edge. With a sigh of something akin to disappointment, he pointed to a parking place next to his nondescript sedan, which the rangers had arranged to have returned from the airport.

He and Jake got out of the Bronco and slammed their doors shut. Zach led the way, pulling a key ring from his pocket as he made his way toward the door, stopping and looking uncertainly at the dozen or so keys in his palm. After only a second's hesitation, he selected the key he knew opened the door to the first-floor apartment.

The key turned easily in the lock, and the door swung open. After being shut up for four days, the apartment already had a stuffy, unlived-in smell. Zach, who liked to sleep with the windows open as long as the temperature was bearable, had forgotten to turn on the air-conditioning before he left the morning of the sting. He asked Jake to leave the door open.

Open miniblinds revealed a fair-size living-dining area—for an average-priced apartment—and a wood-burning fireplace on the outer wall. The dining area, which opened onto a small concrete patio and a hand-kerchief-sized lawn and a privacy fence, was to the right of the living room.

A bar with cabinets above separated the dining area from the narrow kitchen. On the opposite side of the room, directly across from the front door, was a hallway that evidently led to the bedrooms. The walls were white, the furnishings were gray with touches of forest green and brick red, and the pictures on the walls were prints of popular Western paintings.

"Somehow, you don't seem like the flower type," Jake said, one corner of his mouth hitched upward in a droll smile.

Zach's attention moved to a cactus blooming in the sunshine of a nearby window. His face grew hot.

"Shelby—my partner when I was on the police force—gave it to me. She said it went with my decor, such as it was, and it didn't take much maintenance."

Surprised that he'd suddenly remembered that Shelby was his former partner and not his girlfriend, Zach's forehead furrowed in concentration. "She said the place looked like a cell, not a home, so she fixed it up a little." He waved his hand toward the sofa. "She bought the throw pillows and lamps, too."

Jake gave him a strange look, and Zach shrugged. "I don't know how I know that when I don't know much of anything else, but I do."

A mournful, somehow critical meow came from the open doorway.

"There you are, Attila," Zach said, smiling at the Oscar-worthy performance. He couldn't suppress the feeling of relief at seeing the cat well and well-fed, even though he'd rather die than admit he'd been worried about the ungrateful wretch.

The big black cat sauntered in, a regal tilt to his scarred head. He passed right by Zach's twin and proceeded to rub against Zach's legs in a way that expressed his pleasure at his owner's return. A superb thespian, Attila managed to project both a pitiful, neglected air as well as one of reluctant forgiveness, now that his master was back. Zach reached down and scratched the feline's head.

"You don't look like the cat type, either," Jake observed dryly.

Zach straightened. "I'm not," he said, with more firmness than the situation called for. "I like dogs. Big dogs. Attila's not really my cat. He just sort of came with the apartment."

"It's no sin for a man to like cats," Jake said, squatting on his haunches and reaching out to pick up Attila.

Zach opened his mouth in warning, but it was too late. With a hissing snarl that would put Dracula to shame, Attila half turned and gave a vicious swipe of his paw, catching Jake across the back of his hand.

Jake yelped a curse and bolted upright, carrying his blood-streaked hand to his mouth in a gesture as old as time. Attila skedaddled toward the open door.

"Damn cat!" Jake snarled, the look on his face as feral as that on the cat's just seconds before.

"I tried to warn you," Zach said.

"Yeah, yeah." Jake glared at the seeping scratches. "Do you have some antiseptic?"

"Sure." Zach pointed toward the hallway. "Bathroom's through there to the left. There are cotton balls, peroxide and other stuff in the medicine cabinet."

"Thanks."

Jake disappeared through the doorway, and Zach resumed his careful inventory of the room that reflected his life. There was a photo of two people on the mantel, himself and a slender woman with streaky blond hair that brushed her square jaw. They both wore the uniform of the Dallas PD, and, while Zach smiled broadly, the woman's smile was nothing but the slightest quirk of her lips. Her square chin tilted in a way that warned she shouldn't be messed with, and her eyes were hidden by dark sunglasses.

Shelby. Shelby Hartman. His partner before he left the Dallas Police Department and became a Texas Ranger. He knew the woman was Shelby, just as he knew that she wore the dark-lensed glasses more to keep anyone from seeing into her soul than to keep out the sun.

A sudden need to talk to her gripped him. Maybe Shelby could tell him something that would break down the walls of forgetfulness that kept him from getting on with his life. If nothing else, her pragmatic outlook would help him put the whole thing in perspective. But he couldn't see her until it was convenient for her, because Will said she was working undercover.

He put the photo back and turned toward the dining room. A combination answering machine and cordless phone sat on the counter, the red message indicator light blinking persistently. Drawn by the promise of hearing a familiar voice, he crossed the room and hit the replay button.

After the usual whirring of the tape, he heard the voice of the teenage girl at the cleaners who had a crush on him, informing him that, as of the day of the airport sting, his shirts were ready to be picked up. There was a message from Will the same day, telling him that the fishing was great and he and Viki were having a great time.

The next voice he heard was feminine, a wry-sounding voice with a hint of worry lacing it.

"It's just me."

The knowledge that he recognized the voice as Shelby's brought a smile to his lips.

"I called ranger headquarters to see if we could get together one evening when I'm off. Will told me about your accident. I've been worried sick. If you're home, I guess you'll get this. If you're still a guest in no-man's-land, you know I won't rest until I hear from you.

"I stopped by your place and picked up a little. I cleaned out your fridge, too. I swear, Zach, you could supply the CDC with penicillin with all the mold growing in there!

"Attila was out of cat food, so I bought some. That danged cat is weird. He has ESP or something. No matter what time of day or night I come over, he shows up before I leave. Oh, and I watered the cactus. Hope you're better soon. Bye."

The connection was broken and another female voice came on the line. This one was low and husky and had the barest hint of a Mexican accent.

"Hi, Zach. It's Laura. How's it going? I haven't heard from you in ages. Give me a call, will you? We need to get together. I miss you, *muchacho*. Bye."

"Got 'em standin' in line, don't you?"

The dry remark was delivered by Jake, who had entered the room while Zach was listening to his messages. The challenge in Jake's eyes couldn't be misconstrued. It dared Zach to try to add Georgia to his list of conquests.

The machine whirred and buzzed through a hang-up.

"Just a couple of friends," Zach said, and wondered why he felt compelled to justify himself to Jake.

"Hey, Ranger. Sorry I missed you at the airport." The feminine voice that came from the machine made a tsking sound. This woman's Mexican accent was as unmistakable as her sarcasm.

Immediately, the image of a gorgeous, dusky-skinned woman with bleached strawberry-blond hair and an insatiable lust for money rose in Zach's mind.

"My frien's, they say you got spooked after the incident at the airport, but I don' figure you're the spooky kin'. I figure you're still hurt somewhere, but nobody knows where you are, which is good for your recovery, eh?" A throaty chuckle filtered into the room. "I sure hope you're goin' to be better soon, 'cause you're goin' to have work to do. Remember Paco?''

Paco? Who the heck was Paco? Zach's mind raced in circles as he struggled to dredge up a single bit of information about Paco.

''Well, I think it's almos' certain that our mutual friend, Ramon, is goin' to come down with the same thing Paco did unless you do somethin' fast. *Adios.*''

A click signaled that the phone message had ended, and the sound of the tape rewinding told Zach that the messages had ended as well.

''What was that all about?''

Jake's query barely registered. Zach's attention was turned inside, where a dam had broken and wave after wave of memory washed over him, threatening to swamp him in a flood of feelings and emotions. Like a drowning man, he dragged in a deep, shuddering breath.

He'd been at the airport to apprehend Rita Morales, the girlfriend of Kiki Alvarez, an up-and-coming drug dealer who operated too close to the border for the comfort of the United States Drug Enforcement Agency.

One of Kiki's henchmen, Paco Rodriguez, had been sent to prison just before Thanksgiving. Like most criminals, he'd been willing to turn state's evidence for a lesser term and had given the police much valued information about Kiki's operations, including the fact that Rita was responsible for transporting the drugs and the money across the border. Paco's testimony had helped in the apprehension of another of Kiki's lieutenants, Ramon Varga, who was awaiting trial.

Two months earlier, Paco had died in jail, which is how Zach became involved with the case. One of the duties of the rangers was to investigate prison deaths. Zach learned that Paco's demise had been designed and initiated by Kiki and carried out by someone on the inside. His job was to find out who.

Later, the police learned that Rita was coming back into the country, presumably with more drugs. In an assist role, he and a select few peace officers from other branches of law enforcement had been following her, hoping to keep her in sight until they exited the terminal, where there were fewer people and the risk to any innocent bystanders was lessened.

But something had gone wrong. There was another woman there, a woman with a smile as bright and warm as summer sunshine, who'd mistaken him for someone called Jake. She'd latched on to Zach like a leech, and it was at that moment when his attention wavered that all hell had broken loose. He'd been hurt, and Rita had gotten away in the midst of the tussle.

He couldn't believe she'd had the guts to call and—

"Zach!"

The tone and tenor in the voice calling his name jerked Zach from the distressing turn of his thoughts. He looked up, his gaze finding that of a man looking at him as if he'd just taken leave of his senses. A man, Zach realized with a jolt, who looked just like him. His eyes widened in surprise and anxiety. For a brief moment, while the memories still gripped him, he didn't know who the man was.

"Are you all right?" the stranger who looked like him asked.

With the question came another surge of memory…everything that had happened to him since the altercation at the airport. This man was Jake, the man the woman had mistaken him for, the man everyone believed was his twin brother—obviously with good reason. Zach remembered that they'd had blood tests just an hour earlier to see if the belief was true. He reached out a steadying hand toward the bar.

The woman at the airport, the woman whose kisses were as hot as her smile, the woman who'd mistaken him for Jake was Georgia...Georgia Williams. He remembered that she was Jake's fiancée, and he himself was halfway in love with her, though how that had happened was way beyond his comprehension at the moment.

"Is everything okay?" Jake asked, frowning. "Is someone named Ramon in trouble?"

Ramon! Thoughts of Georgia's kisses and Jake's anger fled before a new fear. Zach grabbed the phone from its base. "I've got to call ranger headquarters. That was Rita."

"Who?"

"Rita Morales. Kiki Alvarez's girlfriend." Not bothering to explain, he punched in numbers with his thumb and waved his free hand at Jake in a gesture of dismissal. "It doesn't matter. What matters is that Kiki saw to it that one man was killed in jail, and he intends to do it again."

While Jake and Zach were in town, Ben tried to reach Jack Campbell out at his newest rig to ask him if he remembered anything unusual about the night they paced the waiting room together. Bliss Abernathy, the child of Jack's dead business partner whom Jack had raised as his own daughter, told him that Jack had gone off on one of his "jaunts," and no one had any idea how to get hold of him.

Telling Bliss that he'd try Jack later, Ben called Valerie, Jack's ex-wife, who had remained a good friend to her former husband after their divorce when their boys were eight. Valerie's personal secretary told him that Val was out of town for a few days and that she'd have her return Ben's call as soon as she got back.

Filled with a growing frustration, Ben called the proper administrative department in Austin to see if he could find out more about Jake's and Zach's parentage by getting copies of their birth certificates. The woman he spoke with was pleasant but firm. He was told that certainly the information could be looked up, but that without names of either parent, it would take longer.

"How many babies could have been born in a dinky little Texas hospital on August tenth, thirty-five years ago?" Ben asked testily.

"Not many, I'm sure," she said, "but you also have to remember that if the adoption records were sealed, you'll need to get a court order to have them opened. It takes time."

Feeling that he'd just run into another brick wall, Ben thanked the woman and hung up. He was bound and determined to get to the bottom of this, but for now, his hands were tied.

First things first.

One of Retha's favorite sayings popped into his mind. First they would see what the DNA tests showed. If he had proof that Jake and Zach were twins, then he'd call Tom Barnette, get Lillian Hampstead's phone number and put on the pressure himself. By the time he got through with her, if she had done anything illegal or immoral, she'd wished to hell she hadn't.

Staring disbelievingly at the instrument in his hand, Zach pushed the off button of the cordless phone and set it in its place with the same care he might have used to lay down a newborn.

His call to ranger headquarters was too late. Ramon Varga was dead, just as Rita Morales had predicted. And, as she predicted, he'd died the same death as Paco Rodriguez. His body had been found in the infirmary where he was recovering from food poisoning with huge amounts of narcotics in his system, drugs that were certainly not used to treat his particular ailment.

"I'm sorry."

Zach raised his gaze to Jake's compassionate one, not bothering to hide the defeat he knew was reflected in his eyes. "Yeah. So am I. Ramon was just a kid. Twenty-three or four. I don't even think he was a bad kid, really. Just one who'd been hungry a lot. One who wanted a better life for his mother and his brothers and sisters."

Neither spoke for a few seconds. Finally, Jake said, "Your memory's back, isn't it?"

"Yeah," Zach said with a wary nod. Now that he remembered his past, including his infatuation with this man's fiancée, he felt peculiarly vulnerable...and somehow more guilty than before. His belief about his moral code had been right on target. He wasn't the kind of man who went around luring women away from the men they loved. "How did you know?"

Jake shrugged. "The look on your face. The way you were acting. The way you knew suddenly you had to call your superiors."

Zach's mustache inched upward at one corner. "It was like being run down by a Mack truck, having everything come rushing back like that. One minute I was racking my brain trying to figure out who the hell Paco was, and the next I knew I had to call and tell head-quarters about Rita's threat about Ramon.'' He swal-lowed back the bitter taste of remorse.

"Don't be too hard on yourself," Jake said. "That woman deliberately waited until there was no chance of your getting help in time."

"Intellectually, I know that, but somehow that ra-tionale never seems to make failure any easier to take."

"Then why do you do it?" Jake asked. "What made you want to go into law enforcement?"

"I had a little brush with the law when I was four-teen," Zach said, shrugging. "Nothing too serious, but serious enough to make my mama think I was going to spend the rest of my life in jail and eternity in hell."

"You remember your mother?"

"Yeah. I remember her," Zach said. Unwilling to share any of his newly reclaimed recollections with Jake just yet, he steered the conversation away from that topic, elaborating on the answer to Jake's earlier question.

"Lucky for me, the town cop was a good guy, not one of those hicks who lets the power of his job go to his head."

A slow smile lifted Jake's lips and lit his eyes. "I've had a run-in or two with that type myself."

"You?" Zach asked with raised eyebrows. "The paragon of virtue to the entire Southwestern United States?"

The dig seemed requisite, somehow, a small com-pensation for Jake's earlier remarks about the cat and the cactus. And, as he now realized Jake's comments were, Zach's was meant to needle a bit, not belittle.

"If you weren't already hurt, I'd knock your head off for that," Jake said in a conversational tone with another lazy smile. "Actually, I caused my parents a fair amount of grief growing up. Like you say, nothing serious, just usual boy stuff."

They shared a smile, and then, as if shocked by the fact that they'd trusted each other enough to share a bit of their pasts, neither of them could think of anything else to say.

"What happens next?" Jake asked at last.

"I guess I'll stay here," Zach said. "I appreciate more than I can say what you and everyone at the ranch did for me the past few days, but there's no sense going back now that my memory's returned."

No sense going back and chance meeting up with Georgia again.

"Thanks," Jake said. "We try. The problem is, my dad's taken a liking to you. You'll hurt his feelings if you don't tell him goodbye."

Zach knew Jake was right. Ben Lattimer had treated him with all the consideration of a son. Refusing to thank him in person would be the height of churlishness.

"You're right. I'll drive out in my car later on this afternoon, so you won't have to bring me back."

"Sounds good," Jake said with a nod. "See you later, then."

Jake was at the door when Zach said, "Under the circumstances, I bet you'll be glad to see the back of me, won't you, hoss?"

Both knew just what circumstances Zach was talking about.

Jake turned. Smiled that wry half smile. "You don't threaten me, Zach."

"I'm glad," Zach said with a nod. "It was never my intention."

* * *

Jake thought about Zach's comment and his own answer most of the way back to the Lazy L. He hadn't been exactly truthful. In fact, he'd out-and-out lied. He would be damned glad to see the last of Zach Rawlings. Glad to have his life back, complete with a father who loved him and a fiancée who was going to marry him in just over two weeks.

Truth was, he *was* threatened. Threatened by the fact that the people he loved the most thought he should just accept Zach's arrival into all their lives like the brother they believed he was. It wasn't that cut and dried for Jake. He needed time to process everything that had happened, time to weigh the pros and cons. Time to come to grips with the changes taking place in his life.

Finding out that he'd been adopted was like having the cornerstone of his world jerked away. Finding out that he possibly had a twin brother was another shock. Knowing that both his dad and Georgia were taken with Zach was almost more than his bruised ego could bear. Though he wasn't proud of it, Jake knew he was jealous, too. Jealous of the time Ben spent with Zach, jealous of Zach kissing Georgia.

He pulled the Bronco to a halt in the driveway and shut off the engine. Rubbing his mustache thoughtfully with one finger, he admitted that even though he did feel threatened, he was also intrigued by the idea of having a brother, since he'd always wanted one. He got out of the vehicle, slamming the door behind him. Still, he didn't deny he was genuinely glad Zach's memory had returned so fast.

Jake was about to go into the house when a flash of something inside the Bronco caught his eye. Turning back, he saw a black cat sitting on the headrest, staring at him from amber eyes filled with ancient secrets and arcane wisdom.

Damned if it wasn't Zach's ill-tempered black cat! Jake wondered how the cantankerous critter had managed to stow away, and remembered that Zach had left his window down when they went into the apartment.

What should he do? He sure as heck didn't want to drive back to Fort Worth, and he sure as heck wasn't about to try to lay hands on Attila and put him in the carrier they used to transport Elizabeth to the vet's. He couldn't leave the cat inside the car; he'd be dead from heat before Zach arrived that evening.

Jake sighed. He had no choice but to let the cat out. Zach could round him up and take him back when he arrived. Feeling as if he was about to open Pandora's box, Jake reached for the handle and opened the door. Attila shot out like a black cannonball, streaking past the corner of the house and disappearing.

Jake went into the house, unable to shake the feeling that his life had just undergone another major upheaval, that Attila's stowing away was somehow symbolic of Zach's advent into his life, and that their arrivals would change his world forever.

After Jake left, Zach left a message for Shelby at the police station, and then called Laura Ramirez. He felt compelled to make contact with the people he knew, as if seeing them, doing something with them could somehow validate the return of his memory and his life. If he remembered right, Laura was off the next day. Since he couldn't go back to work until the doctor released him, maybe the two of them and J.R., her five-year-old son, could get together for lunch.

To his surprise, Laura answered the phone on the second ring.

"What are you doing home?" he asked, forgoing a salutation.

"Zach!" Laura cried. "Are you all right?"

"I'm fine."

"Good. When I heard what happened at the airport, and when I found out it was you who got hurt, I called ranger headquarters to get the scoop. All they'd tell me was that you were on medical leave. I didn't have any idea where you were."

"I've been taking it easy out on a ranch," he said. "I'm home now, but I'll be out of commission a few days."

"A ranch? What were you doing on a ranch?"

"It's a long story. If you want to hear it, how about you and J.R. going to lunch tomorrow? Or today, since you're home?"

"We'd love to, Zach, but Rufio's been under the weather the past couple of days, and I hate to take him out."

Rufio, which meant red in Spanish, was auburn-haired J.R.'s nickname, a moniker that fit the ornery little cuss.

"What's wrong?"

"I think they let him play too hard at the day care. You know how hyper he is. He just seems worn-out and listless."

Zach heard the thread of worry in her voice. Even though she was forced by circumstance to work, Laura Ramirez was as good a mother as Zach had seen—not that he'd seen all that many. But there was no doubt to anyone who was around longer than five minutes that J.R. was her pride and joy as well as her heart and soul.

"Don't worry," Zach said. "It's probably some sort of a bug. Kids are pretty resilient. He'll snap out of it in a few days."

"I'm sure you're right," Laura said. "But we have a doctor's appointment tomorrow morning, just to make sure."

"Good idea."

He heard J.R. ask who it was, and, when he was told, heard the child wail, "I wanna see Zach!"

"I guess you heard that," Laura said, laughing. "Both the place and I are a mess, but why don't you come over? I'll fix lunch here."

"I have a better idea," Zach said. "I'll stop and pick up a pizza."

"Great! I can't wait to hear what happened."

"Well, I'll tell you this much, darlin'," Zach drawled. "It's the kind of story that makes the front page."

An hour later, armed with a large pizza with every topping imaginable on it, Zach drove to Laura's. He'd become acquainted with her six years ago, when she, soon to be an unwed minority mother, had first moved to Dallas from San Antonio. A knockout Mexican beauty, she looked more like a flamenco dancer than a reporter. Indeed, she played flamenco guitar as a hobby.

Zach had learned real fast that just because Laura Ramirez came wrapped in a pretty package, her intelligence should not be underestimated. Anyone, especially a man, who was chauvinistic enough to comment on her looks or suggest she cash in on them for a story got set straight faster than J.R. could unwrap a candy bar.

Though Zach had been physically drawn to Laura when they'd first met—and Zach's opinion was that any man whose heart rate didn't accelerate when he looked at her was a prime candidate for a coffin—she'd let him know up front and in a hurry that she wasn't interested in him as anything but a friend and a contact in law enforcement.

Over the years, he'd learned that her relationship with J.R.'s father had blazed so hot and bright that it burned itself out in six short weeks. The man wasn't interested in putting down roots, and she wasn't interested in being his occasional plaything, so they'd parted ways.

When she found out she was pregnant, she hadn't told him. She couldn't stand the possibility of his rejection, or worse, that he might offer to marry her out of some misguided sense of duty. She'd moved from San Antonio to Dallas, hoping to leave the memories behind, start over and carve out a niche for herself in the competitive world of journalism.

She'd partly succeeded. Though Zach knew she'd never fallen out of love with the man who had fathered J.R., Laura was steadily making a name for herself as an investigative reporter, unearthing everything from age-old scams that dated back to the horse-and-buggy days. The stories made fascinating reading when she compared them to their modern-day counterparts.

Occasionally, when she uncovered something that really hit her on an emotional level, she did human-interest pieces. The last time Zach had talked to her at any length, one of the local television stations was wooing her, hoping to convince her to give up regular journalism for a spot in front of the camera. She was gorgeous and quick, and, like Shelby, a good friend, even though their respective careers prevented them from spending much time together.

He'd known that telling Laura his tale was front-page news would pique her interest, as would the mention of amnesia. By the time they'd gotten off the phone, she'd decided to do a series of stories about amnesia victims.

Zach grinned. He couldn't wait to tell her about how Georgia had spotted him at the airport and the whole crazy twins thing.

J.R. met him at the doorway. He looked taller, and his face looked thinner than Zach remembered, but it was wreathed in a smile.

"J.R. My man!"

"Zach, my old bud!" the incorrigible Rufio shot back, catapulting through the open doorway.

Zach knelt, balancing the pizza box on one palm as he braced himself for the impact of the small body hurtling toward him. They hugged briefly, did the high five with a lot of extra stuff Rufio had taught him thrown in—from sliding palms to hooking fingers. Zach had no idea what he was doing, but that he remembered how clearly pleased the boy.

Their usual ceremonial greeting out of the way, Zach straightened and started for the front door where Laura stood, wearing cutoff jeans and a baggy turquoise-hued T-shirt. Her long ebony hair, a riot of waves that he knew grew halfway down her back, was caught up in a ponytail that perched high atop her head. Her dark eyes, with those ungodly long eyelashes, sparkled with laughter, and her full, smiling lips were as naked as her feet.

"I hope you got everything on the pizza," J.R. said, skipping along beside him.

"Have I ever let you down?" Zach replied, reaching down to ruffle the boy's auburn hair. "And by the way, I don't want to hear anymore of that *old* stuff, you hear."

"What do you mean?"

"Don't play dumb with me." Zach pitched his voice to a childish falsetto and said, "Zach, my old bud!"

Both J.R. and Laura laughed.

"Hi, gorgeous!" Zach said, slipping his arm around Laura's shoulders and brushing a kiss to her cheek.

"Hi, yourself," Laura said, smiling at him as she slid her arm around his waist. She searched his face for a moment, then nodded. "You look pretty good, and your wits are as sharp as ever. Are you sure you took a blow to the old noggin?"

"I'm sure," Zach said. "And I've got the goose egg to prove it."

"Can I see?" J.R. asked.

"*May* I see?" Laura corrected with a stern look. "Where's your grammar?"

"In San Antonio," Rufio said with a grin. "With Gramper."

Laura bit her lower lip to hide her laughter, but Zach didn't even try to hide his. The kid was a prize. "How about I let you see when you finish your pizza, short stuff?"

"Sure," J.R. said with a shrug. "Come on, then. I'm starving."

Over several slices of pizza and ice-cold tea, Zach told Laura everything that had happened to him from the moment he'd set eyes on Georgia at the airport four days earlier.

"And how do you feel, knowing you may be a twin? Knowing you were given up for adoption?"

"I feel as if I've been kicked in the gut, that's how I feel," he told her. "What do I do if it's true?"

"You get to know your brother," Laura said. "You told me you always wanted one."

Zach nodded, but he wasn't convinced. "What about my real mother? Should I try to find her?"

Laura's gaze was direct, candid. "Do you want to?"

"I don't know," he admitted, "and even if I did, I wouldn't know where to start."

Laura waggled finely defined eyebrows at him. "You're looking at the woman who can help you."

"What are you talking about?"

"Remember that series I did about the rise in unwed mothers a few months ago?"

"Yeah."

"Some of the girls I interviewed planned to keep their babies, some didn't want to be saddled with any reminder of their mistakes and some didn't really want to give them up, but they were underage and their parents were making the decisions for them."

Laura's eyes took on a glitter of excitement. "Well, one thing led to another, and the next thing I knew I was thinking about a whole new series on adoptions—everything from black-market babies, foster parenting, kids who just basically *give* their babies to their parents to raise, and orphanages, which may be obsolete one day soon."

Zach thought of all the kids abandoned or abused by their parents. "That will never happen."

"You're probably right," she said, "but things are

a lot different than they were a hundred years ago, Zach—or thirty-five years ago, for that matter. Even back then, there were mostly closed adoptions where everything was sealed and the prospective parents had no idea of what they were getting. Compared to today's private adoptions where the couple meets the mother-to-be, and she may have visiting privileges, the old way was like getting a pig in a poke.''

''What are you trying to tell me?''

''Just that I've learned a lot working on this series, and I've made a lot of contacts. If you decide to look up your mother, I may be able to help you locate her.''

Chapter Seven

By the time Zach left Laura's at mid-afternoon, the daily, dull headache he'd come to expect throbbed in his temples, a side effect of the concussion, he supposed. When he got back to the apartment, he took a couple of over-the-counter painkillers, put on a pair of disreputable running shorts and crawled into bed thinking how emotionally exhausting reclaiming a life was. He was asleep in minutes.

He didn't remember dreaming, but as he lay there after waking up, the image of the woman he'd dreamed about at the ranch crept into his mind. The woman who was so similar to Georgia. Abby. His mother. He thought about her patience and how she'd taught him things about respecting and caring for the world around him, how she'd taught him about spiritual things.

Was the conjecture about him and Jake being twins separated at birth really possible? A part of him that he didn't want to listen to whispered that it was not only possible, but probable. His mind roiled with the same questions that had plagued him for the past four days, only now the focus had changed.

Before his memory had returned, everything—including Ben's certainty that he and Jake were brothers—was just one more missing piece to the puzzle of Zach's misplaced memory. The idea troubled him because it seemed to upset everyone else involved, but until his memory returned, it was no more troubling than the fact that he couldn't remember his name.

The return of his memory had flung him into the middle of an emotional morass, and his confusion was compounded by anger at how—if it was true about him and Jake being separated—it could have happened. Like Jake, he didn't want to believe it, because acknowledging it as truth would affect his future in ways he couldn't yet comprehend.

If the DNA testing proved beyond a doubt that he and Jake were twins, coming to terms with that truth would involve sacrifice of the values taught to him by his mother from infancy up, values like reliability and honesty.

As Jake had already experienced, the most painful of these shattered beliefs to accept was not that some unknown woman had given him and his brother up, but that he and Jake had been lied to all their lives by people they loved and respected.

It wasn't hard for Zach to imagine his dad telling him a lie. Dwayne Rawlings's life was built on a series of lies that he hoped would compensate for his weaknesses and general lack of character. On the other hand, it was almost impossible to imagine Dwayne keeping his mouth shut about something of this magnitude for so many years.

Zach stroked his mustache thoughtfully. Of course, if there was some reason Dwayne and Abby couldn't have kids, and obviously there was, his dad was the kind of man who'd take that as a personal blow to his manhood. It wouldn't matter to him where the problem of infertility lay, Dwayne wouldn't go blabbing the news for fear it might make him look less a man.

Zach's mother was different. Though she'd died when he was fourteen, he remembered her whole life as being one based on kindness, honesty and service to others. Dwayne had made good money driving trucks for various local businesses through the years, but he was stingy with his paychecks. Zach and his mom lived frugally, but somehow, Abby always managed to cook extra food to share with some shut-in or someone who was sick.

One of his most vivid memories was standing on a chair next to her—he couldn't have been more than two—as she baked homemade bread to take to various homebound neighbors. Flour and yeast were cheap, she said. Every Tuesday, the house was filled with the scent of baked bread that she'd lined up along the countertop.

She taught him to count with the bread, patiently pointing out the six or seven loaves, each perfectly browned and glistening with the butter she rubbed into the crusty top when she took it from the oven. He remembered her saying that the butter kept the tops soft.

Angrily, Zach rolled from the bed to his feet and went to stare out the French doors that opened onto the patio. How could she have been so generous when she was nothing but a liar? How could she preach honesty and integrity when her lies served as the very foundation of his life?

He felt the sting of tears prickling his eyes. Did he want to take Laura up on her offer to use her contacts to find his real mother? Did he want to pick what was left of his dad's brain to find out the truth?

His dad. Zach let out a deep breath. As much as Abby's lies hurt, Zach couldn't help feeling a bit of relief to know that if it were true that he was adopted, Dwayne Rawlings wasn't his dad. That was something to be thankful for.

When he'd gotten into the scrape with the law just months before his mom died, he'd been so scared of being sent away that he'd taken her tongue-lashing gratefully. She'd cried and begged him not to become like Dwayne.

She made her point. Zach didn't want to be like Dwayne. He'd lived his whole life feeling uncomfortable around his dad, disliking his arrogant, cocky behavior and his treatment of him and his mother. Hating the drinking.

As he'd grown older, Zach had become increasingly fearful that he'd inherited Dwayne's bad blood, that he might be a "bad seed," as his grandma called it. That fear was one of the reasons he'd gone into law enforcement. If he was dedicated to doing good, there was no way he could go bad, was there?

Now it looked as if all that worry had been for nothing. The pain in his head, which had disappeared while he slept, began to throb like an aching tooth. He couldn't have it both ways. Either Abby and Dwayne were his real parents and his mom could stay on her pedestal, or they weren't—in which case, his mom fell from grace, but he was compensated by the knowledge that not a drop of Dwayne Rawlings's blood flowed in his veins.

The Lord giveth; the Lord taketh away.

Zach turned away from the window, his heart heavy. He didn't know what to wish from the DNA tests.

"What do you mean he has his memory back?" Georgia asked Jake that evening as they sat around the pool and waited for Zach's arrival. The news sent her already troubled spirits plummeting. If Zach's memory was back, he'd leave, and she might never see him again...except as her brother-in-law. The thought was sobering, and more disturbing than she wanted to admit. "How could it happen so fast?"

"I don't know, but he was listening to his phone messages, and I could see it taking place right in front of me," Jake told her. He related what happened, and said, "It was weird. When he found out that he'd remembered too late to save that guy in prison, he was pretty shaken up."

The doorbell rang. "That must be him," Ben said, going to answer the door.

Georgia's heart began to race. She hadn't seen Zach face-to-face since Jake caught them in the barn. What would she say to him? What could she say? That the memory of his kisses and the way his hands had moved over her body had been keeping her awake at night? That she'd been so caught up in those same recollections that Kat Bensen had made a crack that afternoon about Georgia being lovesick?

Georgia couldn't deny the sudden nervousness that swept through her when Zach entered the living room. Her gaze went unerringly to his mouth. Memories of that mouth devouring hers blinded her to the greetings going on around her.

Her hungry gaze raked over him from his shoulders to his booted feet. All she could think of was the way his flesh felt beneath her fingertips, warm and supple, with well-defined muscles beneath. That, and the disturbing feel of his hard thighs between hers.

"Hello, Georgia."

The sound of his voice scattered her thoughts like a covey of quail before a dog. Struggling for a composure she was far from feeling, she met his eyes with hers. Though it was probably her imagination, fed by the guilt that had shadowed her since their encounter in the barn, the moment seemed filled with tension. She felt as if Ben and Jake's attention was centered on her reply, as if they were weighing her response, gauging the look in her eyes, reading each gesture to see what her body language had to say about her feelings.

What she said was, "Hello, Zach."

She didn't know what her face revealed and refused to look at Jake to see what was in his eyes. Convinced that there was more she should say, she offered a quick quirk of her lips she hoped passed for a smile. "I heard the good news. I guess you'll be glad to get back to your real life."

Zach's smile wasn't much more successful than hers. "It's nice to have a handle on things again. Not knowing anything about yourself can be pretty scary."

"Well, we'll miss you," Ben said.

"Thanks. I have a feeling I'll miss all of you, too."

His answer was for Ben, but his gaze flickered toward Georgia, whose immediate reaction was to glance at Jake. He was frowning.

"I wanted to thank you for all you've done for me,"

Zach said. "I appreciate your making me feel part of the family."

"I think we all believe you *are* part of the family," Ben said.

Zach's smile didn't reach his eyes. "We'll know soon, won't we?"

"That we will." Ben smiled. "Whatever the outcome, I want you to know you'll always be welcome here."

"Thank you, Mr. Lattimer."

"Ben," he corrected.

"Ben." Zach glanced at Jake. There was a moment's awkwardness when it seemed to Georgia that Jake should say something. He didn't.

"I'll get my things together and get back to town," Zach said after a moment. Georgia wondered if it was her imagination, or if it was hurt she saw lurking in the depths of his dark eyes.

"You'll eat supper before you go, won't you?" Ben asked. "Rosie has an American history class tonight, but Georgia brought stew and homemade bread. I can vouch that they're both delicious."

"You make bread?"

Seeing the surprise in his eyes, Georgia shrugged. "It's no big deal. I have a bread machine."

"Oh."

She thought she saw disappointment in his eyes, but decided that there was no reason he should be disappointed because she made bread in a machine. As she excused herself to go warm the stew, she heard Zach agree to stay and found herself hoping this batch of stew was as good as Ben claimed. She pushed through the saloon-style doors to the kitchen, her palms sweating with sudden nerves. After all, as Meredith would say, the way to a man's heart was through his stomach.

The random thought drew her footsteps to a halt just inside the doorway. Now, why had she thought that? Zach Rawlings was a peace officer. Peace officers in any form were unacceptable, no matter how fast they might make her heart beat and no matter how well they kissed. They were taboo. Out of bounds. Forbidden. She had absolutely no interest in getting to Zach Rawlings's heart...did she?

When dinner was finished, Georgia stayed behind to clean up the dining room and kitchen, while the three men went down to the barn to check on Lucy and water the horses that had been put into the barn for the night.

Jake also expressed hope that Zach could nab the villainous Attila and deport him back to the city where he could mix it up with others of his ilk instead of sparring with the virtuous Elizabeth. Georgia wasn't sure when she'd seen Jake so upset over an animal.

She'd just put the last of the leftover stew into the refrigerator when she heard footsteps on the tile floor. Closing the door and turning, she saw Zach in the doorway. She knew without a doubt it was Zach, not because she knew what he was wearing, but because he looked at her differently than Jake did.

Just now, there was a contemplative, searching expression in his dark eyes. A look that sought her secret dreams and her deepest thoughts. A look that stole her breath and made her painfully aware that she was a needy woman.

"What?" Her voice was breathless, questioning.

"I forgot something."

It was only when he crossed the room and stopped

less than two feet from her that she realized she was trapped between him and the refrigerator.

"What did you forget?" The words fluttered from her lips on a breathless whisper.

"This."

Slowly, Zach placed his palms against the refrigerator on either side of her head. Even more slowly...so that she could stop him if she wanted—which she didn't—he lowered his head. Her lashes drifted down a heartbeat before his lips touched her eyelids, placing a gentle kiss on each one before grazing the crest of her cheek and moving to her ear.

She felt the tickle of his breath before he drew her earlobe into the hot moistness of his mouth. A soft sob of longing escaped her parted lips, and her nails dug into the flesh just above the waistband of his jeans. She quaked like a leaf in a spring breeze, quivering with longing and fear and uncertainty.

When she opened her mouth to tell him that what they were doing had to stop, that it wasn't right, that it wasn't fair to either of them, much less to Jake, he kissed her, a soft, openmouthed kiss as gentle as the brush of a fairy wing, as potent as a sip of white lightning.

The floor seemed to roll beneath her like the sand at the ocean's edge. Dizzy, light-headed, needing something solid to hold on to, she slid her arms around his hard waist. His warmth melted the facade of indifference she'd adopted earlier.

Things had gone too far for Georgia to pretend she didn't know what she was doing. Until now, she'd been able to convince herself that her feelings were simply an infatuation that she'd get over. But she'd been lying to herself, and every time she was with Zach, she grew more convinced that she might never get over it. No, the time for lying to herself was over. She knew exactly what she was doing, and whom she was doing it with.

She was betraying her fiancé with his brother.

The brutal honesty of the thought brought back a measure of her sanity.

As subtle as it was, Zach picked up on her withdrawal. He eased his mouth from hers and straightened, but he didn't let her go. Instead, he took his hands from the refrigerator and drew her close, sliding his palms down to her bottom and fitting her to him in a way that made her excruciatingly aware of the physical differences in their bodies.

Georgia knew she should free herself, but even though his hold on her was gentle and she knew he would release her with a single word, she also knew that she could no more tell him to stop than she could turn the tides.

He looked down at her with a wry, lopsided half smile. "I think that you'll agree that what we have here is a hell of a problem." Zach raked his thumb across the wetness of her bottom lip. "Question is, what are we gonna do about it?"

Hearing him put what was between them into actual words made it more substantive, somehow. Georgia looked into dark eyes filled with a question and a strange combination of desire and uncertainty. She, too, was uncertain, unsure how to answer...torn between what she wanted and what she knew was right.

"Nothing."

His eyebrows drew together. "What do you mean, nothing?"

"We're going to do nothing. I can't hurt Jake by...by—"

"By sleeping with a man who might be his twin brother?" Zach offered in a taut, sarcastic voice.

Aghast at the suggestion, Georgia tried to free herself. "I wasn't planning to sleep with you!"

"What were you planning to do then?" Zach asked. "Keep on teasing me? Keep tying me in knots for the heck of it?"

"I wasn't teasing you," she denied hotly.

"What the hell do you call it?"

Georgia opened her mouth to say that it was just kisses, but Zach's next comment stopped her.

"You don't love Jake."

The words hung in the air between them. Accusation. Condemnation. Denunciation. They stripped her of pretense, exposing her deepest concern with a brutal ruthlessness. Tears pooled in her eyes and trembled on her eyelashes.

"Damn you!" she choked out in a soft voice.

His dark eyes even darker with anger, Zach shook his head. "No, Georgia. Damn *you*."

He moved his hands to her hips, jerking her against him with a roughness that took her breath away. Her gasp of shock was swallowed by his parted lips, which settled on hers with an expertise that sent her senses spiraling out of control.

He kissed her with a greedy hunger that left her helpless to do anything but answer with the same hunger, the same greed. His hands moved over her, touching her in a way that made her body ache for release. After what might have been aeons or mere seconds, he stepped back, distancing himself from her.

The expression in his eyes was as harsh as the ruthlessness in his voice. "You want me."

Uncertain if she was angrier at him or herself, she

managed a short, mirthless laugh. "It's been a long time."

She intended for the statement to convey the idea that any man could evoke a response from her. Instead, good law officer that he was, Zach homed in on the relevancy of her testimony.

"You and Jake aren't sleeping together?"

Realizing her mistake, Georgia did her best to backtrack. "I didn't say that."

"Yes," he said, nodding, "you did. What I'm wondering is why."

"Jake's a gentleman," Georgia said, taking up for her fiancé.

Shaking his head in disbelief, Zach planted his hands on his hips. "He's a lunatic."

She raised her chin. "He respects me."

"He's an imbecile."

Georgia stamped her foot in frustration. "Oooh!" she said through gritted teeth. "Stop trying to make it sound so terrible! He wanted to wait until we were married, so that everything would be perfect."

"Well, pardon the heck out of me!" Zach's voice dripped sarcasm. "Obviously the man's a prime candidate for sainthood! If I were your fiancé I'll be damned if I'd wait."

"But you're not, are you?" Georgia snapped.

The wisecrack didn't faze him. He went on as if she hadn't spoken.

"I'd carry you off to the nearest bed—"

"Over my dead body!"

"—strip you down—"

She gasped.

"—and make love to you until you couldn't move

for a week,'' he finished, glaring at her as if he'd like to beat her instead of kiss her senseless.

They stared at each other for long seconds, each knowing they'd crossed over some imaginary line, but neither knowing exactly what that line was, or what the crossing might mean.

''As if I'd let you,'' she said at last.

Before she realized what he was up to, Zach reached out, grasped her chin in a firm grip, and took her lips in a kiss that was half angry, half frustrated.

In spite of herself, Georgia felt herself responding.

In spite of himself, Zach felt his anger draining.

When he released her, they were both breathing heavily.

Without speaking a word, he released her and, turning on the heel of one booted foot, left her standing there, her lips wet from his kisses, her eyes wet with tears.

He turned at the doorway. His eyes held conviction and sadness.

''You'd let me.''

Georgia had herself more or less under control by the time Jake and Ben came through the kitchen from the barn a few minutes later. She busied herself with emptying the trash to keep them from seeing something in her eyes they shouldn't.

''Zach's leaving. Don't you want to come and tell him goodbye?'' Jake asked.

Georgia felt a sharp stab of pain in her heart. Contrary to what Ben hoped, she had a feeling that Zach wouldn't be spending his spare time at the Lazy L with his newly found brother.

She bent over to lift out the trash sack. ''We said

goodbye when he came in to get his things together.''
The lie tripped from her lips with startling ease.

"Wait!"

The sharpness of Jake's voice made her straighten
and look at him. Their eyes met, Georgia's wide and
questioning, mirroring her fear that he'd suspect what
had happened between her and Zach. Jake's eyes were
calm and considering.

"I'll get that."

The gentlemanly gesture, so much a part of his innate kindness, brought tears to her eyes.

"What's the matter?" he asked, crossing the room
and lifting her chin with his forefinger.

With the memory of Zach's kisses and her response
burned into her mind, it was all she could do to look
Jake in the eye. This lie came with a small smile.
"Nothing. Just tired. And a little headache starting."

Jake turned her around and started to massage her
shoulders. "No wonder. You're as tight as that new
fence in the south pasture," he mused. "Must be something going around."

"What?" she asked, unable to follow his mental
leap.

"Headaches. Zach said he had one and wanted to
come and get something to take before it got worse.
Did you show him where the medicine was?"

Georgia shook her head. "He didn't mention it.
Maybe there was something in his medicine cabinet in
his bedroom."

"Oh, yeah," Jake said. "I forgot. Rosie usually
keeps the guest bathrooms well stocked." He gave her
shoulders a final squeeze. "Better?"

"Much. Thanks."

"Good."

She felt Jake move her hair aside, felt him press a kiss to the side of her neck. She sucked in a surprised breath and tensed.

"What's the matter?"

"Nothing." She forced a smile to her lips and turned to face him. "You just caught me off guard."

"Better get used to it," he said, dropping a brief kiss to her mouth.

Thankfully, the statement didn't require an answer. He lifted the trash from the metal container and tied it with the same deft speed she'd seen him use on a calf at branding time.

"I'll take this outside later," he said. "Come on. Let's see Zach off."

"You go ahead," Georgia said. "I'll be there in a minute. I need to use the ladies' room. Tell Zach I said goodbye and I wish him well."

Jake nodded. "See you in a few minutes."

Georgia watched him go, filled with a sense of relief. She really was getting a headache. Two Jakes—or two Zachs—was one too many for a woman to handle. She wished she'd never seen Zach Rawlings at the airport. No, that wasn't true. What she wished was that she'd met him first. But that wasn't true, either.

Quite simply, she was smack-dab in the middle of a dilemma. She might not be crazy in love with Jake, but she loved him. Yet Zach had been right when he'd said she wanted *him.* She was an intelligent woman. Wanting and love were certainly not the same thing. Everyone knew that a relationship based only on lust was doomed to failure, that if wanting was the only tie binding two people together, the hot flames of passion would soon consume that fragile bond.

It was far better to marry Jake, liking and respecting

him, than to give him up for a fling with Zach Rawlings just because kissing him was like receiving a small jolt of electricity.

How many times are you going to tell yourself that?

A better question might be to ask herself when she was going to start believing it.

Zach left—without his darned cat, which wasn't anywhere to be found. Georgia followed some ten minutes later. Jake sat on the front porch long after they'd driven away and Ben had gone inside to watch television.

Something was going on with Georgia and Zach. He wasn't blind, or stupid. He *knew* it the way a coyote hound knew when a coyote was in the area. Up to a point, he could buy her mistaking Zach for him, but as of tonight, he'd pretty much reached saturation with that argument.

Zach had left him and Ben at the barn with the excuse that he was suffering from one of the headaches he'd gotten often since his accident, and was going to the house to get something for it.

When he'd asked Georgia about it, she said Zach hadn't mentioned it, but when he'd left Georgia in the kitchen and asked Zach, *he'd* said that Georgia had given him a couple of acetaminophen. One of them was lying. The question was, why? Georgia had been jumpy as a jackrabbit in the spring, but at the same time, she'd seemed subdued, almost depressed, something she'd blamed on her own headache.

What had happened between the two of them while he and his dad were still at the barn? If the sinking feeling in Jake's gut was to be trusted, he knew. It was time he recognized his problem for what it was. Georgia and Zach were attracted to each other. Very attracted.

But he and Zach were identical, so what did Georgia see in Zach that she didn't see in him? Was it that Zach's Texas Ranger image was more exciting, more of a turn-on? Or was it just that Georgia was frustrated because he hadn't taken her to bed? If so, maybe he'd better correct that little problem. If his fiancé was suffering sexual deprivation to the extent that another man looked tempting, then by golly, he'd see to it that she got what she wanted.

Women! Zach thought, as he pulled into his parking place at the apartment complex. All they were good for was tying a man into knots and then tightening those knots every chance they got.

He got out of the car and carried his things inside, dumping them onto the sofa, going into the kitchen and popping a top on a can of Coke. It was times like this he longed for something stronger, but because of Dwayne's longtime abuse of the bottle, Zach had sworn off alcohol at an early age. He liked being in control, and he'd vowed never to let excesses of any kind hurt those he cared about.

He pulled off his boots, flung them toward the door and lifted his feet to the scarred coffee table. It felt good to be home, even after being gone only a few days, but he knew that a great part of that feeling was relief at knowing there wouldn't be any more chance encounters with Georgia Williams.

Leaning his head against the sofa, he stared at the ceiling. Georgia. It was time to stop fooling himself and put a name to what was between them.

Lust. Maybe. But lust implied nothing but a basic,

instinctual sexual need. His feelings for her were more than that. He wanted her, but he also liked her. He liked her smile, her impetuousness, the way she treated Ben and Rosalita...heck, everyone she came into contact with, for that matter. He knew she was a good and decent person, the kind of woman who would make any man a good mate.

She was hurting, too, but he didn't know why. Did it have something to do with Jake, or was it just that their two passionate encounters upset her normal equilibrium? Was he the cause of her misery?

He didn't want to be. Something about Georgia roused a desire to shield her from any pain. It was a feeling he hadn't experienced toward a woman since his mother died. Was it because Georgia reminded him of Abby?

No. Other than the gentleness and the innate goodness he sensed both women shared, they were nothing alike. Abby had been salt of the earth, dependable. Georgia was no doubt as dependable, but she was impulsive, spontaneous. Abby could hardly be coaxed off their seven acres. Georgia liked to travel. The differences between them were innumerable, yet they were enough alike that they both engendered the desire to shelter and keep safe.

He took a drink of the cola. It wasn't like him to covet. Abby, who'd been brought up with a strict moral code instilled by her preacher father, had taught him that wanting what another person had was wrong. If you wanted something you worked for it. If God meant you to have it, you would. If not, you wouldn't. Sometimes, she'd told him, what you wanted and what God wanted for you weren't the same thing at all.

What he wanted was clear. He wanted Georgia—

badly, but not at the risk of hurting Jake, and only if she wanted him. That was the problem. He suspected that things weren't right between Jake and Georgia, which is why she was so vulnerable to his advances. What he wanted was to be in Jake's place, to make love to Georgia all night and wake up beside her in the morning. What he wanted was Georgia for his wife.

Zach hardly realized when the half full can of cola slipped from his fingers onto the carpet. He didn't know why it had happened, or how, but somehow, Georgia had smiled her way into his heart, just as she'd bluffed her way into his life.

God help them all.

He'd fallen in love with Georgia Williams.

Chapter Eight

Georgia called Carrie from her cell phone when she left the ranch, but Denton said his wife was at a fund-raiser for a local literacy group and told Georgia to stop by on her way from school the next afternoon.

Disappointed that there was no one to tell her troubles to, Georgia drove home and was soon in bed. Jake called at ten and asked if he could come over, telling her he needed to talk to her, but she put him off, using the excuse of her worsening headache. The lie stuck in her craw, but saved her from a confrontation she knew she couldn't deal with at the moment.

She was so torn between her loyalty to Jake and her attraction to Zach that she couldn't fall asleep and spent her wakeful hours polishing all her brass pieces and writing a thank-you note and wedding invitation to Myra and Ruthie, her rescuers at the airport, who had contacted her earlier.

The following school day was one of the longest she remembered. The students were so rowdy she actually went to the calendar to see if it was a full moon. It was nowhere near. After ruling out the possibility that aliens from outer space had come down and infested their youthful bodies with the sole intention of driving her crazy, she decided that her inability to deal with them effectively had more to do with her state of mind than their behavior.

Her emotions seesawed from a thrilling sort of secret joy whenever she thought about how it felt to be held in Zach's arms to a depressing guilt when she thought of Jake.

Somehow, she made it through the day. At mid-afternoon, she received a dozen red roses from Jake, along with a card so sweet and loving it brought tears to her eyes. Instead of lifting her spirits, his thought-fulness made her more despondent.

She drove to Carrie's as soon as school was out. Her friend greeted her with a hug and a keen look of concern. Georgia wasn't sure when she'd been so glad to see her sharp-eyed friend.

After sipping two cups of coffee, demolishing a huge piece of chocolate cake each and soaking up the ambience of the May afternoon on the Adairs' multilevel deck, Carrie asked, "What's happened?"

Georgia raised her gaze from the café au lait hued liquid in her cup to her friend's concerned blue eyes. "Zach Rawlings."

Instead of the I-told-you-so look she expected, Carrie's eyes held a combination of resignation and sorrow. "You're falling in love with him."

Georgia's eyes widened in shock. She could truthfully say that Carrie's statement was one possibility she hadn't considered. It was even more frightening than the idea that she was just physically attracted to Zach.

"Don't be ridiculous," she snapped.

Carrie held up both hands in a placating gesture. "Okay. You aren't ready to hear that yet."

"I'm not ready to hear it because it isn't true," Georgia said, but she couldn't look Carrie in the eye. She blew out a lusty breath that stirred her too-long bangs. "I admit I'm attracted to him in a way that's totally inappropriate considering that I'm engaged to another man."

"Attracted?"

Georgia shifted her gaze to Carrie's. Tears glittered in Georgia's eyes. "All right. When he kisses me, he makes me feel things I've never felt for Jake."

Carrie's eyes widened. "He's kissed you? Since the hospital?"

Georgia nodded.

"Oh, Georgia! Do you want to talk about it?"

The tears in Georgia's eyes slipped down her cheeks. "If I don't talk to someone, I'm going to go bonkers!"

"Let me go tell Denton to pick up some burgers from the Bearcat for dinner. Then you can tell me everything."

"This is much more serious than I thought," Carrie said when Georgia finished catching her up on what had happened at the Lazy L the past few days—including the return of Zach's memory and the DNA testing. "What are you going to do? Break off with Jake?"

"I can't break off with Jake now. The wedding is just two weeks away."

"Well, you can't marry him feeling this way about another man. It wouldn't be fair to either of you."

"Once Jake and I are married, everything will be fine," Georgia said. "I just have a bad case of infatuation and sexual deprivation."

Carrie's face wore the same stunned expression Zach's had when he'd found out she and Jake weren't sleeping together.

"Why is that such a shock to everyone?" Georgia asked. "Chivalry is not dead. There are still a few bastions of prudence and integrity left in this old world. Jake and I respect each other and the sanctity of marriage."

"Is it respect for marriage or the lack of passion?" Carrie asked with her usual forthrightness.

Georgia frowned. "What do you mean?"

"I mean that maybe you and Jake don't feel any urgent desire for each other because you aren't attracted to each other that way."

"That's ridiculous!"

"Is it? Then tell me why you're having such a hard time with Zach Rawlings."

Georgia had no answer for that. Finally, she said, "It doesn't make any sense, Carrie. They look exactly alike. Why *do* I feel my heart go wacky when Zach comes near me?"

It was as close to an admission as Carrie was likely to get. "It has something to do with chemistry, not looks," she said. "And I don't think there's a scientist or psychologist alive who understands it. It just is. Like sunrise and sunset, tides, that kind of thing."

"Well, it's darn scary."

Carrie nodded. "You still haven't said what you're going to do about it."

Georgia straightened her shoulders and drew in a deep breath. "I'm going to pray that Jake and Zach aren't really brothers. I'm going to steer clear of Zach, which should be easy since he moved back to his place yesterday. And I'm going ahead with this wedding full steam ahead.''

"Oh, Georgia!" Carrie said shaking her head.

"What do you think I should do?"

"Break up with Jake and see if this feeling you have for Zach develops into anything else."

"I can't do that."

"Then you're doing both you and Jake a disservice." Carrie's shoulders lifted in a nonchalant shrug. "The other alternative is to go ahead and sleep with the guy."

"Carrie Adair!"

"Well," she said with an unrepentant shrug, "maybe he'll be terrible in bed and you can go into your marriage with an easy mind."

"If I slept with one man while I was engaged to another, there's no way I could go into the marriage with an easy mind," Georgia said with a shake of her head. "I'd be so guilty I might just as well stamp a big red *C* on my forehead."

"*C?*"

"For cheater."

Neither spoke for a moment. From inside the house came the sounds of Denton and Megan returning with the hamburgers.

"What makes you think I don't love Jake and that I'm falling in love with Zach Rawlings? I could never love a man in law enforcement." The question came out of the blue and was negated by the addendum.

"I didn't say you don't love Jake. I'm sure you do. The same way you love Denton—as a good friend, a nice guy. But you aren't *in* love with him, and I think that if you'll take a look down deep in your heart, you've always known that. I'm not sure Jake is really in love with you, either.''

That idea surprised Georgia.

''I'm sorry if that hurts, but I have to say that I think this engagement came about because both of you reached an age where you wanted a family, and you figured that if Prince or Princess Charming hadn't come along, he or she wasn't going to, so you agreed to settle for second best—each other.''

''Nothing about Jake is second best.''

''I agree wholeheartedly. He's a wonderful man with wonderful qualities that make him a catch for any woman. I know you love and respect him. I'll even go so far as to say that I believe this marriage could have been a good solid one—if a little uninspired—if Zach Rawlings hadn't come along to make you see what's missing.''

''Which is?''

''Passion.''

''A highly overrated emotion.''

''Is it?''

''You know yourself that it burns out.''

''Life dulls it sometimes,'' Carrie admitted. ''We get older. We have other commitments. The daily grind wears us down. But if it's really love, that passion will always be there when you want it, or need it.''

Georgia chewed thoughtfully on her bottom lip, trying to absorb the things Carrie was telling her.

''It still doesn't make sense.''

''For the last time, honey, it isn't supposed to make sense,'' Carrie said gently. She reached out and covered Georgia's hand with hers. ''And I know you have good reasons not to *want* to fall in love with a man in

law enforcement, but you have to realize that our hearts
don't always listen to our heads.''

When Georgia got home, there was a message on
her machine from Jake, asking if he could come over.
What had happened to Jake? she wondered. He was
behaving like a man totally besotted—which was the
last thing she needed right now.

She called him back, pleading last-day-of-school
preparations. She heard the disappointment in his voice
and felt like a dog for being the one responsible for
putting it there. Before they hung up, he told her he
loved her. The knife in her heart turned, bringing a
fresh spurt of pain.

Georgia spent another sleepless night. By midnight,
she'd conceded that Carrie might be right, but even
recognizing that fact didn't alter her dilemma. She
couldn't sleep with Zach and then blithely go ahead
with her marriage to Jake. And she couldn't cancel the
wedding at this late date, either. Jake would be morti-
fied. Ben would be furious. The Lattimer men took
great store in the fact that they were the pillars of the
community, above reproach, above scandal....

By the time dawn slipped silently into her bedroom,
she'd convinced herself that Carrie had lost her mind
by suggesting that the feelings Zach's nearness generated were based on the first stirrings of love. She'd also
convinced herself that there was nothing to do about
the situation but bury those feelings under an avalanche
of last-minute preparations for the wedding.

The next day, Friday, was the last day of school,
which would leave a lot of time on her hands. Georgia
knew her mother could use the help, and keeping busy

would keep her mind centered on her future with Jake and not on a few stolen kisses from his brother.

When Georgia walked into her first hour class, the trio of girls she'd nicknamed the Three Musketeers were standing near her desk. Meredith, who was munching on a chocolate bar, and Sabrina, who held a copy of Premiere magazine clutched to her breasts, were listening with rapt attention to Kat. Georgia paused in the doorway, her attention caught by the provocative situation.

"He's a great kisser, and he's positively gorgeous," she all but groaned. Georgia saw her shoulders lift with a sigh. "And he's hot for me. He's called me every night this week."

"You've *kissed* him?" Meredith asked, around a mouthful of Milky Way.

"A couple of times," Kat admitted with studied nonchalance.

Sabrina's snort of disgust barely registered. Kat's situation with Joey and some other guy was so similar to Georgia's with Jake and Zach that she made a sound of surprise.

"Oh, hi, Ms. Williams," Meredith said, looking up and spying Georgia in the doorway.

Feeling like a kid caught with his hand in the cookie jar, Georgia summoned a smile and struggled for an innocent nonchalance she was far from feeling. *Eavesdropping.* "Hi! I hope I'm not interrupting."

"It's your classroom," Sabrina said. "You can do what you want."

Yes, Georgia thought. But, like Kat, she wasn't sure just what that was.

* * *

Zach hardly slept for two nights, either. Inactivity didn't suit him, but the doctors refused to let him go back to work for at least another week. He was bored, and he was lonely. Laura was busy. Shelby was working. He found himself listening for Attila's scratch at the door, but even the cat had defected, leaving the stress and grit of the city for the leisurely country life. Zach's only pastimes were watching television and thinking. He grew tired of the first after a day. He couldn't escape the second.

His thoughts were divided equally between the idea that he'd been given up for adoption and how Abby had managed to fool him so well for so many years. Yet the more he thought about it, the less sure he became that he *was* adopted.

He knew that part of this skepticism was a perfectly normal form of denial that this kind of thing could happen to him. But the more he thought about his past, the more memories he was able to pull from his mind and the farther back those memories went. He remembered his mother telling him about the night he was born on more than one occasion.

He'd been born on a stormy night in a small Texas town called Brownsboro. Three women were in labor. The phone lines were down and the doctor couldn't be reached. Abby told him that she was scared until her mother told her to pray. Laughing, Abby had told him that the nurse on duty kept humming "Love Me Tender." She'd smiled when she told him what a beautiful baby he'd been, with his head full of dark hair sticking up all over. But even now, he remembered that her smile looked sad, somehow.

Was Abby his mother or wasn't she? The memory of Laura's offer to look into things for him slipped into his mind. Did he want to open this particular can of worms? He didn't think so. Not just now.

Frustrated, his head aching, he lay down, hoping he could sleep away the headache and the problem. Instead, his thoughts shifted to Georgia and the guilt gnawing away at him. But even though he was suffering a fair amount of self-imposed condemnation, the more he thought about Georgia and Jake not sleeping together, the more certain he became that Georgia and Jake had become a habit with each other, that they weren't really in love. That's why—whether she admitted it or not—she was drawn to him.

That settled to his satisfaction, it was a natural conclusion that the upcoming marriage was a mistake, and that if Jake and Georgia went through with it, they would only wind up hurting each other. Zach decided that, as Jake's probable brother and Georgia's future brother-in-law, it was his duty to talk to them and convince them of their error. Well, maybe he'd talk to Georgia. Jake hadn't been very friendly since catching him and Georgia in the barn.

While Zach was trying to figure out how to wangle her address out of Rosalita without stirring up her suspicions, he recalled the Lazy L housekeeper telling him that Georgia taught French at one of the private schools in Fort Worth. He knew the school and its location.

Maybe if he drove over there about the time school let out, he could make her see that going ahead with her marriage to Jake was a mistake. Maybe she could see that whatever it was between them deserved closer examination. It might even deserve exploring.

Georgia shoved a batch of papers into her burgundy leather briefcase and latched it. Her eyes were grainy from lack of sleep. All she could think of was getting home, taking a warm, rose-scented bath while she drank a cup of cappuccino, eating a frozen dinner and falling into bed. If there was a God, she'd be asleep before the six o'clock news came on.

As she exited the double doors at the front of the native stone building, she heard a chorus of girlish laughter. The sound drew her gaze to the knot of girls standing near the parking lot. She recognized Meredith, Sabrina and Kat with several others from her last period class. In the midst of the laughing females stood a tall man in Western garb and a black hat.

Jake. A frown drew her eyebrows together. What was he doing here? She thought about his phone calls and her refusal to see him the past couple of days...thought about the roses he sent that sat in a vase on her desk.

She sighed. He was making an all-out attempt to do what she'd asked of him before she went to France. He seldom came to town, and she remembered only two other occasions he'd deigned to step foot on the school campus. He was trying to be what she said she wanted him to be, so why did she feel irritated instead of happy?

She saw him smile and heard Kat's voice, though she couldn't hear what she said. The responsive laughter rankled. He claimed he didn't feel comfortable with all the kids gawking at him, but here he was smackdab in the middle of a gaggle of giggling girls and looking as if he were having the time of his life. This wasn't like Jake at all.

She drew in a sharp breath and drew to a stop.

Oh, no! He wouldn't, would he? She slung the long strap of her briefcase over her shoulder and marched toward the group, disbelief battling with exasperation. As she drew nearer, he looked up. The blatant sexuality slumbering in his eyes caught her off stride.

One corner of his thick black mustache inched upward. "The bride cometh," he misquoted.

Resolutely, her eyes never leaving his, she proceeded. The cluster of girls parted, allowing her access to him. She forced a smile to her lips. "Hi."

"Hi, sunshine," he said, sliding an arm around her shoulders. Sunshine. Not sugar. Any lingering doubts she might have had about his identity vanished with the greeting. She didn't miss the devilment in his dark eyes as he dipped his head to kiss her.

She knew she shouldn't allow the kiss, but she could have no more stopped him than she could have denied herself her next breath. And, as much as she hated herself for it, she was helpless to do anything but kiss him back.

It was less than the desperate, greedy kiss he'd bestowed on her in the Lattimer kitchen. It was more than a welcoming brush of hard lips. Compared to their other kisses, this one was brief, but even the abridged version conveyed his hunger...and her own.

"Wow!"

The single word, uttered in an awed whisper, came from Meredith. It brought Georgia back to her senses with a vengeance. She drew back from Zach and put the relative safety of a few inches between them. Then, donning her most schoolmarmish expression, she faced her students and said, "Girls."

The single, stern word sent them scattering like a bunch of marbles that had been hit by an exceptional shooter, but as they glanced over their uniformed shoulders, she saw their smiles and heard their snickers of laughter. Thank God tomorrow was the last day of school, not the first. She didn't think she could take a whole year of those sly looks and the innuendo she knew to expect.

Feeling the revival of her exasperation, she looked at Zach and said, "How did you find me?"

"I didn't know you were hiding."

"You know what I mean."

He smiled, a flash of white teeth against the darkness of his mustache. A glimmer of humor lurked in the depths of his dark eyes that crinkled at the corners. "I wanted to talk to you, and I remembered Rosalita saying you taught here." His observant gaze roamed over the building and the grounds. "Do you like it?"

"Very much."

"You teach French, right?"

"And history."

"History? Great. I love history."

"Look," Georgia said, her agitation rising, "you didn't come look me up to talk to me about my job. What's up?"

Zach's grin was slow, naughty, unrepentant. "My blood pressure...among other things."

The admission, followed by an intimation she couldn't help noticing, sent her gaze winging to the front of his jeans. His low chuckle sent color flying to her face. He was *enjoying* this! She forced her eyes to meet his. "You really like making a fool out of me, don't you?"

He shifted his weight to one muscular, jeans-clad leg, crossed his arms over his wide chest and shrugged. "I like watching your face, yeah. As a matter of fact, I like everything about you...." He paused, the mischievous gleam back in his eyes. "What I've seen, anyway."

Georgia's reaction wavered between indignation, embarrassment and a distinct pleasure. Indignation won, but only marginally. "You've seen all you're going to see."

The look in his eyes sent a scorching heat throughout her body. He shook his head. "Now that's a shame."

"Will you stop it!" she cried in a low voice. "What do you want from me?"

"No, I won't, and everything you'll give me," he said, answering each question in turn.

Stunned into silence, unable to even think of a comeback, Georgia dragged her gaze from his, brushed past him and stalked toward her car. She didn't need this. Didn't want it.

Liar. You do need it. You want it. You want him.

No. What she wanted was to go back to the way things were before she mistook Zach for Jake at the airport. What she wanted was to hurry up and marry Jake so she could get over this ridiculous, schoolgirl infatuation with Zach Rawlings and get on with her life.

Liar. What you want is for Zach to make wild crazy love to you so that you'll have something to remember when you marry Jake.

A sob of outrage escaped her. Damn Zach Rawlings, anyway! How dare he come here and upset her routine this way. How dare he try to bully his way into the life she was trying so hard to build with Jake.

She was so wrapped up in her anger and self-loathing that she had no idea Zach followed her. She unlocked her car door and started to open it when a big hand reached over her shoulder and pushed it shut.

She whirled, righteous in her fury, ready to cuss him out, dress him down, tell him what he could do with his teasing winks and his cocky grins and his unwanted advances.

The expression in his eyes stopped her. Instead of the self-confident amusement she expected, she saw tenderness, uncertainty and something that looked very much like fear.

Her hostility dwindled to aggravation. She felt the stinging threat of tears. "Why are you doing this?" she asked, her voice hardly more than a whisper.

"What?"

"Why do you keep kissing me when you know I'm engaged to Jake? Why did you come here?"

"I can't seem to help myself." The answer sounded flip, but the look in his eyes was dead serious.

"What do you want?"

"I already answered that question, but you ran away from the truth."

Georgia closed her eyes and sagged wearily against the car door. Where was her backbone? Why couldn't she just tell this guy to take a hike?

"I'm marrying Jake in two weeks." It was the best she could do.

"You'll be making a big mistake."

"Why? Jake's a wonderful man. Quite a catch."

For the first time since he'd shown up, she saw a hint of exasperation in his eyes. "I'm sure he is, but that doesn't change the fact that you don't love him."

"You have no idea how I feel about Jake."

"Maybe not, but I know how you feel about me."

It was territory they'd covered before. Every time he put it into words it was like taking an unexpected blow to the stomach. She raised her chin. "Oh? And how do I feel about you?" Her voice held a definite chill.

He narrowed his eyes. "You want me." When she started to speak, he pointed a finger at her. "Don't insult me or yourself by denying it. Deal with it."

He was right, and Carrie had pretty much said the same thing, but that didn't make it any easier to take. "I'm dealing with it the best way I know how," she snapped, realizing too late that the statement was tantamount to a confession.

"How's that? By ignoring it—and me—in hopes that we'll go away? Well, I'm not going away and neither is what we feel when we're together."

The fragile hold Georgia had on her dignity slipped. "All right. You want me to face it. I'll face it. Yes, I like it when you kiss me. Yes, it's exciting. Maybe—" Her courage and her voice faltered. She glared at him. "Maybe I even want you, but I'm not stupid enough to throw away my future happiness for a few kisses and a quick roll in the hay."

"Throwing away the happiness you might find with someone else is exactly what you'll be doing if you marry Jake."

"Are you saying Jake can't make me happy?"

"I think you and Jake might manage contentment together, but you both deserve more. You deserve honest-to-God love. Wild passion. Don't get married just because you think life is passing you by and you want a husband and a family. Don't ignore what's going on between us."

"There's nothing going on between us!" she cried.

"Because you won't let it."

She closed her eyes and pressed her fingertips to her temples. "I can't believe this is happening," she said almost to herself. "This whole conversation is crazy. You're crazy."

"Maybe."

The simple concession caused her eyes to fly open. He looked as upset as she felt. "What are you asking me to do?" she said. "Drop Jake and experience that wild passion with you?"

He nodded. "It's for your own good."

She laughed, a harsh, bitter sound. "What do I do when it's over? Go back to being the schoolteacher? Sit around and wait another thirty-odd years for someone to offer to marry me?"

"What makes you think it'll end?" he asked.

"What makes you think it'll last?" she countered.

"I'm more attracted to you than any woman I've ever met."

"Not good enough," she said. "I think the same thing of you, but I wouldn't base a long-term relationship on it."

"I want you," he said, his eyes moving over her face like a gentle caress. "I want you more than any woman I can ever remember wanting."

"Still not good enough."

"What do you want me to say?" he asked, his exasperation on the rise once more. "I'm trying to be honest and up-front here. You know you don't love Jake the way you should love him, you don't even *want* him, so all I can figure is that you're marrying him for his money."

"Jake Lattimer's money is the last reason I'm marrying him." She shook her head. "You just don't get it, do you? Women are different than men. We don't just jump into things without thinking about the long term. First, you're a cop. I could never get seriously involved with a man in law enforcement.''

"Why?"

"My grandfather was a sheriff's deputy, and he was killed by some alcohol-crazed thief when I was just a kid."

He started to make an objection, but she stopped him with a raised hand. "Let me finish. If I were to do what you're suggesting, I'd have to believe with all my heart that there was more to what I felt for you than lust. I'd have to believe that there was a commitment on at least my part and something permanent somewhere in the near future."

"You're talking love and marriage."

"You rangers are *so* smart," she said derisively. "Are you willing to offer me that, Zach? Because time's passing, and you're right. I do want a family as well as a husband."

"If you want me to say that I'll offer you marriage, I have to say I can't."

"Then as much as I might want to, I can't crawl into bed with you, either."

Chapter Nine

The results of the DNA tests came back in ten days. It was a Friday, a day Zach would never forget, one week and a day since he'd talked to Georgia in the school parking lot, exactly one week until the wedding.

He was supposed to return to work the following Monday, but in the meantime, he pretended to watch mindless talk shows while he thought about Georgia, whom he hadn't seen or heard from since their confrontation at the school.

Ben had called a couple of times, asking him to come to the ranch for a meal, but Zach had declined, using any excuse that came to mind. There was no way he could build a brotherly relationship with Jake when he wanted to steal his bride-to-be, no way he could be in the same room with Georgia and act as if everything were okay.

So he stayed holed up in the apartment, only going

out to get food, marking off the days until he could go back to work on his calendar, and hoping that Georgia would think about what he'd said and call him to say she'd changed her mind.

Zach didn't know what else he could say or do to convince her that she and Jake were making a mistake, even though he had to admit that she had a right to be angry that he himself wasn't willing to offer her anything but a roll in the hay, as she so bluntly called it.

Deep in his heart, he thought it could be more, wanted it to be more...but there was a part of him that had always shied away from the idea of long-term commitments, a part that was afraid to offer more because he was afraid of Dwayne's blood running through his veins.

Then there was this twin thing. It had shaken his self-confidence. Until the past couple of weeks, he'd always known exactly who he was—Abby and Dwayne Rawlings's son. He'd cherished the traits he got from Abby and had done his best to suppress any qualities he thought he might have inherited from Dwayne, but since Georgia had dragged him to the Lazy L and the theory that he and Jake were twins had come up, his conviction of who he was had been shaken to its core.

Even if he wanted to, how could he, a man with a dangerous job and a checkered past, offer a woman like Georgia—a woman who wanted the security of a nine-to-five husband and a stable marriage—a future based on uncertainty and lies?

The ringing of the phone was a welcome relief from his troubled thoughts. It was Shelby, who was calling to check on him.

After telling her about the return of his memory and

filling her in on the latest installment of his life, Zach asked, "What's the matter, Shel?"

Though they hadn't worked together for years, he knew her well enough to recognize the edginess in her voice.

"I don't know," his former partner said. "There's nothing I can put my finger on, you know? I've just have this funny feeling the past couple of days."

"Cop paranoia," Zach said. "You know as well as I do that undercover work is hell on a good day."

Shelby laughed. "You can say that again."

"I remember a couple of long-term gigs that stretched my nerves to the limit."

"Yeah, I remember, too. I hope we nail the bad guy soon. I could use a little R and R to recharge the old batteries." He heard her sigh. "Well, I've gotta go. I have a jillion things to do before I go back. I just wanted to check in with you. I'll give you a call next time I get a chance, okay?"

"Sure. Take care of yourself, Shelby."

"You, too. Bye."

Zach was cradling the phone when the doorbell rang. The postman had a letter for him to sign for. When he saw the return address, his heart skipped a beat. It was from the lab that did the testing on him and Jake. It seemed too soon to have results, but they'd requested an answer as soon as possible.

His heart beat out a slow, heavy rhythm as he closed the door and slit open the official-looking envelope with his pocketknife. He unfolded the paper and scanned the results with a combination of eagerness and apprehension.

Involuntarily, his hand clenched, crumpling the paper that he let fall to the floor. He scrubbed his hand over his face, blinked several times and drew in a deep, calming breath.

He and Jake Lattimer were brothers. Twins. He'd thought about this possibility for endless hours, and, viewing all the evidence at his disposal, it was the result he expected. So why did he feel as if he'd just taken a hard right to the gut?

He sat down, picked up the paper, smoothed it out and read the results again. What did it all mean?

You know what it means. Yeah, he did, but even though he'd considered the possibility on at least one occasion, it was a scenario he'd refused to consider seriously. Now, he had no choice but to take a hard look at the facts. Simply put, he and Jake had been given away and adopted out to different families, or Abby had given birth to them both, and for some reason known only by herself, God and Dwayne, she'd kept only one child, him.

Why? He thought again about Laura's offer to help him unravel the mystery. Initially, he'd wanted to wait for the results of the tests, and now that he knew for certain he and Jake were brothers, he felt an urgency to know the truth. He reached for the phone and dialed Laura's number, telling her about his conviction that Abby had been his birth mother, not his adoptive mother.

"Wow!" she said. "If that's true, it means she gave Jake away."

"Yeah. But why would she do that? It doesn't make sense. She was a great mother."

"I'd be glad to look into it for you," Laura said. "As a matter of fact, you're not going to believe this, but I ran an ad in several papers a few months ago, asking to hear from people who wanted to share their

unwed mother stories. If I remember correctly, someone wrote in about a woman—a nurse—who ran a
home for unwed mothers several years ago. I'd have
to check my files to be sure, but I think the name of
the place was Brownsboro. It may take a while, with
all these doctor's appointments for Rufio.''

"No problem. I appreciate anything you can come
up with," Zach told her.

"What about your dad—Dwayne? Do you want me
to try and locate him?''

"No. You don't have to bother with that. I'll get
hold of Dwayne myself."

Laura laughed. "Well, he ought to know whether or
not you and Jake were adopted, and he sure ought to
know if he fathered a set of twins.''

"He should," Zach agreed.

Laura said she'd do some preliminary snooping and
get back to him as soon as possible. Before they hung
up, Zach asked Laura about her son.

"The tests they ran didn't show anything conclu-
sively. We're going to do some more in a week or so.''

Zach could tell that she didn't want to talk about it,
and he wasn't one to press.

"I hope they come out okay," was all he said. After
he'd thanked her again for her help, they hung up.

Suddenly anxious to get to the bottom of things, he
looked up the number of the last trucking company he
remembered Dwayne working for, but the woman he
spoke to said Dwayne had quit almost two years previously. She had no idea who he was driving for now.

Zach hung up and stroked the corner of his mustache. Tracking down his dad might be hard, but he
intended to do it.

Zach's gaze wandered to the paper with the lab results. He read them again. A part of him was pleased. If it weren't for his feelings for Georgia, the news that Jake was the brother he'd always wanted would have brought tremendous pleasure. But if Georgia married Jake, Zach knew his feelings for her would always stand in the way of him and Jake building a relationship.

He folded the paper and put it in the envelope, wondering if Jake had gotten the results yet, and, if so, how he was taking the news.

"Well?" Ben asked.

"We're brothers, all right." Jake handed the paper to his dad and walked to the window of the office that looked out at the pool.

Ben read the document. As far as he was concerned, the news was good news, but if the look on Jake's face was any indication, he was none too pleased.

"Jake?"

"What?" he snapped, turning from the window.

"You don't seem very happy about this," Ben said.

Jake's eyes held an unmistakable coolness. "Can't say that I am."

Ben frowned. "You must have at least suspected this would be the outcome. You've had plenty of time to get used to the idea."

"I don't think I'll ever get used to the idea."

The genuine distress in his son's gaze surprised Ben. He thought Jake was more confident about who he was than to feel threatened by Zach Rawlings.

"Are you afraid this is going to change how I feel about you?" Ben asked. "Because if you are, you can stop worrying."

"Everything's changed since Georgia brought him here," Jake said in a voice tinged with bitterness.

"You're wrong. Just because I feel I was cheated out of being a father to Zach and I'd like to pursue some sort of relationship with him in the future doesn't change my love for you."

After several long seconds, Ben thought he saw the fury in his son's eyes fade the slightest bit. "I still wish to hell Georgia had never seen him," he said. Without offering any further explanation, he turned and walked out of the room.

Helpless to do anything but watch him go, Ben went to the window Jake had stared out of just seconds ago. How could he believe that anything could change or diminish their relationship? Ben blew out a deep breath. Maybe he was reading more into this than there really was. Maybe Jake would feel differently after he'd had some time to think about it.

Every fatherly instinct Ben possessed told him something was wrong between Jake and Georgia—had been ever since she came back from France. There was nothing he could put his finger on, but Jake seemed over-anxious to please her whenever she came around. Georgia, on the other hand, seemed edgy, irritated...even, he realized now, unhappy.

Was she having second thoughts about marrying Jake? Ben's heart sank. He hoped not. He knew, had known from the first, that while Jake and Georgia loved each other in many ways, they weren't wildly in love. That had never bothered Ben. His grandparents were virtual strangers who married as a matter of financial convenience. But they'd had a good marriage, and according to Ben's parents, a happy one.

It would break his heart, as well as Jake's, if Georgia

backed out at this late date. He and Retha had always doted on her. Had she met someone in France? Had this attraction raised doubts about the wisdom of marrying Jake?

"I still wish to hell Georgia had never seen him."

The words leaped into Ben's mind. No. Surely Jake didn't think Georgia was interested in Zach.

The timing is right.

True. Things had started going sour between Georgia and Jake about the time she brought Zach home from the hospital. Was it possible that Georgia's attraction was for Zach, not some Frenchman?

Ben's heart ached with a dull empathetic pain for his son. It was not only possible, it was probable.

Zach Rawlings was his brother. His twin. How lucky could one man get? Jake left the house and went straight to the barn to saddle his horse. He'd take the dogs and see if he could round up that crazy heifer still hiding out over in the stand of willows down by the creek. He couldn't stay inside and listen to Ben try to persuade him that having Zach Rawlings for a brother was the best thing to happen since sliced bread.

Jake believed Ben when he said that taking Zach under his fatherly wing wouldn't affect their relationship, but that didn't alter the fact that things *had* changed since Zach had come into their lives, and the changes—good or bad—would continue.

Jake swung the teal and black saddle blanket onto the gelding's broad back. Ever since Georgia dragged Zach home from the hospital, Jake's emotions had been as unpredictable as a roller-coaster ride.

He'd thought Zach's leaving would restore the status quo, but he was as wrong about that as he was about his decision to drive Zach from Georgia's mind by consummating their upcoming nuptials. That tack had met with a hard-line resistance. Georgia, who'd begged him to take her to bed before she left for Paris, was now the one saying they should wait, that she was too stressed with tending to the last-minute wedding preparations to enjoy a romantic liaison.

He knew she was tired. Since school let out for summer vacation the previous Friday, she had thrown herself into the wedding preparations with a fervor that approached frenzy.

He finished saddling Dusty and whistled up the cattle dogs he'd borrowed from a neighbor. The blue heeler and the cur dog came trotting out from their cool napping places—one from under the bunkhouse steps, the other from the crawl space beneath the machinery shed. He gave the dogs a treat he kept in his pocket, swung up into the saddle, and headed out across the pasture that stretched to the horizon.

The farther away from the barn he went, the more he felt the subtle influence of the land around him. The clear air filled his lungs and the joyous sounds of birdsong eased the ache in his heart. He realized that he was bone tired. Knew, too, that his exhaustion was a weariness of the soul, not the body.

Jake gave the buckskin his head, and the gelding moseyed through the dense saplings. He knew from experience his excursion might be an exercise in futility. Just because the heifer had been spotted in this area a couple of days ago didn't mean she'd still be there, although Jake's guess was that the water supply would at least make this a place to come back to between grazing sprees.

He'd been trying to catch her ever since she'd been

delivered to the Lazy L six months ago. Jake had taken one look at her wild eyes as she'd banged around in the stock trailer and known she was trouble, just as he'd known Zach Rawlings was trouble the first time he'd set eyes on him.

Hoping to give her time to settle down, Jake had suggested that they unload the brindle cow into a holding pen until she calmed down. Once in the pen, the big heifer had taken one look at the wide open spaces beyond the barn and lunged toward the aluminum gate securing her. After making three swipes at the gate that left it bent like a taco shell, she'd headed out across the pasture like a scalded terrapin.

Jake had almost gotten his lariat on her the last time he'd gone looking for her, but she'd ducked at the last minute, and all he'd caught was a loop full of air.

After that, the standoff had become personal. Knowing he needed some help, he'd borrowed the two cattle dogs from one of his neighbors to help catch the ornery slab of beefsteak. Duncan Ledbetter had assured him the dogs could do the job.

Jake's sharp gaze scanned the area, looking for any sign of the heifer, hoping to spot her, daring the ornery critter to come out of hiding. He was feeling more than a little ornery himself, and was just a little tired of being done in by females. He meant to find the heifer, rope her and send her off to the nearest auction barn—today.

Ben was paying some bills and wondering where the heck Jake had gone off to when the panicked sound of Rosalita's little girl's excited voice broke his concentration. "Señor Lattimer! Come quick!"

He bolted up from the chair and hurried down the

hallway, where Leza met him halfway, her dark eyes wide with concern and excitement.

"What is it, Leza?" Ben asked abruptly. "Is something wrong with your mother?"

"No, señor. It's Mister Jake."

Ben's stomach clenched in fear. "Jake? What's the matter?"

"I don't know. My daddy said for you to crank up the chopper. Mr. Jake needs to go to the hospital."

"Dear God!" Ben said, as panic filled him. Brushing past Leza, he hurried down the long hallway to the French doors that led outside, covering the distance to the barn in record time. Leza followed close on his heels. He slid open the barn door, stepped inside the dim interior and struggled to focus as his eyes adjusted to the darkness.

"You're movin' pretty darn fast for an old man."

The droll comment went a long way toward calming Ben's trepidation. He turned toward the sound of Jake's voice. His son leaned against the wall of a stall, one arm cradling his middle. His shirt and jeans were filthy and blood-streaked and torn, and his face was covered in sweat and grime. His eyes held an unholy satisfaction and an edge of pain.

"You all right?" Ben asked.

"Never better," Jake said, but he grimaced as he spoke the words.

"Leza said you needed to go to the hospital."

"Aw, hell. You know what a worrywart Ernesto is. He took one look at me and went bananas."

Ernesto did rattle easily, but Ben thought that this time his alarm was founded. Jake looked like he'd been dragged through a knothole backward.

"What the heck happened?" Ben asked.

"I tried to bulldog that eight-hundred-pound heifer that's been out so long."

"Seriously," Ben said.

"Seriously," Jake countered, sketching a Boy Scout salute. "I knew she was hanging out down by the creek. Duncan's dogs found her where she was bedding down and made her life hell for an hour or so. When they finally wore her down, I got a rope around her neck, cinched her up to Dusty and dragged her home."

"Looks like you're the one who got dragged home."

"Everything was just dandy till I got to the barn," Jake said. "I'd just dismounted and was going to load her up when that black reject from Hades came running out of nowhere and spooked Dusty and the cow."

"What reject from Hades are you talking about?" Ben asked with a frown.

"That damned cat of Zach's."

"Attila?"

"Yes, Attila," Jake growled. "Dusty whirled and knocked me down. The heifer tried to do a tap dance on my head, but I managed to roll out of the way. When I got up, she was like a wild beast. She charged me, knocked me up against the trailer, then—I swear to God she knew exactly what she was doing—she rolled her eyes and blew a face full of slobber at me, spun around and slammed her whole body into me. If Dusty hadn't been trying to keep the tension on that rope, she'd probably have finished me off."

Though Jake made light of the accident, Ben's experience with cattle told him the incident could have had a far different ending. "You could have been killed."

"The Lord giveth, the Lord taketh away," Jake muttered, pushing himself away from the wall and grunting with discomfort.

Ben's immediate concern was for his son's well-being, but something about the sarcasm threading the cryptic statement triggered Ben's temper. "What the hell's that supposed to mean?"

"Zach could move into my room. You'd never miss me."

Too shocked to say anything, Ben blew out a disgruntled breath. He thought they'd straightened this out. "Feeling a little sorry for yourself, are you, son?" he asked, pinning Jake with a pointed look.

Jake seemed startled that Ben had grabbed the bull by the horns. He scrubbed a hand over his face, which donned a hangdog expression. "Yeah, I guess I am. I'm acting like a ten-year-old instead of a grown man."

"You won't hear any disagreements from me."

"I'm just a little on edge right now."

"I've noticed," Ben said. "Is there something wrong between you and Georgia?"

"Big weddings are tough on everyone," Jake said, answering Ben's question with an indirect comment. "Everything will be fine once we get past the wedding."

"Yeah," Ben said.

Jake started toward the barn door. Even through his bravado, it was obvious to Ben that he was hurting.

"Hold on a minute," Ben said, rushing forward. "Let me and Ernesto give you a hand." He glanced around. "Where is Ernesto, anyway?"

"I told him to go get a couple of the other guys and take care of that heifer. I want her off this place by sundown."

Ben slid a supporting arm around Jake's waist and

offered him a mocking grin. "What's the matter? Four thousand acres not big enough for the both of you?"

Jake's voice and expression were grim. "You got it."

"I think you need to go in to Fort Worth and let someone in the emergency room check you out."

"I'm all right," Jake groused, but Ben noticed that he leaned on him as he walked.

"Humor me."

Jake shook his head. "You're a stubborn old cuss. Anyone ever tell you that?"

"A time or two," Ben acknowledged. "Mostly your mama."

At the mention of Retha a sudden tension sprang up between them, along with the realization that Retha wasn't Jake's mama at all.

"I'll let you drive me into Aledo and see Doc Masterson," Jake said, breaking the distressing silence.

"That'll work," Ben said. It wasn't what he wanted, but it was better than nothing.

Georgia drove to the ranch, her irritation with Jake warring with her fear that his injury would necessitate delaying the wedding. They couldn't call off the wedding or postpone it. They couldn't!

As ridiculous as she knew it was, the wedding had become a talisman, her only defense—however flimsy—against her unwanted feelings for Zach Rawlings. She had convinced herself that once she became Jake's wife, those feelings would miraculously disappear.

The week since she and Zach had squared off in front of the school had been the longest of her life. She saw his face in every restful moment, heard his pleading voice at random, inopportune times. The disturbing memories of their kisses threatened to destroy both her sanity and her resolve.

She combatted those memories by throwing herself into all the last-minute details of the wedding, from making intricate ribbon and lace flowers that would hold the birdseed she and Jake would be bombarded with after the ceremony, to washing crystal and polishing silver to a blinding brightness. Only when she was too tired to see or even think could she close her eyes without seeing Zach's face.

Even then, her dreams betrayed her, tantalizing her with forbidden fantasies of her marching down the aisle to find Zach instead of Jake waiting for her, freeze-frame images of her and Zach washing dishes, walking along the streets of Paris, making love....

"Darn it!" The softly uttered words banished the onslaught of memories. How could she think such things when Jake was hurt? In fact, according to Ben, Jake could have been killed. That thought brought another pang of guilt.

Ben met her at the door, taking her hands in both of his and brushing her cheek with a friendly, paternal kiss. "He's okay," he assured her again. "It could have been bad, but he's just banged up a bit."

"What happened?"

Ben related the incident as Jake had recounted it to him, finishing by saying, "His thigh's all bruised where the heifer stepped on him, and he's got a couple of cracked ribs and a lot of bruises on his chest, but he's going to be fine."

"Thank God!" Georgia said. "Where is he?"

"Watching television in the den and waiting for you to get here."

With a smile of thanks, Georgia went in search of Jake. His usual pose for watching TV was to slouch in the recliner, but she found him sitting ramrod straight in the wing chair. She crossed the room, leaned down and pressed a kiss to his cheek. "How're you feeling?"

"Like my ribs have been put in a vise," he grumbled.

Her tender heart ached. She knew her behavior the past few weeks had caused him no small amount of pain. If she could go back and change things, she would, but since that wasn't an option, she had no choice but to try to make it up to him.

"You could have been killed," she said, her eyes flooding with more of the tears. If he'd died, she knew she'd never have found a way to assuage her guilt.

Jake's penetrating gaze met hers. Sorrowfully, she wondered what he saw. "Might have been better all the way around," he told her.

A tear slipped down her cheek and fell onto his hand. "Don't ever say that!" she told him in a fierce whisper. "Don't even think it."

The tension she felt in him drained away, and he reached out and stroked her shining hair. "I want you to be happy."

Georgia knew it was the truth. The trouble was, she wasn't sure at that moment exactly what would make her happy. Before she could think of a suitable reply, Ben came through the doorway, carrying a tray of coffee and cookies. "Rosalita said this is a new recipe. She wants us to try them out."

Realizing that he was intruding, he paused in the doorway. "I'm sorry. I'll just get a cup of coffee and leave the two of you alone."

Knowing that the moment when she and Jake might

have been able to talk seriously had passed, Georgia stood and forced a smile. "No problem. We were just getting to the mushy stuff, and there's plenty of time for that."

"Yeah, Dad," Jake said, gesturing toward the sofa. "Join us."

They talked about Jake's mishap and the fact that the heifer had already gone to the sale ring. They discussed Rosie's cookies and what tasks still needed doing for the wedding. For the first time in a week, Georgia began to feel a sense of something close to satisfaction as they chatted away the minutes.

"Have you decided what to do about your best man?" she asked. "Will Kevin be back from Argentina by then?"

Kevin Mitchell had been Jake's best friend since elementary school. Though Kevin had moved to Houston and they'd gone separate ways since college graduation, they kept in close contact. Georgia knew that unless it was absolutely impossible for Kevin to get back in time, there was no one else Jake would even consider letting stand up with him.

He let out a lusty breath. "I heard from him yesterday, as a matter of fact, and he doubts he'll be back in time."

"What are you going to do?" Georgia asked.

"I don't know."

"What about asking Zach?"

Ben's suggestion fell into the room like a ticking bomb. Fighting the urge to scream, Georgia waited for Jake's explosion. Her dismayed gaze skittered from Ben to Jake.

"He is your brother."

"Whom I hardly know," Jake reminded him, an unmistakable edge in his voice.

"Time's getting short."

"It's my problem." Silence dominated the room for several seconds before Jake turned to Georgia. "How do you feel about Zach being my best man?"

Georgia almost choked on the piece of cookie she'd just bitten off. She used the time it took to chew it up and wash it down with a swallow of coffee to gather the remnants of her scattered wits. It took every ounce of resolve in her to meet Jake's eyes.

"I think it's your decision," she said, choosing her words with care. "Zach is your brother, but the two of you don't share a past the way you and Kevin do. It's understandable that you don't feel close enough to him to want him to stand up with you."

"Well said," Jake replied with a nod and a cryptic smile. He looked at Ben. "I'll think about it."

"Fair enough," Ben said.

The doorbell rang, Rosalita hollered that she'd get it, and a couple of minutes later Zach stepped through the doorway into the living room. Georgia's heart leaped into a higher gear. Her first, involuntary instinct was to gauge Jake's reaction. That he looked less than thrilled by Zach's arrival was an understatement.

Zach, wearing black denim jeans and a striped rugby-style shirt that exposed his muscular arms, said a brief hello to Ben and gave Georgia a brief nod.

"I called to see if you got the news about the DNA tests and Rosalita told me you'd been hurt," he said to his brother. The genuine concern in his eyes was as unmistakable as Jake's sudden discomfiture.

"I'll live."

"Glad to hear it."

Another deadly silence fell on the room.

"Georgia, girl, why don't you pour Zach a cup of coffee and get him some cookies?" Ben said, ever the genial host.

"Surely." Sparing Zach the briefest of glances, she went to do Ben's bidding. "Cream or sugar, Zach?"

"Just black, thanks."

She offered him the cup and saucer. He took them with a soft thanks.

He was taking a sip of his coffee when out of the blue, with no more concern than if he were discussing the weather, Jake said, "We were talking about the wedding and discussing whether or not I should ask you to be my best man. What do you say, brother? Do you want to stand up with me?"

Ben looked shocked.

Georgia gasped.

Zach almost choked on the hot brew. When he got his coughing under control, he glanced at Georgia and then met Jake's eyes. Though the expression there was bland at first glance, Georgia detected an underlying intensity in her fiancé's gaze.

There was no doubting Zach's sincerity as he said, "You do me an honor, Jake, but I think you should choose someone who's shared more of your life."

Jake nodded. "Maybe you're right. Maybe by the time you tie the knot, we'll have made some memories between us, and I can be *your* best man."

Zach allowed his eyes to meet Georgia's again. Was it her imagination, or was that pain she saw reflected there? There was definitely pain in her heart—excruciating pain at the thought of Zach marrying someone else. How could she ever be content to be his sister-in-law when she wanted to be his wife?

The unexpected thought caught her completely unprepared. Right there, in the middle of the Lattimer living room with three pairs of eyes fixed on her, she realized what she should have known all along. Carrie was right; she was in love with Zach Rawlings. If she hadn't been sitting, her legs would have buckled beneath her.

Oh, she'd admitted she was infatuated with him, even that she *wanted* him. She had toyed with the notion of sleeping with him. She'd even goaded him by asking him if he was willing to offer her marriage, but never in the wildest of her dreams had she imagined her feelings were love. It had all happened too fast for her to believe what she felt was anything so serious. Dear, sweet heaven! What was she going to do now?

"Are you all right, Georgia Lee?" Jake asked.

Urging a smile to her lips, she said, "I'm fine." Wanting nothing more than to escape for a few moments, she stood up. "If you gentlemen will excuse me, I'll go refill the coffeepot."

Attuned to her every mood, Jake watched her go, wondering what had upset her so.

"Well, what do you think about the news?"

Zach's question drew Jake's attention from Georgia. "I figured it would turn out this way."

"Yeah, so did I." Zach munched on one of Rosalita's cookies and wiped the crumbs from his mustache with his brightly hued napkin. "I need to tell you something, Jake. I know now might not be a good time, but I suspect there'll never be a better one."

Jake frowned. "Spit it out."

Zach smiled at Jake's wordage. "Ever since I got

my memory back, I've been thinking a lot about the past, about my childhood and my mother.''

Something in Zach's expression set alarm bells off inside Jake. What else could possibly go wrong? ''What?''

Zach sighed a heavy sigh, tipped back his head and stared at the ceiling as if seeking divine guidance before he answered. Then he lowered his gaze to Jake's. ''My mom told me a lot about the night I was born, things I don't think she could make up.''

''What are you saying?'' Ben asked.

''I may be wrong. I have a good friend trying to track down some answers for me, and I'm trying to—''

''Damn it, Zach, spit it out!'' Jake commanded again.

''Okay,'' Zach said. ''I might be dead wrong, but I think the woman who raised me is the same woman who gave birth to me. I think she's my real mother.''

Jake had been in denial for so long, he hadn't even considered that. Zach's premise sat uneasily on his mind for a minute. ''But if you're right, it means that...'' His voice trailed away.

''If I'm right,'' Zach said, ''it means that for some reason she decided to give one of us away.''

''Yeah,'' Jake said in a bleak voice. ''Me.''

Chapter Ten

Georgia was a woman with a mission.

A woman with a mission and a dull, nagging headache that no over-the-counter painkiller could rid her of. The wedding was a little over thirty hours away, and Georgia, whose final stop was the mall, was tackling the last-minute tasks with an admirable and enviable composure that her mother had commented on the night before. What Ginny Williams didn't know was that what she deemed composure was actually the shutting down of all emotions except those necessary to carry out the tasks connected to the wedding.

Zach had called every day—sometimes twice a day—since the previous Friday when she'd seen him at the ranch. After the first two days when she'd hung up shaking and on the verge of tears, she'd let her answering machine pick up all her calls for fear it would be him.

His arguments made sense. His pleas broke her heart. He was right. But she couldn't stop the wedding. Not with Jake hurting physically from the injury with the heifer and with his ego smarting over Zach's belief that the woman who'd raised him was their birth mother who had chosen, for some unknown reason, to give Jake away.

Zach's theory had knocked the emotional props out from under Jake even more than finding out he'd been adopted. Georgia wasn't sure when she'd seen him so vulnerable...so unsure of himself as he had been this past week.

Though her reasons were different, the feelings and emotions she was experiencing were the same as Jake's. Georgia didn't know how he was coping, but thankfully, at some point about five days ago, a blessed numbness had set in, anesthetizing her aching heart and paralyzing every emotion except a driving need to get through the wedding. If it ever occurred to her that her dogged determination was joyless, she pushed the thought away with the same steadfast resolve she tackled her lists with.

Victoria's Secret was doing a brisk business when Georgia passed by and a table of frothy underwear caught her attention. She glanced at her watch. She had one more stop to make to finish with the "positively, absolutely" last-minute shopping for things that she and her mother had overlooked.

Georgia scanned a rack of tastefully naughty nighties, her gaze drawn to one of creamy ivory. Her sorority sisters had given her a lingerie shower, but in the purely feminine way that only another woman could understand, she was drawn by the promise of forgetfulness that a few minutes of fondling silk and satin and lace could deliver.

She chewed on her lower lip, debating whether or not she should take the time to indulge herself. Drawn by a pull as old as time, she stepped through the doorway and headed for the rack of lingerie, locating her size with no problem.

She was halfway to the dressing room before she realized she already had a gown for her wedding night and that there was absolutely no reason for her to buy another. Still, there was something about the nightwear that intrigued her, and without another thought, she found herself inside the small cubicle, kicking off her shoes and tossing her dress aside.

She wasn't aware that she'd been holding her breath until she turned and looked at herself in the mirror and heard the soft suspiration of air as she released a sigh.

On the hanger, the antique white gown with its lacy, capped sleeves had looked demure and old-fashioned. On, it had a whole different look. The ribbon and laced-edged hemline of the scalloped skirt dipped from mid-thigh to knee in silky folds that parted enticingly as she stepped nearer to the mirror.

On closer inspection, the floral pattern of the close-fitting, lacy bodice was cobweb sheer, hiding nothing, promising everything. Feeling strangely exposed, even in the privacy of the dressing room, she brought up her hands and fitted her palms over her breasts, wondering, as she continued her visual exploration, how the gown managed to look both demure and seductive.

The front closure was scalloped, held tenuously together by tiny pearl buttons placed in four strategic spots. Clearly, the small buttons could be liberated with the slightest touch.

Georgia's eyelids drifted shut and she envisioned Zach standing behind her, imagined his head dipping and his mouth touching her shoulder...pictured his hands circling her waist and moving up to cover the hands on her breasts with his. Caressing...stroking...

Desire raced through her like a jolt of electricity. Suddenly she felt a button pop free. Her eyes flew open. The blush-pink nipples that peeked through the fragile lace had constricted to tight, aching buds beneath her palms.

With one last lingering brush of her fingertips, Georgia began to strip the gown from her body. She was putting it back on the hanger when she heard a familiar voice.

"That's all I've heard for two weeks, and I'm sick of it. Make up your mind. Either break up with Joey or tell Brad to bug off."

"I can't do that." Genuine sorrow infused the words.

The voices belonged to Sabrina and Kat, whom Georgia hadn't seen since school let out. Their discussion was obviously an extension of the one she'd overheard the day Zach surprised her at school.

Aware that she was eavesdropping—again—Georgia thought of making her presence known, but curiosity kept her as still as the proverbial church mouse.

"You're leading them both on."

"I am not!"

"Yes you are. You pulled the same stunt with Joey when you were going with Jimmy Jessup. Are you at all familiar with the word *faithful?*" Sabrina asked.

"Of course I am. Joey and I have been together for six months, and I've been faithful to him."

"In your own inimitable way." Sarcasm infused Sabrina's voice. "Look," she said with her usual bluntness. "Put yourself in Joey's place. If you're interested in this Brad dude, you should be up front with Joey and end it."

"Tell him about Brad?" Kat asked in an incredulous tone. "I can't. I'm crazy about Joey, but something about Brad really turns me on."

"Joey's a nice guy, Kat," Meredith reminded her, speaking for the first time. "And he's cute and intelligent and mature. He deserves better than to be cheated on."

Like Jake.

"Who said I was going to cheat on him?" Kat demanded.

"Well, you must be thinking about it," Meredith said, "or we wouldn't be having this discussion."

"I'm not going to cheat on Joey," Kat denied hotly, adding, almost as an afterthought, "but it has crossed my mind. Maybe I *should* go out with Brad a time or two—"

"Kat!" Sabrina and Meredith chorused together.

"Well, I could...sort of...you know...see what he's like...get him out of my system, so to speak."

A feeling of déjà vu gripped Georgia. The conversation was remarkably similar to the one she'd had with Carrie a couple of weeks earlier.

"Are you out of your ever-lovin' mind?" Sabrina's query and Kat's reply faded as the trio moved past the dressing room and out of earshot.

Georgia's fingers unclenched from around the plastic hanger. Feeling as if she were in some sort of time warp, she left the dressing room and went to pay for the gown, hardly aware of what she was doing. She finished her errands and drove to Aledo, her weary mind filled with thoughts of the conversation she'd overheard.

After calling her mother and telling her that she'd finished her shopping and intended to take a nap before the rehearsal and dinner that were scheduled for seven than evening, Georgia changed into a T-shirt and a pair of faded shorts and fell across her bed.

Despite—or maybe because of—her inner turmoil, she was asleep in minutes. But even there, she found no respite from her dilemma. She dreamed of a judge in black robes who looked like Ben and demanded that she make a choice—Jake or Zach. When she couldn't decide, he made her draw straws. She drew the short straw, but neither she nor the two men in question had any idea which one of them it represented.

When Judge Ben banged his gavel and sentenced her to life without either of them, Georgia woke up, her heart pounding and a terrible feeling of doom hanging over her. With her head throbbing and a painful ache squeezing her heart, she got up and began to dress for the rehearsal and dinner...her last night as a single woman.

Much later, after the rehearsal at the church and the dinner that followed, Jake thrashed around in his lonely bed, trying to get comfortable, which was an impossibility since his discomfort came more from his mind than his cracked ribs.

His temperament lately was a cross between that of a wild animal whose foot was caught in a trap and a man who'd just lost his best friend. His mood fluctuated with each dip and rise of the emotional roller coaster he'd been on the past few weeks. He had no idea what other unpleasant little surprises life had in store for him, but he knew with a sense of fatalism that it wasn't over yet.

He wouldn't begin to feel really secure again until he slipped the wedding ring onto Georgia's finger. A part of him whispered that even then, he would never be the same...never be certain of anything—especially who Jake Lattimer was. Zach Rawlings's entrance into his life had seen to that.

Jake doubled up a fist and punched the down pillow. He knew it was unfair to place the blame on Zach who was as much a victim as he was, but because of Georgia's attraction to his brother, Zach was the person Jake had singled out to bear the brunt of the anger that by rights should be directed at his birth mother.

As they had so often the past week, his thoughts turned to Zach's statement about believing that Abby Rawlings, the woman who'd raised him, was the same one who'd given birth to him...and thus, Jake, too. As Zach had, Jake wondered what kind of woman could choose between identical babies. Had she done the old eenie, meenie, meinie, mo thing or drawn straws—short for Jake, long for Zach?

He flopped to his back and threw a forearm over his eyes. Maybe the fact that they were identical had made choosing easier. She hadn't had to decide whether she wanted a blond or brunet, dark or blue eyes. Hell, maybe Abby Rawlings had just tossed a coin, and Jake had come out the loser, but as Georgia had pointed out, no one who wound up with Retha and Ben Lattimer for parents could ever be a loser.

Jake glanced at the clock. Ten past midnight. His wedding day. He rolled to a sitting position and rested his elbows on his knees. He wondered if Georgia was lying awake thinking of the past and the future, or if she was fast asleep, dreaming away this last night before their lives became forever intertwined.

Georgia rolled to her side as the red numerals on the clock jumped to midnight. She was tired to the bone and her head still ached, but sleep eluded her. The dull throbbing in her temples had settled in a week ago and showed no sign of letting up. Everyone said she had too much on her mind, that she was stressed. She knew that the pain was caused by the battle raging inside her head, the never-ending concern that she was doing the wrong thing by going ahead with the wedding and her equally disturbing fear that if she called things off Jake would be crushed and might never forgive her.

She flopped to her side and prayed for peace of mind. The rehearsal had gone smoothly. So had the dinner that Ben had catered by one of the most posh restaurants in Fort Worth. If she and Jake were both a little quiet, not one among the joyous assemblage seemed to notice.

Jake had driven her home an hour ago, leaving her at the door with a kiss that, to her, held more desperation than passion.

Desperation. It was an emotion she was fast becoming acquainted with. She was desperate to marry Jake and consummate that marriage in hopes that doing so would rid her of the craving to feel Zach's lips on hers, a craving she denied by the light of day, a craving she'd been running from as fast and furiously as she could. She'd run so fast and hard that she didn't think she could go much farther. Thank God it would all be over by this time tomorrow.

She brushed at the sudden spurt of tears. Beneath the sheet, she rubbed the sole of one foot up and down her leg in a gesture that betrayed her restlessness. The silky fabric of the gown she'd bought earlier that afternoon brushed against her thighs with the softness of a lover's touch.

She had known for weeks that her restlessness was based on her uncertainty about what to do with her unwanted attraction to Zach. Her mouth curved into a bitter smile. Time had run out. It was too late to do anything now...even if she wanted to...even if she could dredge up the courage to hurt Jake.

"You're leading them both on." Sabrina's accusation to Kat pushed itself into Georgia's troubled mind. *"You should be up front with Joey and end it."*

Sabrina was right. Kat should do the right thing, Georgia thought, just as she should.

"Maybe I should go out with Brad a time or two...sort of get him out of my system, so to speak."

Maybe Kat was right. Maybe there was some merit to her crazy idea. Maybe for once in her life she should follow her heart instead of her head. Maybe she should call Zach and tell him to come over and join her in her lonely bed.

"You've got to be crazy, Georgia Lee," she said to the darkness.

The whole idea wasn't just crazy, it was insane. There was no way that spending one night with Zach Rawlings would get him out of her system, not since she'd realized she loved him. If anything, it would just make her want more of what she would never be able to have.

It would make a beautiful memory, though, a bright and shining moment in time to take out and look at when the thought of the long years ahead threatened. Threatened. She shook her head. Like Jake's desperation earlier, *threat* was not a good word to think of in connection with your upcoming married life.

Georgia chewed on her lower lip. Surely she wasn't seriously considering going to Zach's and throwing herself at him, was she?

Oh, but she was. Seriously.

She'd always done what was expected of her. As a teenager, she'd never gotten into any trouble. Heck, she'd never even stayed out past curfew. Ditto for her life as an adult. She'd never picked up a man in a bar, or let herself be picked up. She was the model citizen, the dutiful daughter, the perfect fiancée—and just look at her! She was as boring as last week's news.

Jake would never have to know. *Of course, he'll know.*

"How?" she said to the darkness. "Zach and I won't tell."

You'll know. If you do it, you'll never be able to be in the same room with the two of them without feeling guilty.

Then she'd just have to learn to live with it. With any luck at all, Zach would be too busy with his own life to spend much time at the Lazy L except for the occasional holiday. Surely she could handle that.

She flung back the sheet and slipped her feet into the house slippers sitting next to the bed, unaware that she had actually made a decision. Pulling a lightweight raincoat from the closet, she dragged it on over the nightgown with no thought to what she'd say if she got into an accident on the way...with no thought to anything except getting out the door and into her car. Thinking was not allowed. If she let herself consider the ramifications of what she was about to do, she'd reason herself out of it.

She would have one night with Zach Rawlings. Not to get him out of her system. Not to lead him on or to hurt Jake. But for herself.

Sleep was impossible. All Zach could think about was that by this time tomorrow night, Georgia would be his brother's wife. The thought filled him with anger—at Georgia and at himself. She knew she shouldn't go through with it, but she was so damned stubborn, she wouldn't listen to reason, or her heart.

When he heard the tapping, his first thought was that the guy next door had locked himself out again. The second time he heard the sound, he bolted upright. No one came knocking at this time of night unless something was wrong.

Was it Will needing him to go out on a case? Had something happened to Shelby or J.R.? He pulled on the jeans he'd taken off earlier, dragging the zipper up just enough for decency's sake before he strode through the small apartment and flung open the door.

Whoever he imagined he might find standing there, it wasn't Georgia. Yet there she stood, her arms crossed over her breasts, wearing the unlikely combination of house slippers and a raincoat, her eyes filled with uncertainty.

Zach scowled. There wasn't a cloud in the night sky, and he didn't recall any rain in the forecast. "What are you doing here?"

The gruff question caused her eyebrows to draw together. Distress pushed the uncertainty from her eyes. "I should go," she said, half turning to do just that.

He reached out and caught her arm, pulling her around to face him. Her teeth worried her bottom lip in an appealing, familiar gesture. Neither of them spoke. He couldn't quite read the expression in her eyes as she looked at him, and she offered no explanation about why she'd come.

Afraid to trust the fragile sprout of hope unfolding inside him like flower petals beneath a summer sun, he let go of her arm and asked, "Why did you come, Georgia? What do you want?"

"You."

The word was little more than a soft exhalation of breath hanging in the noisy silence of the city night like a drop of moisture clinging to the fragile web of a spider, shimmering with the promise of quenching a need as old as time itself.

For an instant, Zach thought his ears were deceiving him. He wondered if she'd really spoken, or if the answer was nothing but his ears hearing what his heart wanted to hear.

He crossed his arms over his chest. "Why now?"

She shook her head. Golden glimmers in her strawberry blond hair danced in the light of a nearby security lamp. "I couldn't before now."

"Why?"

She reached up and tucked her hair behind her ears, blowing out a breath that stirred her bangs. He noticed they'd been cut. For the wedding. The realization hardened the heart that had gone unexpectedly soft when he noticed the sheen of tears in her eyes.

She tried to smile, but it came out looking more like a grimace. "You aren't making this easy."

"Why should I?" he asked in an uncompromising tone. "You haven't made it easy for me."

"I know. I'm sorry."

He thought again that she looked as if she were about to cry. "Why?" he asked again.

"Because you're right. We owe it to ourselves to see what this is between us."

His short bark of laughter held no humor. "Don't you think it's a little late for that?"

She shook her head. "I'm not asking for anything from you except what's left of tonight."

"What if I want more?"

She looked surprised by the question. She shook her head. "We can't have more. Whatever this is, it happened too late. I can't hurt Jake any more than he's already been hurt."

He wanted to ask her what he would do with his hurt come the dawn of her wedding day and what she would do with hers, but he already knew what the answer to those questions would be, and he wasn't sure he wanted to hear them vocalized.

"So you just want a last fling, huh?" he asked, hiding his pain behind a shield of sarcasm. "One last roll in the hay. One last one-night stand."

"This will be my first one-night stand," she said in a soft voice. "And what I want is a memory of you...of what you make me feel...to keep me..." She paused, searching for the right word. Not finding it, she finished, "To keep."

Her truthfulness disarmed him. His mask of mockery cracked and crumbled, leaving him feeling exposed and vulnerable, the way she looked.

"Please, Zach," she said, reaching out and placing one small palm and then the other on his crossed arms. "Give me one night."

Her touch sparked the wanting he'd tried hard to suppress since the kiss they'd shared that night at the hospital, a forbidden wanting that grew every time they

were together. There was no way he could deny her—
or himself.

Knowing he was about to cross into uncharted territory and that the way back would be long and pain-
filled, he reached out and slid his hands beneath the
collar of the raincoat to her shoulders. He let his
thumbs rest lightly on the delicate crest of her collar-
bones and was struck again by her apparent fragility.
His thumbs began a slow stroking. She closed her eyes
and let her head fall back the slightest bit, as if his
touch took all the starch from her.

Unable to resist the offering, he leaned over and
pressed his parted lips to the place just below her jaw-
line where her blood pulsed in time with the rapid beating of her heart. He heard the sigh that fluttered from
her lips, felt her breath, hot against his cheek.

Slowly, as if he had nothing to do but stand in his
open doorway and feast on her soft, willing flesh, Zach
cradled her head in his hands and crowded her throat
with kisses, inching his way down and around, then up
over her chin, moving inexorably closer to her parted
lips. Even though she must have known what was coming, she drew in a sharp breath the instant before his
open mouth found hers.

He had forgotten how pliable her lips were and how
well her mouth fit his. He had forgotten the way she
tensed up when he first kissed her, and how, after a
moment, the tension seemed to drain from her body
and she went boneless against him. He had forgotten
the little sounds she made deep in her throat...tortured
groans that spoke of a rising hunger. Aching whimpers
that told him his kiss was both pain and pleasure.
Yearning moans that said she wanted to prolong the
delicious agony even while she longed to end it.

His hands moved down to grasp the lapels of the coat. He slipped it from her shoulders, sucking in a stunned breath at the sight he beheld.

Georgia wore nothing but a wisp of gown made of white lace and satin, a gown made for a wedding night. For the first time, the reality of what they were about to do hit him. If they made love—and only an act of God could stop them now—and Jake found out, Zach knew they would both lose him as brother, husband, friend. He knew Georgia had spent weeks counting the cost and made her decision. He knew she was thinking of it now.

She whispered his name, and the single word was filled with so much longing the doubts and fears vanished.

His eyes feasted on her, hungry to see every sweet curve, every silken slope, every tantalizing valley. The gossamer bodice might have been spun of moonbeams, so airy was the lace that covered her small, shapely breasts. Even with nothing but the security light and the last rays of a waning moon for illumination, their shadowy tips were clearly discernable. His body responded with typical masculine appreciation.

Slowly, afraid he would do something to frighten her away, Zach put his hands on her narrow waist, slid them down over her hips and drew her close, so close that there could be no doubt in her mind about what was in his. So close that not even a breath of night air could find its way between them.

Georgia drew a deep, contented breath that popped the top button free of its flimsy anchor. His immediate instinct was to undo the others, but he battled the urge, covering her breasts with his hands instead.

Her eyelids drifted shut and she caught her lower lip

between her teeth, covering his hands with hers, pressing harder. A look of intense pleasure played across her face. He felt the tips of her breasts grow hard against his palms.

Faced with her utter surrender, he was powerless to do anything but stoke the fire, which he did by taking her mouth in a series of hungry kisses. Her mouth was sweet, eager and surprisingly, she matched him kiss for kiss, thrust for thrust.

He felt her hands on his waist, felt her fingers slip beneath the loosened band of his jeans, felt her go still when she realized he wore nothing beneath the wash-softened denim. Then, when he half expected her to pull away, to stop him, her mouth opened wider and her hands moved down. Her touch was gentle, almost tentative, her hesitancy as drugging as an aphrodisiac, as heady as a fine wine. Need was an ache in his loins. Love was a pain in his heart.

The sound of a siren reminded him that they were making out on his doorstep. He dragged his mouth from hers. Her usually animated face held a dreamy slackness that spoke of surrender and desire.

Without a word, he took her mouth in a heated kiss and lifted her so that her legs were around his waist. She wore nothing beneath the scalloped skirt of the gown. The feel of her flesh against his sent his libido over the edge. Thoughts of and worries about the future vanished beneath the need to fill her with his love and end the aching emptiness inside them both.

He carried her inside and kicked the door shut behind them. Then, turning, he backed her against the door and pinned her there, holding her securely with one arm while he made the necessary adjustments in his clothing.

For long seconds after he eased inside her moist warmth, they were still, reveling in the feel of their joined flesh, delighting in the closeness of being fore-head to forehead...breath to breath...heart to heart.

Finally, when he thought she was ready, when he couldn't wait any longer, his hips began to move in the ancient, arcane dance of love.

He wasn't certain how long it took for them to reach the climax together, but the end came far too quickly. As he reached a final, shattering crescendo that ex-ploded throughout him in a burst of feeling so intense he felt the hot rush of tears, his mind whispered that he was a fool—or worse—for settling for this one sto-len moment in time.

His heart said it didn't care.

It wanted a memory, too.

Georgia awakened to the sound of birdsong. Day-light had crept into the corners of the room, softening the darkness to a muted gray. Her cheek lay against the back of a man. Her arm was curled over his waist. Her first panicked thought was that she had missed the wedding.

Then she remembered.

This wasn't Jake. She had spent the early morning hours of her wedding day with Zach, an action she could in no way justify in the cold light of her wedding day. The full weight of her weakness bore down on her in huge waves of guilt.

What had she been thinking? Simple. She hadn't thought. She had acted, giving in to impulse again with no thought to the consequences. But those conse-quences couldn't be ignored any longer. They came rushing at her like a swarm of angry bees.

Knowing she couldn't face Zach, fearful she couldn't face Jake, she eased away from Zach's warmth and inched toward the edge of the bed. She found her gown lying in a creamy white puddle on the carpet and slipped it on over her nakedness.

A quick, furtive search turned up only one house slipper. Her raincoat was nowhere in sight. She fought back a momentary panic before recalling that Zach had taken her coat off on the front porch. Gripping the shoe like a club, she tiptoed from the bedroom to the front door.

He hadn't locked it, so there was no click of the dead bolt to wake him. She prayed the hinges wouldn't squeak and breathed a thankful sigh when her prayer was answered. She found her raincoat on the concrete porch, wet with dew, and pulled it on over her gown. Her car keys were in the pocket. Clutching them in one fist, she raced barefoot down the sidewalk and across the parking lot to her car.

She unlocked the door, got inside and jabbed the key into the ignition. She had to get home before someone called and realized she wasn't there. The thought that she might get caught filled her with horror. What would Jake say if he found out?

What will Zach say when he wakes up?

Would he be angry that she'd slipped out without a word after the wonderful night they'd spent together? Would he have regrets?

Regrets. Oh, she had them, plenty of them, but her sorrow at the thought of causing Jake heartache at some distant time in the future was nothing compared to her sorrow at knowing that she could never, would never, have another night with Zach.

Chapter Eleven

A soft click awakened Zach. He stirred and breathed deeply. The scent of lavender and roses filled his nostrils...his pores. Georgia's scent. Remembering, he rolled to his side, only to find that the place next to him was empty. Numbed by a stunning jolt of pain, he couldn't move.

She'd meant it, then. She had no intention of calling off the wedding. All she'd wanted was one night. Even though she'd said as much, he'd clung to the hope that the time they spent together, that the love they shared, would change her mind.

An alarm clock buzzed in the apartment above him, and something in his brain connected the click that had awakened him to the closing of the door. Georgia! Leaping from the bed, he dragged his jeans over his nakedness again.

Barefoot, he ran to the living room where the sight

of one of her house slippers lying near a small table stopped him cold. He picked it up and carried it to the door, stepping out onto the small cement porch and peering over the too-tall shrubbery.

There was no sign of her car in the parking lot. With a sinking heart, Zach looked at the slipper in his hand for long moments before he turned and went inside.

It promised to be a long day.

And an even longer life.

Outside the old stone church, thunder rumbled in the distance, a bass accompaniment to the clear soprano laughter and chatter of the bridesmaids getting dressed in the next room. Georgia, who wore nothing but an old-fashioned crinoline and a form-fitting bustier, cocked her head to one side and stared at her reflection in the long mirror hanging in the ladies' room, trying to ignore the nausea churning in her stomach, trying to summon up the joy she knew she should feel. But no matter how she tried, the stranger in the mirror just stood and looked at her, unsmiling.

Her usually straight hair had been moussed and rolled and teased into a becoming Gibson-girl style with soft, curling tendrils at her temples and the nape of her neck. The upswept hairdo was the perfect complement for her Victorian wedding gown.

Her ivory complexion was freckle free. A palette of soft taupes and browns dusted her eyelids and brow bones, heightening the blue of her eyes. Mascara extended her lashes to unbelievable lengths. Dusty rose enhanced the sweep of her cheekbones. The same color shaped the outline of her mouth, giving her lips a full, ripe look.

The hairdo and makeup application—both by the renowned François—were a wedding gift from Valerie Campbell, and although Georgia felt as if she had on enough makeup for three people, she had to admit that the man had done a superlative job of transforming her from a rather plain-looking schoolmarm into a gorgeous bride.

For the first time in her life, she knew she looked stunningly beautiful. Even without the added elegance of her wedding gown, she looked like a fairy-tale princess...or a movie star.

She didn't look anything at all like a cheating fiancée.

There wasn't a trace of guilt in her eyes. The blue eyes staring back at her held a dull lifelessness that, thankfully, could be attributed to an understandable weariness. After all, putting together a wedding of this magnitude was a major undertaking.

The papers were calling it the wedding of the year, and Ben had proudly told her at the rehearsal dinner the night before that the governor—whose family the Lattimers had known since the depression—had cleared his calendar so he could attend. The governor, for criminy's sake!

The doorknob squeaked. Georgia, who could see the door in the mirror, didn't bother to turn around. Carrie, who'd gone to get her camera from her car, stuck her head inside. Her eyes were wide and her mouth hung open in amazement. In all the years Georgia had known her friend, she'd never seen her look so flustered.

Georgia's stomach took another sickening dive. "What?" she asked.

"There's a television crew outside!"

Georgia swallowed sickly. Television. Great. Just what she needed.

* * *

"Jake, old buddy, I don't know any easy way to break the news, but there's a television crew outside." Kevin Mitchell, who had pulled some strings and made it back to the States in time to stand up with his best friend after all, made the announcement with an apology in his voice.

Realizing that he had no interest in taking part in the ribald joking that flew fast and furiously from the lips of his groomsmen, Jake, dressed to the nines in a black tuxedo complete with tails, had withdrawn to a window where he could watch the dark clouds gathering outside. He spun around on the sole of a gleaming dress shoe. "A television crew?" he echoed. "Why?"

"Maybe because when a Lattimer does anything it's news."

Jake's reply was a disgruntled snort that caused a dull pain to pulse through his still-sore ribs. He was in a hell of a shape for a wedding night.

"You'd better wipe that frown off your face," Kevin suggested. "If Georgia gets a gander at that, she's liable to cut and run."

"Television crew?" Georgia echoed, fighting the impulse to hike up her petticoat and run as fast and as far as she could. The menacing growl of approaching thunder rumbled, rattling the windows.

"Television crew," Carrie affirmed in a tone that was a cross between disbelief and awe. "They're setting up out by the curb, so they can catch you and Jake on film as you burst joyously through the double doors. Their words, not mine," she added hastily.

Joy. There was no joy, Georgia thought. Not in her, anyway. She felt more like she was going to the gallows than to the beginning of a new, and supposedly happy, life. There was nothing but this sickening certainty that she was about to make a huge mistake....

Kevin's innocent comment about Georgia cutting and running deepened the depression that had settled on Jake the minute he'd opened his eyes. Things had gone downhill from the moment he'd seen the revised weather forecast that predicted severe thunderstorms from two hours before the time of the ceremony until an hour after.

"Stuff it, Mitchell," he said, his attitude saying without words that there was slim chance of that happening.

If only he believed it.

At the thought of television cameras pointed at her, expecting to see a happy couple descend the church steps, the pounding in Georgia's head increased tempo. She swallowed back the sickness rising in her throat and clutched the vanity until her knuckles turned white.

Marrying Jake wouldn't end her doubts about the rightness of their marriage, it would only increase them—and her misery. Saying vows that she knew she couldn't promise from her heart would only augment her guilt.

"Two wrongs don't make a right, Georgia, honey."

One of her mother's favorite sayings fell softly into the noisy chaos of her mind. One wrong was spending the eve of her wedding in another man's arms. The other was marrying a man she didn't love.

"Are you all right, Jake?" Kevin asked.

"I'm fine."

"You look funny."

"So you've told me all my life," Jake said with dry wit.

Kevin Mitchell smiled. "Seriously," he said. "You look like you just lost your last friend."

"I'm fine," Jake reiterated. "Just nervous."

Shrugging, Kevin left him standing there.

Jake wondered if Georgia was as edgy as he was, wondered if she shared his doubts and would rather have Zach saying the vows with her. Far off on the horizon, a bolt of vicious-looking lightning split the darkening sky.

"You look like you just lost your last friend." Funny. That's exactly how he felt. Like he'd lost his best friend. And maybe a brother, too.

"You look pale," Carrie said. "You okay?"

Georgia forced her attention away from the doubts in her mind and urged a sick smile to her lips.

"I'm fine." She realized her friend was still standing half in and half out the door, the same spot she'd been in since the announcement about the television crews a minute or so before. "You can come in, Carrie."

In possibly another first of her life, Carrie blushed a bright red. "I was so excited I forgot to get my camera. I'll be back in a flash." A quick, wry smile tipped up the corners of her mouth. "No pun intended."

Carrie vanished, and Georgia sighed. If only she could feel nervous. If only she could feel anything but this numbness and an occasional surge of nausea.

Thunder grumbled. Her stomach rolled.

Squeezing her eyes shut to halt a sudden bout of tears, Georgia raised a hand to her mouth to hold back a sound of despair. She wasn't the kind of person who could live a lie. Not well, anyway. She'd found that much out the past few weeks.

"You look gorgeous."

The compliment sent her eyes flying open. Valerie Campbell crossed the room, a smile on her dark, patrician features. Valerie and Jack Campbell were old friends of the Lattimers. Ben and Jack had paced the waiting-room floor together the night Jake was born. The night Zach was born.

Jack and Valerie had been divorced for years, citing the fact that they couldn't live together without one or both of them considering mayhem, yet since their divorce they'd maintained a close friendship that had always fascinated Georgia. Though she didn't see either of them often, she liked them both.

"Thank you," Georgia said. "François did a great job. I don't even look like myself." She didn't feel like herself, either, but she didn't say it.

Valerie smiled. "Jake has always been special to me, so it was my pleasure to help make his wedding day special." She reached for the wedding gown hanging on a padded hanger beneath a protective plastic sheath. "Your mother wanted me to tell you that she'll be here in a minute. It's time we got your dress on."

Georgia lifted a hand to her temple where the blood beat painfully. "Already?"

"Already." Valerie paused in removing the plastic and glanced over at her. "Are you all right?"

Georgia tried to smile. "I have a headache, and I feel a little queasy."

"So did I when I married Jack," Valerie said with a sympathetic smile.

"Almost ready, honey?" Georgia's mother's question preceded her into the room by a heartbeat. Carrie, camera in hand, followed close behind.

"Almost."

"Can you two give me a hand?" Valerie asked, taking the dress from the hanger. "We don't want to mess up her hair."

Georgia stood stock-still and with her eyes closed as the trio held the skirt out of the way and lifted the gown over her head. She heard the soft whisper of satin over crinoline as the fabric drifted down over her petticoat.

"Sleeves."

Opening her eyes, Georgia held out her arms obediently, thrusting first one and then the other into the tight-fitting sleeves. Minutes later, she stood in front of a floor-length mirror the ladies of the church had installed for just such an occasion, zipped, snapped and hooked into the gown that had cost almost a month's salary. Ginny carefully placed the veil on her daughter's head. The froth of tulle drifted to the floor like Rapunzel letting down her hair.

Before Georgia could do more than realize that the woman looking back at her from the silvery depths of the mirror could pass for a stranger, the door burst open and the eight women who made up her wedding party surged into the small room. Georgia stood silent while they oohed and aahed, touching lace and fingering satin in a ritual of appreciation as old as weddings themselves.

"It's a stunning gown," Valerie said in complete satisfaction as the first muted strains of the wedding march wafted down the hallway. "And you're a stunning bride."

"Thank you," Georgia said, near tears.

"Where's her bouquet?" Ginny asked in a shrill voice.

"Settle down, Mrs. Williams. It's right here," Carrie said, her control once more in place as she shooed the purple- and lavender-frocked bridesmaids from the room.

Frank Williams poked his head through the doorway as Carrie pressed the wrapped stem of the white rose and violet bouquet into Georgia's cold hands.

"Ready?" he asked, beaming at her.

She was marginally aware that he followed the question with a comment about how beautiful she looked, but all she could think of was his question. Was she ready to walk out that door and become Mrs. Jake Lattimer? Ready to take Jake into her heart and her body?

"Come on, Georgie, girl," Frank Williams said, holding out his elbow in a courtly manner. "They're playing our song."

Without being aware she was doing so, Georgia placed her hand in the crook of his arm. Together, they walked through the door and down the long hall that led to the foyer where they took their place behind the line of bridesmaids mincing down the petal-strewn aisle one by one.

A sudden, severe panic gripped Georgia—not at the thought of going through with the ceremony, but at the thought of making love with Jake. How could she pretend to be in the throes of passion with Jake when memories of the night she'd spent with Zach flashed through her mind at unexpected times, sort of like old, jerky movie frames? How could she hide the lack of love in her heart?

She couldn't.

Even though she'd made a valiant try at convincing

herself otherwise, the hours spent with Zach had shown her clearly what her heart had known all along. A marriage to Jake would fail. Maybe not in a year or even two or ten. But it *would* fail. And when it failed, she would lose Jake not only as her husband, but as one of the best friends she'd ever had.

But if you don't go through with the wedding, you'll lose him anyway.

"Come on, honey."

Frank Williams's words of encouragement ended her mental seesawing. She was surprised to see that she was standing at the entrance of the auditorium. Every eye was turned toward her. Every lip held a smile. She hardly noticed. Her attention was focused on Jake, standing so straight and tall and handsome—waiting for her....

Drowning in an emotion that was more like grief than anger after Georgia had run out on him, Zach had gone through his morning ritual of showering and fixing a breakfast he couldn't swallow past the clot of pain in his throat. After he'd dumped the remains into the garbage disposal, he'd made the bed, stripping off the sheets and cramming them into the dirty clothes hamper so that the next time he crawled into it, he wouldn't be surrounded by the scent of lavender and roses.

By one in the afternoon the apartment was clean from top to bottom. Then, uncertain what to do next, he found himself standing in the living room, staring at a picture Shelby had picked out for him, totally unaware of his surroundings.

Thankfully the phone rang, saving him from the necessity of making a decision about what to do with the rest of his day...the rest of his life.

"Rawlings!" he barked into the receiver.

"You been looking for me, boy?"

If he didn't recognize the cigarette- and whiskey-roughened voice as his dad's, Zach would have known who it was anyway. No one but Dwayne had ever called him boy in that insolent, superior tone. Apparently, the messages he'd left at various places had finally caught up with his dad.

I'm just fine, Dwayne. Thanks for asking. As usual, there was nothing in Dwayne's attitude that said he cared a whit about the boy he'd called son.

"Yeah, I have," Zach said. "I need to talk to you about something."

"Talk away."

"No," Zach said. "I don't want to do this on the phone. Where are you?"

"What's this about, anyway?" Dwayne grumbled.

Zach knew better than to lay out all his cards. If there was anything remotely shady about the deal, Dwayne's skinny rump would be out of the state as fast as his rig and the speed limit would allow.

"I'm in sort of a switch," Zach fabricated instead. "I need to get your opinion about something."

After voicing his surprise that Zach would come to him for anything, Dwayne gave Zach the name of a truck stop just outside Fort Worth and said he'd be there a few hours. He needed to get some shut-eye.

As Zach got into his car to meet Dwayne, Jake stood with the preacher and his best man, waiting for his bride-to-be to make that slow walk down the aisle. She stood poised in the doorway, holding her father's arm, and even though her face was shadowed by her veil, Jake knew he had never seen her looking so beautiful. The dress, some old-fashioned style in a creamy, antique white satin, was exquisite.

A low murmur of approval tittered through the crowd that waited, collective breaths bated as they anticipated her first step. Or maybe it was only he whose breath was held in uncertainty.

Jake saw Georgia look at her father and say something. Saw the stunned look on Frank Williams's face as he glanced toward the trio at the front of the church and then back at his daughter.

Then, accompanied by a combined gasp of surprise, Georgia lifted her skirts, whirled and disappeared from sight. Jake knew then that the pain squeezing the blood from his heart was only a preview to what was to come.

Horrified by what she was doing, yet finally understanding that marrying Jake would be as bad as her betraying him with Zach, Georgia sped down the long hallway toward freedom, her skirt and veil billowing out like a nimbus while tears rushed down her cheeks.

Knowing she couldn't face the questions, the accusations, the whys that were bound to come, she swept past the rest room that held the jeans she'd worn to the church and pushed open the door that led to the side parking lot.

She wrenched open her car, thankful that her keys—from habit—lay in the ashtray were she'd tossed them earlier. Not caring that she was ruining the hairdo Valerie had paid an exorbitant price for, Georgia pulled off the garland of flowers attached to the long veil from her head and tossed it into the passenger seat.

Crushing the skirt of her gown, she climbed into the

car, rescuing the trailing veil from the pavement a heartbeat before she slammed the door shut. In seconds, she was backing out of her parking place and negotiating her way through the parking lot.

As she pulled out into the tree-bordered street, a feeling of déjà vu struck her. She'd run away like this before, this morning when she'd fled Zach's apartment and the certainty that she loved him, that she was marrying the wrong man.

Now, in a complete reversal, she fled from Jake and whatever future they might have had together. She didn't know which hurt most, forsaking the man she loved, a man who had offered her nothing, or abandoning a man who loved her, a man who had offered her his all....

The truck stop was like many others, Zach thought forty-five minutes later as he pulled into a parking place in front of the eatery. A neon sign touted a twenty-four-hour motel, café and on-duty mechanic, all for the convenience of the truckers who transported goods from one side of the country to the other.

Zach saw—or rather heard—Dwayne as soon as he walked through the door. The hoot of laughter that greeted Zach's ears hadn't changed much over the years, except maybe to get louder and coarser.

Dwayne, who shared a booth with three other truckers, spied Zach standing in the doorway and waved him over. He'd aged, Zach thought, noting the receding hairline and the road map of lines radiating from the corners of his dad's dark eyes and over gaunt, whisker-roughened cheeks.

Grinning, Dwayne made the introductions, calling Zach "my boy, the Texas Ranger." That done, he excused himself from the group, and he and Zach adjourned to an empty booth. After stirring two spoonsful of sugar into a fresh cup of coffee, Dwayne asked, "So what kind of trouble are you in, boy?"

Zach met his dad's eyes steadily. "I lied," he said. "I'm not in any trouble. I just had some things to ask you about Mama."

Surprise and something that looked remarkably like apprehension leaped into Dwayne's eyes. "What about her?"

"I want to know what happened the night I was born."

Suspicion overtook the apprehension, but Dwayne managed a short bark of laughter. "That's ancient history. Why on earth do you want to know after all this time?"

"Because I just found out something important about that night, and I need to hear your version."

Dwayne's gaze skittered away from Zach's. He reached into his shirt pocket for a cigarette, a gesture Zach remembered that signaled nervousness.

"What do you want to know?" Dwayne flung a quick glance at Zach at the same time he flicked the top of a worn lighter and thumbed a flame.

"I want to know if Abby Rawlings was my real mother...my birth mother."

As a peace officer, Zach had spent the better part of his adult life in the company of liars and cheats, and he'd grown pretty savvy about spotting one. His gut reaction told him that the righteous indignation on Dwayne's face couldn't possibly be bogus.

"Hell's bells, boy, of course she is. What makes you think she isn't?"

"I found out a couple of weeks ago that I have a twin, an identical twin, who—"

Dwayne interrupted with another brief laugh. "A look-alike, maybe."

The objection, though familiar, was rapidly becoming tedious. "No, Dwayne. We're twins, and we have the blood tests to prove it."

The smile on Dwayne's face didn't falter, but the humor in his eyes did. "Pull the other one, boy," he said. "It's got bells."

"I'm not pulling your leg. His name is Jake Lattimer, and according to some blood work we had done, we're identical twins."

Like the indignation of seconds before, Zach didn't think the confusion in Dwayne's eyes was fake, either.

He shook his head. "That can't be," he mumbled, almost to himself. "She'd have told me."

"What do you mean, she'd have told you?" Zach said, picking up on the strange comment. "You were there, weren't you?"

Dwayne didn't speak for as long as a minute. It was almost as if he were trying to put things together in his mind, trying to make Zach's claim mesh with his version of the truth.

"Dwayne." The softly spoken word brought the older man back to the present. His eyes held confusion, and more than a hint of anger. "This is important," Zach said. "Were you there, or were you on the road somewhere?"

"How could I have been on the road? I wasn't driving a truck back then. Hell, I was barely out of high school."

Zach dragged in an irritated breath and tried another tack. Obviously, Dwayne wasn't going to cooperate.

"Look, I haven't got all day. I just want to know if Abby was my birth mother or if the two of you adopted me, because if she's my real mother, she's Jake's, too, and for some reason no one knows, she gave him up for adoption."

The intensity of his voice and the look in his eyes must have warned Dwayne that his patience was wearing thin.

"Yes."

"Yes, you adopted me, or yes, she's my real mother? Our real mother?"

Dwayne's gaze was as steadfast as the Rock of Gibraltar. "She's your real mother. I'm sure of that. Positive." Then he shook his head. "But believe what I'm tellin' you when I say I don't know nothin' about no twin brother."

Zach pinched the bridge of his nose. He felt a headache coming on. Facts were facts. He and Jake were brothers. Dwayne said Abby was his real mother, but claimed he knew nothing about Jake's existence or that he had been given away. "Damn it, Dwayne! How could you not know?"

"I don't know nothin' about any twin brother or any adoption 'cause I wasn't married to yer mom when she had you, that's why. I ain't your daddy, Zach, and that's a fact."

Jake's first reaction when Georgia picked up her skirts and hightailed it out of the church was one of stunned surprise that was echoed en masse by the murmur of astonishment that rose from the guests.

That emotion was fast followed by a feeling of resignation that grabbed his heart like the powerful jaws of a pit bull. His first dismal thought when she disappeared and her dad turned to him with a helpless look was that deep in his heart, he'd known things weren't right.

With her face red with mortification, Ginny Williams rose and came to him, murmuring something about "bundle of nerves" and "cold feet." Jake nodded, but hardly heard. Then, with a pat on his arm, she slipped out the side door, presumably to go and talk some sense into her daughter.

Jake wanted to tell her not to waste her time, but couldn't seem to find his voice. Instead, he glanced at his dad. The stunned, vacant expression in Ben's eyes gave him the look of someone who'd gone a few too many rounds with Mike Tyson. Valerie, who sat between him and her ex-husband, Black Jack Campbell, wore an anxious look on her pretty face. Her sons, Logan and Russ, sat stoically on Jack's right. If they thought their childhood buddy was looking like a number-one sap, there was nothing on either of their faces to give their feelings away.

The governor, who sat behind Ben, glanced at his watch with more irritation than surprise. That look, combined with one of sympathy from Mattie Maples, the widow woman who owned the spread adjoining the Lazy L, drove the numbness from Jake and ushered in a sudden surge of embarrassment.

Keeping his eyes focused straight ahead, not daring to look left or right to observe the pity he knew he'd see on the faces of the wedding guests, Jake started down the aisle toward Frank Williams, who looked as flustered as his wife had moments before.

At the doorway of the lobby, Frank took Jake's arm and propelled him out of view of the people turning in their seats to look at them. Just one man stood in the foyer, and when he saw Jake, he ducked out the front door. Out of sight and he hoped out of earshot, Frank yanked the decorative silk hanky from the pocket of his tux jacket and mopped his perspiring brow.

"I'm sorry, Jake," he said in a breathless voice. "I'm sorry."

"What happened?"

"Nothing that I know of. She seemed distracted, but I thought it was just nerves."

"What did she say?"

"She said she couldn't go through with it, but it's probably just nothing but a bad case of nerves," Frank repeated, as if by saying it often enough, he could make it fact.

"She's gone!" The breathless, disbelieving statement accompanied Ginny Williams's headlong flight into the vestibule.

"What do you mean, she's gone?" Frank snapped.

"She wasn't in the rest room," Ginny said, "so I looked outside. She was driving away."

Frank swore. A cold dread filled Jake. It wasn't nerves. It wasn't cold feet. Georgia had no intention of marrying him.

She doesn't love you. She loves Zach.

The words fell into his mind like lead weights. A crazy kind of relief flooded him at the admission, but it in no way dulled the escalating pain or the fury that turned his clenched knuckles white. Why had she waited until the last possible minute to make the break? Why hadn't she come to him before now? He'd have understood.

Would you, Jake? Would you really?

Probably not. He'd have been angry and hurt no matter when and how she broke the news, but if she'd come to him sooner, they could have been spared this public humiliation.

"Do you want me to go tell the guests the wedding has been called off?" Frank Williams asked.

Noting the tears in Ginny Williams's eyes, Jake shook his head. Frank needed to console his wife. "I'll do it."

Frank nodded. "I don't know what to say, Jake. I'm sorry doesn't begin to cover it."

"It's not your fault," Jake said. As he turned to make the long trek down the aisle to the front of the church, the doors burst open and a man with a minicam on his shoulder stepped inside. Jake recognized him as the man who'd been in the lobby when he and Frank began to talk. A woman in a teal suit thrust a microphone in his face.

"Mr. Lattimer, can you tell us what's happening here? Why did your fiancée leave you at the altar?"

Frank swore. Ginny burst into tears.

Jake's comment—totally unfit to air on the local news—was accompanied by his suggestion as to what the television crew could do with their expensive equipment. Without another word, he strode to the front of the auditorium and faced the curious, waiting crowd.

Every eye was on him, everyone waited expectantly. Jake looked directly at his dad and said quietly, "I'm sorry to inconvenience you this way, but the wedding is off. It seems the bride has had second thoughts."

Lightning cracked and a loud boom of thunder shook the church. It began to rain, great sheets of water that fell from the sky as if the lightning had split it asunder. Chaos erupted around him as guests broke into a spate of questions directed at the person sitting next to them.

Cursing Georgia, cursing Zach, Jake turned and headed toward the side door.

His heart was shattered, broken into so many pieces that there was no chance of anyone ever putting it back together again.

Chapter Twelve

By the time the church was cleared of people and the Lattimers and Williamses stood looking around at the flower- and ribbon-bedecked auditorium wondering what to do next, Zach had bade Dwayne goodbye and started home through a hellacious storm that had blown through as he listened to Dwayne's account of the past.

According to Dwayne, he'd always had a crush on Abigail Pickett, the preacher's daughter, but Abby hadn't been interested. It wasn't that she was snobby or anything, but Dwayne was three years older than she was and ran with a different, older crowd. And, as all the girls seemed to, she liked the popular boys, the jocks—especially the football players. Hell, Dwayne had said, he couldn't blame her. There wasn't anyone in the little Podunk community they lived in who didn't want to better himself.

When she'd left town without a word that summer,

Dwayne had heard the gossip about her being pregnant, which was the standard reason girls like Abby went away for extended periods of time. He'd never thought she was the kind of girl who'd put out for a few promises from a guy in a football jersey, but the consensus was that that's just what had happened.

Then, to everyone's shock, she'd shown up a few months later with a baby in tow. Unlike a rare few girls who'd had the courage to do the same thing, there was no far-out tale about a marriage that hadn't worked out. She'd just come back to town with Zach in her arms and gone on to pick up the pieces of her life.

At this point in the saga, Dwayne had reiterated again that he was not Zach's father, and he had no idea who was. He even confessed to badgering Abby about it often through the years, but stubborn woman that she was, she'd taken that secret to her grave.

Of course, there was more talk when she came back—more than usual—since she was the preacher's daughter. Dwayne said he remembered how stern and quiet the Reverend Pickett had become after that and how people in town talked about his passionate hellfire and damnation sermons about the sins of the flesh. Abby had stopped going to church. Later, she told him it wasn't her choice. Ashamed to have her and her baby there, the reverend had requested her absence.

Though she lived at home, her parents hardly spoke to her, and all her so-called friends had abandoned her. She'd been ashamed of what she'd done, he could see that, and she was hurting, badly. She kept to herself, mostly.

He'd been working at the grocery store back then, and she came in several times a week to buy things for her folks. Barely twenty himself, Dwayne hated seeing her so heartbroken. She'd needed a friend, and he had become that friend.

Over a period of a few short weeks, he'd persuaded her that he wanted to take care of her and her baby, and, much to the eternal gratitude of her father, Dwayne had married her when Zach was just over five months old.

"She married me to put an end to an intolerable situation," Dwayne said, as he stared at his reflection in the black coffee in his mug. "I tried to tell myself that she cared for me, and I guess in her way, she did, but it wasn't love. It was never love, and after a while, that started eating at me, and—"

"You took it out on both of us."

Dwayne raised his gaze, and Zach knew that he'd never forget the misery in those dark red-rimmed eyes. Misery that, even masked by a fine sheen of tears, went soul deep.

Dwayne nodded. "I did. It's not something I'm proud of, but I couldn't seem to help it. I took to drinkin', and the drink made it worse," he tacked on thoughtfully. "It was easy to blame your mama for our problems, but the truth is, I didn't try hard enough."

Soon after that confession, Zach had left the man he'd called Dad and started home. He'd drawn a tremendous comfort in knowing that Abby was his mother—Jake's, too—and he couldn't deny the intense relief in knowing that Dwayne Rawlings wasn't their father.

Even so, Zach's heart was unexpectedly heavy over recognition of the older man's sorrow. Though he'd expended a fair amount of energy hating Dwayne Rawlings, he left the café feeling sorry for the older man.

At the very least, he owed Dwayne a debt of gratitude for keeping a roof over his head.

Truth really was stranger than fiction. The more he thought about Dwayne's tale, the more intriguing he found Abby's refusal to name the man who'd fathered her sons. But even that question paled in significance compared to why Abby Pickett had chosen to give away one of her sons, and why she'd chosen to relinquish Jake. If Dwayne knew nothing—and Zach believed he was telling the truth about that—and Abby was dead, how would they ever find out?

Zach had no idea, but he had a hunch that if anyone could ferret out the truth, that person was Laura Ramirez. He'd give her a call as soon as he got home. Jake, too, would have to be informed of this newest development as soon as possible. As soon as he got back from his honeymoon.

A fresh rush of despondency mingled with the anger simmering just below the surface of Zach's subconscious. Noting the entrance to the apartment complex, he flipped on his turn signal.

Then his gaze strayed to the clock on the dashboard. Georgia and Jake were probably drinking champagne toasts and cutting cake about now. In another hour they'd be on their way to Colorado and their wedding bed.

The memory of Georgia's body next to his, all warm and soft and willing, flashed through Zach's mind. He swore. For a while there, with Dwayne, he'd managed to forget that he'd fallen in love with his brother's intended wife.

As he pulled into the apartment parking lot, he noticed that the rain had stopped and the clouds were breaking up. Bright afternoon sunshine peeked through, creating a brilliant rainbow. Recalling the tale of Noah his mother had read to him on numerous occasions, Zach thought it looked like an omen, but maybe it was just wishful thinking on his part. Maybe he just wanted some sort of closure on this thing with him and Jake...and him and Georgia.

You'll have closure on your feelings for Georgia the day they bury you. It was a terrifying, but true, admission.

There were no empty parking spaces at the front of his apartment, and Zach was forced to park several places down from his front door. He locked the car and headed across the wet asphalt, relinquishing his frown long enough to smile at the shenanigans of a trio of kids playing in the shallow puddles.

Mrs. Brewer, one of his neighbors who was out walking her pug, Tobias, waved him to a halt and asked how he was feeling. He said just fine, thanks. The woman asked about Attila, and Zach told her his bad-tempered buddy had found a new home out on the range. When Mrs. B. said she sort of missed the ornery cuss harassing Toby every day, Zach realized that he missed Attila, too.

He was lonely. As lonely as old Mrs. Brewer.

On the pretext that he had to make a phone call, he excused himself and, with his eyes downcast, he thrust his hands palm outward into the back pockets of his jeans and crossed the last few yards to the sidewalk that led to his apartment.

Just steps from his front door, his troubled gaze encountered a huge puddle of white that spilled off the damp sidewalk and onto the wet grass. No, not a puddle, a pile. A pile of fabric. Creamy white satin, to be exact...the skirt of a wedding gown.

With his heart thumping in his throat, Zach let his gaze climb upward. Small feminine hands—ringless hands—were clasped around legs bent at the knee. At the peak of the satin-shrouded hill was a pale face with wide melancholy eyes—Georgia's face. She was sitting slouched forward, her chin resting on her updrawn knees.

As he stood unspeaking, just staring at her, she straightened her spine, but kept her arms clasped around her legs. Maybe it was the tentative and unexpected joy sprouting in his heart, but she looked more beautiful than he'd ever seen her.

Strands of her strawberry blond hair had eluded the curly knot atop her head and straggled around her face in attractive disarray. Beneath her artfully brushed on blush, her cheeks were pale. Smudges of mascara underscored the brilliant blue of her eyes. She'd been crying. Had Jake found out about the night they'd spent together? Had she told him?

Dozens of questions tumbled through Zach's mind, but he couldn't have said anything if his life depended on it...and maybe, he realized with a sudden clarity, it did. He was afraid to speculate what her presence might mean, terrified to attach any significance to it.

Finally, when the silence had stretched to an unbearable decibel, Georgia stood and clasped her hands behind her back. Rocking up on her toes and back down again, she said, "I've been waiting for you."

The simple words banished the last traces of anger that had held him in its grip since he'd awakened and found her gone. In its place bloomed an intense, almost giddy sense of relief and a humbling thankfulness.

His macho side told him to make her sweat, told him that he was giving in too easy, but his heart didn't give a darn what his machismo thought. He compromised by offering her a noncommittal reply. "I had to go see Dwayne. My dad."

"Oh." He offered no further explanation, and, after a moment, she said bluntly, "I couldn't go through with it."

"Why?"

Instead of answering, she waved at someone behind him. Turning, Zach saw Mrs. Brewer and Tobias. Mrs. B. was looking at Georgia in her wedding gown with flagrant curiosity.

"Maybe we should go inside," she said after the woman passed. "I'm attracting a lot of attention, and I need to say what I have to say before I lose my nerve."

Wordlessly, he unlocked the door and she preceded him into the apartment, her satin skirts swishing with each step. In the middle of the living room, she turned to face him, her knotted, twisting hands belying the blue flame of determination blazing in her eyes.

"I did what you wanted." The words were whisper soft and filled with so much emotion he wasn't sure the walls of the small room could hold it.

The same shock that had stunned Zach to silence now exploded in an astonished, "What?"

Afraid that any faltering would send her resolve into a nosedive, Georgia marched to within a foot of him and tilted her head back until their eyes met. It was time to lay her cards on the table. "You heard me. I called off the wedding. It's time to put up or shut up."

Zach frowned at her. "What are you talking about?"

She reached out and poked his chest with a rose-tipped index finger. He took an involuntary step backward. She followed.

Her memory flashed to the day in the barn when she'd used much the same approach and backed him onto the tack box. She knew she was being a pushy hussy, but she had to make her point before Zach gathered his wits and told her to go take a hike. After the way she'd treated him, she wouldn't blame him if he did.

"I'm talking about your *unrelenting* pursuit of me these past few weeks, even though you knew I was going to marry your brother." She pushed with her finger. He took two steps back. "I'm talking about your calling and calling and calling, to try and make me see that marrying Jake was a mistake."

Poke. Push. Step. Step.

Zach's back hit the front door. He'd retreated as far as he could.

"Why were you so all-fired certain that my marrying Jake was the wrong thing to do?" she demanded, tapping her finger against his chest.

Zach's face wore a dazed look. "Because I knew you didn't love him."

"And you were right." Georgia heard the softening in her voice, a softness suffused with sorrow. "I don't love Jake. Not the way a woman is supposed to love the man she plans to spend the rest of her life with. And do you know why?"

Zach shook his head.

The last bit of defiance drained from her, and with it most of the counterfeit attitude that was the only thing that stopped her from bursting into tears and begging him to forgive her.

"I don't, either," she told him, remorse and the

slightest hint of exasperation in her voice. "He's a wonderful man. Smart. Handsome. Honest. Kind. But he..." Her voice trailed away. She took a deep breath and a firm grim on her faltering determination. "He doesn't make my heart beat faster, and he doesn't make me crazy with wanting the way—" she swallowed "—the way *you* do."

Zach still didn't say anything. Georgia knew that he could read every emotion in her eyes, knew he saw the love she could no longer deny. She realized that letting him see into her soul was tantamount to giving him a license to break her heart, but she didn't care. All she wanted was to let him know the truth about her feelings for him. She'd deal with the heartache whenever that became necessary.

"Say something!" she cried. "I've just dumped my whole future and made myself and a very good man a laughingstock because I...I'm in love with you." Her declaration ended in a whisper. "At least tell me why you wouldn't leave me alone."

For several seconds, she thought he was going to ignore her, but just as she picked up her skirts to leave, he said, "I couldn't help myself."

Georgia raised her troubled eyes to his.

"From the first time I saw you smiling that gorgeous smile at me in the airport—even in the middle of that sting—I was attracted to you. That smile was like a punch in the gut, or the heart. And then, when I woke up in the hospital and saw you leaning over my bed, I felt something I'd never felt before."

Happiness began to flood Georgia's heart.

"When you kissed me I figured I was as close to heaven as a guy like me might ever get." A small, bitter smile flickered across his lips. "When I found out you were Jake's fiancée it felt like someone had pulled out the rug from under me. Then—''

"Stop rambling, Zach," she said, a smile trembling on her lips, "and just spit it out. Do you love me or not?"

"I do," he growled.

He didn't sound too happy about it, but Georgia didn't care. Allowing any softness into his life was hard for a man like Zach Rawlings. The smile, full-blown and as bright as the sun going down in the west, curved her lips as she moved to stand in front of him. She reached out and began to twist a button on his shirt. "So...since you love me, I guess you're going to marry me—right?"

The button slipped free, and she insinuated her fingers inside his shirt. Zach grabbed her wrist in a gentle hold. His bemused expression had been replaced by one of need.

"If that's what you want."

"No, Zach. It has to be what we both want. Do you want us to spend the rest of our lives together or not?"

"What about my job?" he asked. "You said you'd never marry a cop."

"You're evading the question."

"Of course I want to marry you, but you said—"

"I know what I said, but never is a long time." Her bottom lip quivered, and tears thickened her voice. "I won't deny that I'm scared to death, but when that cow hurt Jake, I realized that none of us has a guarantee for tomorrow. All we have is now, and I want to spend all my nows with you."

She looped her arms around his neck and Jake lowered his mouth to hers in a kiss of thankful reverence. When they were both breathless and trembling with need, she pulled away. "If anything happened to you, I—"

He put his finger over her lips. "It won't."

"Promise?" she asked with a hesitant smile.

"Promise." She knew even as he said it that it was a promise he might not be able to keep, but she intended to give him excellent reasons to try.

Zach lifted a hand and cupped her face, grazing her cheekbone with the pad of his thumb. "What about Jake?"

Georgia drew in a trembling breath. "I hurt him, and I'm sorry. I think that one day he'll thank me, but I don't think either of us will be his favorite person for a while, though."

Zach's eyes reflected his sorrow. "I imagine not."

Georgia laid her palm against his cheek. "I'm sorry I came between you."

Zach gave her a rueful smile. "There wasn't much to come between. That's the saddest part. Someone, someday should pay for that."

"It'll work out, Zach. In time." But like his promise a few seconds before, she knew there were no guarantees. Unable to offer him any comfort but the solace of her love and the haven of her body, Georgia pressed closer against him.

"Hold me."

Instead, he swept her up into his arms, and carried her toward the bedroom, her wedding gown whispering softly as he went.

Though Georgia and Zach wanted to get married as soon as possible, there were things to be settled before they could go into a new life together. The first thing Georgia did the next morning was call her parents and assure them she was okay, that she hadn't lost her mind—not even temporarily—and that she'd come later that morning to help them rid the church of the wedding paraphernalia.

She found her parents on the back porch, drinking coffee and wearing frazzled, worried looks. Georgia didn't want to tell her folks about Zach. It didn't paint her in the most positive light, but she had no choice, since they planned to be married as soon as they could make some sort of order out of the chaos she'd unleashed by walking out on Jake.

Her dad, who looked as if he was still in a state of shock, leaned his head against the cushion and stared at the sky when she announced that she'd fallen in love with Jake's twin brother. A horrified Ginny Williams was more vocal about her disappointment that her only daughter would cheat on her fiancé and that she could have "pulled such a stunt."

Knowing she deserved it, Georgia listened quietly to Ginny's railing all the way to the church and turned a deaf ear as she helped her parents vacuum the drying rose petals in the aisle, take the ribbons down from the ends of the pews, and box up the crystal and silver in the fellowship hall. She watched with a keen sense of sorrow as the florists loaded the candelabra and flowers in their van.

Ginny stood at her daughter's side as the van roared away, bemoaning the unnecessary expense and all the hard work. Her main concern seemed to be what she was going to do with all those fancy little finger sandwiches and the wedding cakes and *all* those bottles of champagne.

Georgia's answer was to freeze them, eat them and

return them. Ginny looked at her as if she'd suddenly sprouted horns.

"I know I've disappointed you, Mom," Georgia said, her exasperation showing for the first time. "But can't you be glad that I didn't make a mistake? Can't you be happy for me and Zach?"

Ginny's eyes filled with tears. "I've never even met the man, and you're going to marry him!"

"He's Jake's twin, Mom. He's like Jake and not like Jake. You'll love him."

In the end, her parents reluctantly agreed that Georgia had made the only choice she could—better a called-off wedding than a divorce with innocent little children involved—and wished her happiness. Georgia left Aledo with a lighter heart. Now if she could only get that same blessing from Jake and Ben.

After the first day, she stopped counting how many times she'd tried to talk to Jake. Rosalita was cordial if not friendly, which was understandable since her loyalties lay with the Lattimers. Invariably, the housekeeper said Jake was out and that she'd tell him Georgia had called.

After the first half dozen times, Georgia realized that he had no intention of talking to her—perhaps ever—but she needed to explain. She needed to hear him say he'd forgiven her, or that he would one day soon....

Unable to make contact with Jake, Georgia finally convinced Ben to meet her for lunch. Once they placed their order, Ben cut right to the chase.

"It's Zach, isn't it?"

Georgia forced herself to meet his gaze. "Yes," she said, knowing lying would only add to her sins. "I never meant for it to happen. I never meant to hurt Jake. Surely you know that."

"I do believe you, and I don't blame you," Ben said, his voice heavy with the pain he bore for his son. "I blame Zach."

"It isn't his fault," Georgia insisted. "I was having doubts about me and Jake before I went to France. It seemed like something was...I don't know...missing from our relationship." Seeing Ben's skepticism, she added, "Ask Jake."

"So Zach was just the catalyst, the last straw."

"I guess so." Georgia blew out a troubled breath. "I'm not sure I understand any of it. I love Jake, but I love him like a brother or a good friend. I don't feel any wild all-consuming passion for him. I knew it when I accepted his proposal, but I wanted to get married and start a family, and so did Jake. To be honest, I think Jake feels the same way about me."

"Why do you say that?" Ben asked.

Georgia felt a hot blush creep into her face. "Because we never slept together. He never even *tried* to get me into bed. At least not until lately, when he finally saw that things weren't what they should be between us."

Another flicker of surprise crossed Ben's face. "Unlike Zach Rawlings," he said at last.

The heat in Georgia's face deepened, a sure sign of her culpability. "That isn't important," she said. "What is important is how I almost convinced myself that mutual caring and respect could take the place of love."

"It might have worked if Zach hadn't come along and seduced you."

"Maybe it would have, and maybe it wouldn't. But Jake and I would have both been settling for second best, Ben, don't you see?"

Ben's fingers tightened around his water glass. "I see that Zach Rawlings has convinced you of that. Darn it, Georgia! If you were going to break it off, why didn't you do it sooner? Why wait until the last possible minute?"

Tears filled her eyes. "Partly because I'd persuaded myself that it could work, and partly because I knew Jake was upset about this twin thing and the possibility that his mother had given him up and kept Zach. I didn't want to add to his worry."

"So you waited until half the county was at the church and then left him at the altar. That sure as hell makes sense," Ben said with a brutality that made Georgia wince. "Do you have any idea how embarrassed he was? How embarrassed he still is? Not to mention that he's pretty ticked off."

"I know that. I know you're both furious with me. You think I've betrayed you both, and I admit that maybe, in some ways, I have. But in another way, it was the noblest, best thing I ever did."

"I don't know how you can say that."

"Didn't you hear what you said? You said Jake was embarrassed and angry. Not that he was heartbroken. His pride is bruised, not his heart, and one day, he'll realize it and thank me for what I did."

Ben regarded her steadily, as if he were weighing the things she'd said.

"He just needs time," she said. "We all do." When Ben didn't reply, she decided to change the subject. "Zach talked to his dad."

"About Jake?" Ben asked, his voice sharp with sudden interest.

Georgia nodded. "It seems Dwayne Rawlings isn't his biological father."

"What!"

Georgia nodded. "He told Zach he married Abby when Zach was about five months old. She was nursing him, so she must have given birth to him. Dwayne swears he doesn't know anything about a twin."

"Did she say who the birth father was?"

Georgia shook her head. "When Abby died, she took that bit of information with her."

Ben rubbed his thumb through the moisture on his glass.

With a sigh, Georgia reached out and covered his hand with hers. "I know this troubles you, and I know you're worried about how Jake is taking all this. And you should. But don't let what I've done rob you of the feelings I know you have for Zach. He's a special man, Ben—like Jake—and he needs the caring you can give him. He'd never admit it, but he needs Jake even more. And Jake might not want to admit it right now, either, but he needs Zach, too."

Almost two weeks passed before Georgia felt as if she'd done everything she could to try to make amends with Jake. Unable to speak to him or see him, she'd written him a letter explaining her feelings and her reasons and begging for his forgiveness.

Knowing there was nothing else she could do except pray that time and circumstance would soften his heart, she married Zach on June 17, twelve days after her previous wedding date.

This time, Georgia wore a waltz-length dress of creamy white lawn and carried a simple tussie mussie of violets and daisies. This time, there was no crystal and silver, because there was no reception. This time, the ceremony was performed by a justice of the peace in the shabby austerity of his office.

The only people in attendance were Ginny and Frank Williams, Carrie and Denton Adair, Will James—who acted as Zach's best man—Laura Ramirez, whom Georgia liked instantly, and Laura's son, J.R., who performed the duty of ring bearer.

As happy as they both were, an aura of sadness dampened the happiness of the ceremony. Neither Zach nor Georgia could halt the thoughts of Jake that sneaked into their minds as they promised to love and cherish each other for the rest of their lives.

After bidding everyone goodbye, they drove in silence to the Anatole in Dallas where they planned to spend the night before leaving the next day for a two-week trip to Florida.

The door was barely closed behind the bellhop before Zach pulled Georgia into his arms almost roughly. "You're thinking about Jake," he accused.

"So are you," she said with a bittersweet smile.

"Regrets?"

"None," she said with a shake of her head, "except that I purchased my own happiness at the expense of Jake's. It's going to take us both a while to get over that."

"Yeah," Zach said. "It will."

He hugged her so close she could hardly breathe. "I love you," he told her in a voice thick with tears. "And I promise you'll never regret giving up all the things Jake could have given you."

She brushed her thumb across one heavy dark eyebrow and regretted the sadness she saw in his eyes. "I know," she said softly.

Slowly, tenderly, they unbuttoned, unzipped, and

tossed various articles of clothing to the floor. Stripped of everything but the love shining in her eyes, Georgia knelt on the bed and drew him down beside her.

Facing each other, seeing the heat of Zach's passion blazing in his dark eyes and feeling the tenderness of his touch wherever his fingers strayed, Georgia offered a silent prayer for the man lying beside her.

Later, after she'd met Zach at the crest of a passion unlike any she'd ever experienced, and they lay in the lethargic aftermath of lovemaking, she knew without any doubt that she'd done the right thing, that in spite of Jake's anger, everything would work out for them all....

Epilogue

Later that evening, Laura Ramirez sent J.R. off to his room to watch cartoons while she caught the evening news to scope out the woman who would be her direct competition if she decided to take the television job she'd been offered. She also wanted to think about the wedding she'd attended earlier that afternoon.

All it had taken was one look at Zach's face as he gazed into Georgia's eyes to know he was crazy about her. Laura sighed. She was thrilled that her good friend had finally found someone, but if she were honest with herself, she'd admit that she was just a little jealous of Zach and Georgia Rawlings.

Their happiness brought a sense of sadness Laura could no more deny than she could deny the memories stealing over her, memories of a russet-haired man she didn't often allow herself to indulge in...memories of J.R.'s father.

She was deep into those forbidden remembrances when Paula Dennison announced the lead story for the evening—a female police officer had been seriously injured while doing undercover work.

Since anything involving law enforcement intrigued her, Laura's attention was hooked immediately. She turned up the volume.

"Shelby Hartman, an eight-year veteran of the Dallas police force, was almost killed this afternoon when the undercover assignment she'd been working on for five months suddenly went sour."

Laura listened with rising horror as the perky anchor detailed the afternoon's happenings. Those details were sketchy at best. No one would know exactly what had happened until Shelby was able to tell her side. The segment ended with the statement that Shelby was in serious condition at an undisclosed local hospital.

Without a moment's hesitation, Laura switched off the television set, reached for the phone and dialed information for the number of the Anatole.

Zach answered the phone on the second ring.

"Zach, it's Laura. Georgia's going to hate me for interrupting your wedding night, but—"

"What's wrong?" he asked sharply. "Is it Rufio?"

"No. Shelby." Laura told him what she'd heard on the news. "They didn't say what hospital she's in, but I know you have ways of finding out those things."

"Darn right I do. I'll do some checking around and Georgia and I will go see how she's doing."

"Georgia—"

"Don't worry about Georgia," Zach said. "I appreciate your calling. Shelby means a lot to me, and I'd never forgive myself if I wasn't there for her."

They said their goodbyes, and Laura hung up the

receiver. Zach Rawlings was a good man, a good friend. She was lucky to have him in her life. Georgia might not know it yet, but she was lucky, too. Men you could trust, men you could lean on, men who put other people's well-being above their own didn't come along every day. She should know. She'd been looking a long time.

Knowing she was allowing herself to sink into that terrible trap of feeling sorry for herself—something she didn't allow often—Laura admitted that she wanted a man in her life: She needed one, especially now, when she was so worried about J.R.

So far, the tests were inconclusive, and she was thinking about finding another doctor and getting a second opinion. It would be nice to have a husband to help make the hard decisions. Nice to have a man to snuggle up to at the end of the day when Rufio was tucked away in his room. Nice to talk to someone over five years old. Rufio needed a brother or sister, too. Like her, he was often lonely.

With considerable effort, Laura dragged herself up from the pit of self-pity and determinedly focused on the things Zach had learned from his conversation with his dad. The news that Dwayne Rawlings wasn't Zach's and Jake's father was as intriguing as the fact that Dwayne had no knowledge of the existence of a twin.

Why had Abby been so secretive about the father of her babies? Why had she given one of them away? Why had she chosen to keep Zach instead of Jake?

Laura knew the answers to those questions wouldn't be easy to find, since Abby had taken the name of her babies' father to her grave and every avenue Ben Lattimer had followed seemed to be a dead end.

But she wasn't a quitter. This was just the kind of puzzle she liked, the kind that kept a person like her interested, which was why her career was taking off. First thing tomorrow morning, she'd take another look at the information they had and see if something jumped out at her that she hadn't noticed before. If it didn't, she'd go over her facts with a fine-tooth comb and look for that elusive, sometimes nagging bit of information that just didn't fit, some small, insignificant something that often led to a breakthrough.

This was too intriguing to quit now.

Like Zach, she wanted some answers.

* * * * *

*For all of you rooting for Jake to find
true love and happiness— Look for
THE COP AND THE CRADLE
by Suzannah Davis (SE#1143),
book 2 in the exciting SWITCHED AT BIRTH
miniseries…coming your way in December—
only from Silhouette Special Edition*

Share in the joy of yuletide romance with brand-new stories by two of the genre's most beloved writers

DIANA PALMER

and

JOAN JOHNSTON

in

Diana Palmer and Joan Johnston share their favorite Christmas anecdotes and personal stories in this *special hardbound edition.*

Diana Palmer delivers an irresistible spin-off of her **LONG, TALL TEXANS** series and Joan Johnston crafts an unforgettable new chapter to **HAWK'S WAY** in this wonderful keepsake edition celebrating the holiday season. So perfect for gift giving, you'll want one for yourself...and one to give to a special friend!

Available in November at your favorite retail outlet!

Only from

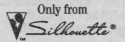

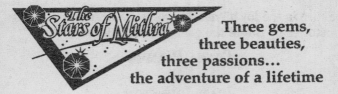

The Stars of Mithra

Three gems,
three beauties,
three passions...
the adventure of a lifetime

SILHOUETTE·INTIMATE·MOMENTS®
brings you a thrilling new series by
New York Times bestselling author

Nora Roberts

**Three mystical blue diamonds place three close
friends in jeopardy...and lead them to romance.**

In October
HIDDEN STAR (IM#811)
Bailey James can't remember a thing, but she knows
she's in big trouble. And she desperately needs private
investigator Cade Parris to help her live long enough to
find out just what kind.

In December
CAPTIVE STAR (IM#823)
Cynical bounty hunter Jack Dakota and spitfire
M. J. O'Leary are handcuffed together and on the run
from a pair of hired killers. And Jack wants to know
why—but M.J.'s not talking.

In February
SECRET STAR (IM#835)
Lieutenant Seth Buchanan's murder investigation takes
a strange turn when Grace Fontaine turns up alive. But
as the mystery unfolds, he soon discovers the notorious
heiress is the biggest mystery of all.

Available at your favorite retail outlet.

Welcome to the Towers!

In January
New York Times bestselling author

NORA ROBERTS

takes us to the fabulous Maine coast mansion
haunted by a generations-old secret and introduces
us to the fascinating family that lives there.

Mechanic Catherine "C.C." Calhoun and hotel magnate
Trenton St. James mix like axle grease and mineral
water—until they kiss. Efficient Amanda Calhoun finds
easygoing Sloan O'Riley insufferable—and irresistible.
And they all must race to solve the mystery
surrounding a priceless hidden emerald necklace.

Catherine and Amanda

THE Calhoun Women

**A special 2-in-1 edition containing
COURTING CATHERINE and A MAN FOR AMANDA.**

Look for the next installment of
THE CALHOUN WOMEN with Lilah and Suzanna's
stories, coming in March 1998.

Available at your favorite retail outlet.

by two of your favorite authors
Penny Richards and Suzannah Davis

Four strangers are about to discover the true bonds
of brotherhood...with a little help—and love—
from four terrific women!

THE RANGER AND THE SCHOOLMARM
by Penny Richards (SE #1136, 11/97)

THE COP AND THE CRADLE
by Suzannah Davis (SE #1143, 12/97)

LITTLE BOY BLUE
by Suzannah Davis (SE #1149, 1/98)

WILDCATTER'S KID
by Penny Richards (SE #1155, 2/98)

Thirty-six years ago, in a small Texas hospital, four
adorable little boys were born. And not until they were
all handsome, successful, grown men did they realize
they were SWITCHED AT BIRTH. Find out how this
discovery affects their lives. Only in

Silhouette ® SPECIAL EDITION ®

SILHOUETTE WOMEN KNOW ROMANCE WHEN THEY SEE IT.

And they'll see it on **ROMANCE CLASSICS**, the new 24-hour TV channel devoted to romantic movies and original programs like the special **Romantically Speaking—Harlequin™ Goes Prime Time.**

Romantically Speaking—Harlequin™ Goes Prime Time introduces you to many of your favorite romance authors in a program developed exclusively for Harlequin® and Silhouette® readers.

Watch for **Romantically Speaking—Harlequin™ Goes Prime Time** beginning in the summer of 1997.

If you're not receiving ROMANCE CLASSICS, call your local cable operator or satellite provider and ask for it today!

Escape to the network of your dreams.

See Ingrid Bergman and Gregory Peck in *Spellbound* on Romance Classics.

Daniel MacGregor is at it again...

New York Times bestselling author

NORA ROBERTS

introduces us to a new generation of MacGregors
as the lovable patriarch of the illustrious MacGregor
clan plays matchmaker again, this time to his three
gorgeous granddaughters in

THE MACGREGOR BRIDES

From Silhouette Books

Don't miss this brand-new continuation of Nora Roberts's
enormously popular *MacGregor* miniseries.

Available November 1997 at your favorite retail outlet.

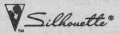